F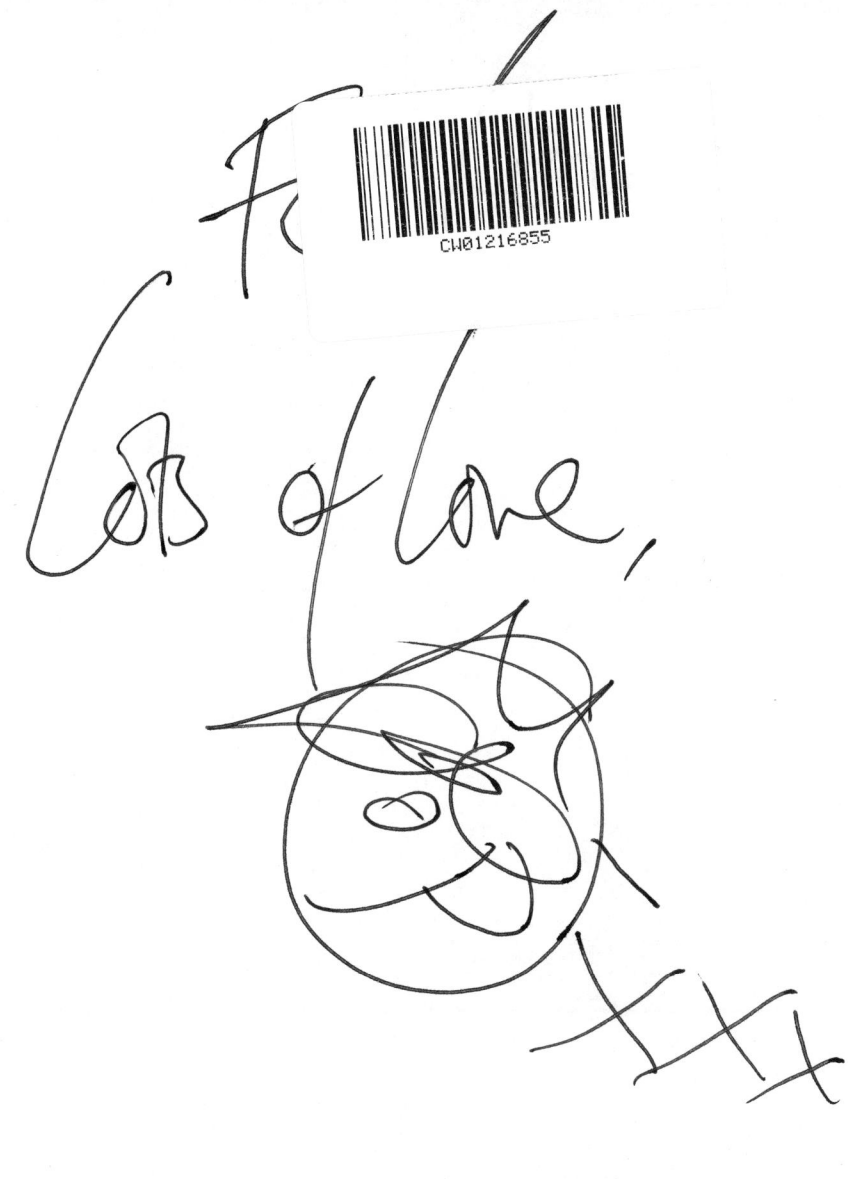

Lots of love,

xxx

The Morning Parks

Dominic Ryan

AuthorHouse™ UK Ltd.
500 Avebury Boulevard
Central Milton Keynes, MK9 2BE
www.authorhouse.co.uk
Phone: 08001974150

© *2008 Dominic Ryan. All rights reserved.*

No part of this book may be reproduced, stored in a retrieval system, or transmitted by any means without the written permission of the author.

First published by AuthorHouse 1/7/2008

ISBN: 978-1-4343-5819-6 (sc)

Printed in the United States of America
Bloomington, Indiana

This book is printed on acid-free paper.

Chapter One

Bombs and Butterflies

OBLIVIOUS to the weight of Holy Night, the skin of her shoulder is open-pored, soft and warm, though hard-boned against me. I rest my cheek and chin in my hand and watch a breast rise quick, slow fall. The nipple stands in the cold of the bedroom.

I tug at the quilt and cover her chest.

Her face is stone dead, blue lips pouting against the dark, dark-lashed eyes closed to the night, and around her throat is a chain of bruise-red wildflowers.

She is beautiful, I realise, surprised.

The window frame rattles, shivering in the January gale, clinging dearly to the walls of the old tenement building.

What is behind those eyelids? What does she dream?

I have known Anna every day now for two years, give or take those long nights when her voice becomes so loud and hammering I cannot find the strength to answer her calls.

My silences seem to make her want me more.

Silence has inspired our lovemaking to become more urgent. Tonight she wrapped her fingers around my hands around her neck. I pressed hard, squeezed and she gasped and writhed, but I was horrified inside myself.

But she knows little of my thoughts, asks less.

She is focused on her work. She has an important job. Legislation, she says, is not only the new religion, it is the only legitimate currency for a world that is destitute.

No, she knows little of my thoughts because they are such ghosts that when finally I speak, after too many hours drinking meatbeer, I tell her only what I hope will not haunt her in the morning.

My hip falls into the hollow of the mattress as she rolls away from me on to her side, pressing warm buttocks into my groin, thrusting her arms up underneath the pillow then just as suddenly turns again on to her back and an elbow stabs my chest bone.

I cup her arm away and around the softness of her small, round belly.

She is still asleep.

All is calm when outside in a distant somewhere someone shouts against the winter. The voice is snatched at once and flung away, flapping at the edges but never unfolding.

Who could be out so late on Holy Night?

Who does Anna dream of?

Eyelids tell me nothing, yet her breasts push again against the quilt. Perhaps she is thinking of the senior in her firm. Peters? Paterson. Paterson, the one who wants to take her to New York.

What does he look like? There is no face, yet I imagine he is tall, with square-suited shoulders, and there is a voice, loud, level, confident, hailing a yellow buzzcab, a hand reaching out to lead her away.

Anna sighs, squirms her shoulders deeper into the bed.

Where will she sleep in New York? Some say you can still taste the death in the air after so many Hits. Anna says the Hits mean nothing. What's important is the city is legally bankrupt. Paterson believes the whole of the States needs laws, a seller's market.

I sense a tingling in Anna's skin and the room fills with a growl that grows until the tins of potion on her dresser tremble.

I listen alone until the vibrations are joined by the distant whine and grind and wheeze of huge machines. The net veil against the window is lit and a rectangular slab of pure and clean white slides across the ceiling, as quickly disappears back out into the night.

I know if I could tug the quilt out from beneath Anna's hip, and if I braved the cold floorboards, and if I looked outside through the grimy pane, I might glimpse the searchlights of the diggers.

In the first hours of the night I had listened to the whistle of the wind as it wrestled with the window and counted seven Hits. Now the diggers are busy. I imagine them charging ruined buildings, filling in smoking holes with entrails of stone and metal, soothing the scars with black soil, plugging gaps in the city by planting shrubberies and spiking the fresh, churned earth with mature trees.

When the sun rises tomorrow there will be more than one Morning Park.

Anna has slept through it all.

Only once did I ask, what did she think of the Holy Nights?

"Do you never think, what if? What if they actually bombed us here in this building?"

She shrugged her shoulders, said: "What's new, Jimmy Blue, what's ever new? No-one knows, no-one cares. Anyway, next year we'll be covered in weeds and trees and grass, that's all I know."

"It's not that bad. You make it sound as though we're being covered in countryside."

"Countryside? You're so quaint," she said and laughed. "Not bad? Every year it's like sitting through the last big act, except every Holy Night is bigger and bolder than the last one. Maybe next year we'll reach the grand finale in a theatre of natural cruelty. Before we know it, your dreadful little cottage will be our last bastion of civilisation. How do you like that for an image, Jimmy Blue? Do you like my green apocalypse?"

I smiled.

"Jimmy, really, I don't know. I don't even know where to step any more out there. Look at these new boots, ruined they are, scraped to the second skin. I'm the laughing stock. Do you know what it was? Mud! Right here in the city. From soil!"

"Soil! No, no, not the soil?" I wailed.

She laughed. A belly laugh so warm I hugged her there so that she was tickled into bending over, and when she stopped the smile was still strong on her lips and so I kissed her to test it.

I know I'm still the only one who can do that. Paterson can't do it.

A long, indistinct whine fills the air again, falls slow and sure into a distant scream and ends in a muffled kerrupmh.

For an instant, the winter holds its breath amid the horrible rumble of falling masonry.

Ten miles away, I reckon.

Anna stirs and her hair brushes my cheek.

"Mmm, yes, is it?" she asks.

I know not to reply. She isn't talking to me. She is asleep.

I wonder where she is.

For a while there is silence again and then the wind tugs at the window in its creaky frame. And the diggers rumble back into life.

****

EVERYTHING seemed fresh after Holy Night. As I walked behind Anna, down the scrubbed steps of the lobby that always smelled of bleach and out into the granite canyon, I felt the air beaten clean after last night's storm.

I held it empty and cold inside my chest before setting it free in joyful white plumes.

There were only a few early morning others in this grey half-light, white-suited runners, the kind who set their alarms for a minute after the end of Holy Night curfew, when the machines would be gone but the streets quiet.

Anna hurried and I ambled, content to watch her walk. She wore her tight black suit, the one that made her feel professional and made me feel proud as the skirt slid up around a stockinged thigh with each step. Around her throat was a white silk scarf that I knew she would not dare take off today.

We had not spoken of last night. The wild flowers were blue and black this morning.

She turned to me once on this block, urging me to hurry, and I smiled back, twice on the next and so I waved, and on the third she turned abruptly on her heel, too far from me to see if she had looked for my face, and disappeared down into the Mole Hole.

I sighed, told her I'd see her later, as a sudden gold lit the windows of the building beyond, making me blink. It took a second before my new corneas darkened. I blinked again.

The Morning Parks

There was a shadow on the reflection of the rising sun. An alien bird with vast wings. There were so few allowed now. The aeroplane arced above me until my neck ached. I closed my eyes and listened to the faraway, virile drone of the engines.

For half a dozen blocks, as the streets grew busy with commuters pinballing for the Mole, I traced the escaping vapour trail across the blue sky before discovering myself by a Morning Park.

There was neither railing nor wall, just patterns of circles where the brushes had scoured spilled soil from the paving, then an abruptness of frost-glazed grass. A path of shaved brown bark split the man-high clumps of yellow-flowering bush and taller trees that stood to attention like grey-skinned sentinels, waxy green leaves nervous in the light.

The path arrowed to a depression in whose concave an eye of black liquid gazed at the sky. That must be the crater. Perhaps the Hit was too deep for the machines to fill before curfew was lifted. It would be easier to pump the hole full of water.

The aeroplane scalpelled across its lens, leaving a blurred white cataract.

The park was the exact width of the space between McWhirter's Knowledge Store and a Siren Supermarket. What was missing? A sign had hung here? I should be able to remember the sign, at least. An aeroplane? Of course, the park had been the Global Travel Shop.

"What a waste!" gasped a ghost at my side.

I turned to the runner who wheezed between white breaths, wiped his pasty bald head with a sleeve of his white tracksuit, said, "Just what we need."

I nodded, turned back to the nearest tree and watched a droplet of water form on the tip of a bell. Its feathery pink tassels were thawing with the morning. Beyond the bell, between the branches, seated on a bench on the far side of the pool, I spied a figure.

He was dressed in a dark blue pin-striped suit and overcoat. His face was hidden below a black bowler hat. On his lap was a long black tube, an umbrella perhaps.

"What are they anyway? The trees, they smell like mouthwash," said the runner.

"I don't know" I replied, "And I don't know how can they live like this, I mean, bloom in the middle of winter? Where do they come from?"

I had not taken my eyes from the figure on the bench. He had produced a large pipe from his jacket pocket and, setting the bowl alight, proceeded to puff on it from below the brim of his bowler, sending out a thin wisp of blue smoke.

"Where, who cares?" said the runner. "Let's just hope next Night they don't get the Siren or we'll be eating the leaves. Here, what's that madman doing? Is he smoking?"

The droplet grew and grew and the plume of smoke ballooned bigger and bigger and drifted towards us until I could almost imagine I smelled its aroma, a strangeness of sweet, moist bark, when suddenly, from behind, there was a terrifying electronic howl.

We turned and I almost stumbled backwards on to the grass as a small brown animal lolloped into the middle of the street on huge paws, with eyes like black and white marbles, tongue lolling, flanks heaving hollow under blood-matted hair.

A second later a dozen buzzscoots raced around the corner, the riders' faces hidden by outsized goggles, red coats flapping behind. Their prey spied, a dozen crackling shockers were held aloft and the leader let out another blast from his horn.

The creature did not pause but ran straight towards us. It was only yards away. If it could make it past us, make it into the Park.

Instead it stopped, jerked back into the air with a strangled yelp, stifled as the wire lasso tightened. The thing lay gasping on the ground, its eyes on me, a front paw clawing for me.

The runner clapped and skipped forward for a closer view.

"Oh good, oh good!" he cried.

Immediately, I lost both runner and creature behind a wall of red backs but could hear a crackle and singe. I was surprised to find myself disgusted.

It must be hunger making me feel queasy. I turned back to the Morning Park but the bench was empty. The stranger in the bowler hat had disappeared.

I made my way the hundred yards to Osama's Pause, away from the smell of burning flesh and the hunters' chanting and the confusion in my stomach.

The cafe was empty post-curfew and for once there was no line for the Vendor. I pressed my thumb to the plastic fascia and listened for the klunk and hiss as the door opened to reveal a black flask.

I took my breakfast to a table by the window and right-ended a cup before plunging the cafetiere. There was a crunch of small bones as the contents mixed with the caffeine capsule. I hated that sound, could never bring myself to peer too closely into the glass.

I strained breakfast into the cup and sipped the hot, sweet blackness.

I knew I should head for the Mole.

Instead I watched a butterfly land on the window, inches from my face. A butterfly in January, with wings that were a diaphanous violet and yellow, dabbed with two spots of indigo, and legs that trembled under the nothingness of its own weight, and shiny blue globes that twitched on long, grey antennae.

I gazed at the wings and into the swirls of the colours until all I could see was their black-eyed centres and suddenly it was the dying creature's eyes that were staring back at me, rolling and pleading.

I jolted, spilling my cup over the table, and the butterfly rose and fluttered away across the road, flitting among the first of the day's buzzcars, over the red-streaked faces of the redcoat riders, and disappeared into the depths of the Morning Park.

****

IN the Mole Hole a green moss grows on the walls. It appears first in the cracks between the black, blast-proof tiles nearest the floor but spreads quickly, crawling to larger areas, corroding the plastic sheaths of the neon advertising boards, even fingering its way around the metal pillars of the bomb detection gates, until entire sections of tunnel are decorated entirely in a faintly luminous green sponge.

I'd always thought plants only grew where there was sunlight. As if I could know that for sure, and yet there has never been sunlight down here, where the moss was warm and wet beneath my fingers.

The stench of offal fled from the Mole and spewed forth from the tunnel ahead of its greasy white light and the shuddering of the ground.

It would take five minutes to reach Glasgow in the west of the city. Five minutes of hanging from the strap, inhaling other people's stale nerves. Five minutes staring at the white collar of the man in front of me as he mumbled figures into his wrist.

This morning, however, above the heads of the commuters, was a cloudless blue sky and into this firmament rose a solitary tower of grey rock, lapped on all sides by a sea of monstrous, cauliflower-headed treetops.

"Batavia: gateway to your dreams!" declared the banner's slogan.

My dreams? When sleep had rescued me from the Hits, I'd woken in an ancient city of archways, alleyways and impossibly angled buildings of polished jade. It was eternally night in my city and the rain had been falling forever. A man with wild, wet hair stood before me, a thin blade held low by his thigh, dripping red that swirled with the sapphire in the pools. We stood for a long time, saying nothing. The rain would not stop.

I'd woken to the sound of Anna running her shower.

Dreams. I gazed at the advertisement as a single marshmallow floated slowly across its sky and tried to remember more. Nothing. I wondered if the mountain, the trees, the cloud, any of Batavia was real.

I was wondering how anyone could reach the gateway of dreams when there were so few aeroplanes and no Global Travel Shop any more, when my attention was diverted by a black bulb bobbing through the heads, away from me, just as the Mole shot into the sudden white of Zero Station.

I pushed through for the opening doors but by the time I had alighted the man in the bowler hat had disappeared again.

No, there he was, just yards away, surrounded by another forest of Batavia, the rim of his hat turning upward, about to reveal his face, when the crush of the crowd swept me onward.

When, finally, I was able to look back all that remained was the peak of the grey giant left naked and alone in an empty blue sky.

****

I was late and Charlie Blake III was in one of his bullet moods.

"What's a barbecued spaniel gonna do for the points?" he cried. "Folks expect vermin to be burned off the streets. It's called hygiene."

I erased the first line from my screen, wrote the word spaniel, and waited for the next volley from across his desk.

"What else you got, Blue? What about this junkie actress with the transplant face. Do the old owner's family get a stake in the box office? What happens to the Oscar? Now there's juice!"

"Tizzy Carmen. She's filed for exclusive rights," I said.

"Another bloody plugger! What about the family?"

"Bought their story too. Double bill."

Charlie's face was a wrinkled red balloon that deflated a little more daily. He got up and paced the office floor like the air was even now leaking from him, his voice disappearing into a wheezy whisper.

"So what you got, Blue? What you got?"

He slumped back in his seat and I watched the golden cylinder spin through his fingers.

"What about the man I told you about, the smoker?"

"No, not the Parks again?" cried Charlie, clutching his bald brow, pulling his cheeks out. The golden cylinder fell on to the desk. We both stared as the bullet rolled against the edge of the vid-screen.

"But, Charlie, there are things growing wild and no-one cares. And, well, he was sitting there, in broad daylight."

"You know what, Blue, take the hint," said Charlie, picking up the bullet and testing its point. "No-one cares about the Parks. And if you feel that bad about a bloody pipe smoker make a complaint. Stop an Abidar and tell him to shoot the bastard on sight. Just move on."

I nodded and Charlie put the bullet in his shirt pocket.

"Right, Siren's opening something or other, place at Brunswick, so get it sorted. And don't forget to file a Box for Monday. Okay, you out, Stiles in."

"Stiles went a month ago, remember?"

"Yeah, yeah right, another bullet boy. So send in the fresh one," said Charlie, slumping further into his chair.

"Sam's day off, Charlie. Just you and me."

"Well, get out, Blue. I can't think with all your noise."

I closed the door behind me and walked across the empty office, past row upon row of blue pulsating screens. Charlie once told me that in the days of Blake I this place was full of coming and going, huge voices and manic energy rebounding off the glass walls. Now only the mute computers were busy, hounding stories from the pluggers, putting them into house style, slotting everything into pages.

I ran the day's InfoDat from Siren, a series of stat graphs and holopics of smiling customers. I thought again about the man in the Park. I looked up spaniel. It was a kind of dog. I thought about last night's Hits and wondered again why I'd never been able to read any survivors' stories.

Finally, before leaving, I filed a Fame Box. The programme selected an accidental hero story, the one where a child is saved from a virused buzzcar by an unwitting bystander, and pulled a name from the city register. Congratulations, Mark Hume, Monday's hero and big cash prizewinner.

I stopped briefly by Charlie's office. There was no noise. I poked my head around the door to find him asleep on the sofa in the corner. He wouldn't be going home tonight.

****

THE night was especially cold and I wanted to walk with my thoughts through the streets, but the lamps pre-empted me, directing me to the Mole Hole. I stopped and waited until the last white light had timed out, then phoned Anna.

"I saw a spaniel killed on the way to work. It's a kind of dog."

"A what? Listen, it's hard to hear you."

"Where are you, it sounds like a party?"

Cut off.

There was soft pop as the nearest lamp relit, urging me onward and home. Instead, I veered down an alleyway on the right, away from the sudden whoosh of a buzzcar behind me, and made my way to McNabb's. There I listened to the drone of city workers and sipped an acrid meatbeer. And another.

Above the bar a spider's eye screen was showing the huge orange blossoms of the Hits, followed by serene images of the Morning Parks.

My phone lit but I ignored the call. I was annoyed at Anna, though I wasn't sure why. I thought I might go home and listen to music, the antique discs I'd discovered in The Strand, but knew I'd stay.

After an hour I returned Anna's call.

"I told you weeks ago I had to be here. Anyway, listen, Jimmy, I'm going to New York. It's been agreed at last, the sales mission."

I saw Paterson caressing Anna into the back of a buzzcab.

"Mission? Look, do you want to meet me at McFab's? We can eat here."

"It's McNabb's and it's near ten. And, no, you're not listening, there's a work thing. Listen I've got to go. Tom wants me to meet some people. I'll phone, okay?"

"It's Tom?"

I cut the link and thumbed the bar until the Vendor hissed at me and delivered another meatbeer. This one tasted smoother. New York. I recalled the aeroplane and how so incredibly far away the engines had sounded. I thumbed the bar.

A long time later my phone rang so I ignored the call. I didn't want to hear her shouting down the line to tell me about Tom. Not tonight. Anyway, it would make her think I was hurt and miss me. Like the way I was hurt and missed her.

Later, hours and miles away in the cottage, I woke and fumbled automatically for the phone by my bed. The history showed I'd tried to call twice but her link was off.

I think my silences made me miss her more.

****

Chapter Two

The Art of Silence

I HAD always believed the wonder of a story begun could still spellbind the way it did when we were children, wide-eyed and without too many fingerprints on our brains. When long dark nights and a disembodied voice meant the whole, wide world was an adventure just beginning and the impossible was only that sleep should come too soon.

I long believed a story was a treasure, more precious than urns of fire stolen from the Sun on pirate ships, more rare than silver apples grown in the orchards of the Moon, that, though we cannot hold its weight in our hands, a story would surely fill our ears with the beyondness of things, spill an exotic melange on the tongue, drum alien thunder home into the heart. That's what I believed.

Charlie Blake III set me straight.

"We don't need stories any more, Blue, we only need their juice. Doesn't matter where you wring it from, the roots, the shit, the mess, just so long as readers like its flavour."

Charlie told me, too, that Anna preferred her juice served neat and always, always on time.

By then the silence between us had grown more than two weeks old.

I screen mailed her but even then I did not tell my story. Instead I told her to pick up the phone because we needed to talk, that my story needed to be heard, that some stories should not be kept alone in the dark too long, they can affect us so much we have to expose the truth clawing at our insides, regurgitate it and re-examine it, pass it on for someone else to taste. In other words, I told her: welcome to my vomit.

Maybe I thought Anna would like such straightforwardness. She was a law broker, after all, albeit one who didn't like mud on her shoes. She was not one of those people, despite her outbursts, who could have sympathy for on-your-knees emotion.

She was, I know now, a girl whose heart might be made of secrets, like the former boyfriend she refused to discuss, the Abidar. Her smile, however, told everyone here was life alive, fluttering and exciting and glossy, and, hey, if you weren't a subscriber, she'd know and smile all the same. But only because it was your loss.

I'd signed up the moment she set eyes on me two years ago.

"Jimmy, this is Anna, a friend of someone or other," pants Charlie, in passing, pursing the bristles around his mouth.

"Hi," says she.

High, says I, as a kite without string, smiling at my own clever image, reaching out to take her hand. But she stumbles, and, giggling, upsets the table of drinks laid on by our hosts at the Siren Stars Singalong. I steady her, my fingertips sliding against the wet silk of her dress, into the softness of her side, as she slips by me.

It's been two weeks since she told me of New York and I am beginning to wonder when I will touch the softness of her again, cup both hands around the back of her head and curl my fingers into her hair, like running your fingers through a spill of cool fire, I told her on our first night, and feel the heated strain of her breath against my face as I close my fist.

Now I trace my fingers through a holopic, making the image fizz and blur, and ask myself how it can be that suddenly I've been losing this girl for such a long time.

Around me are the ancient stone walls of Carmelwood Cottage. The agent told me they were built for a farm worker hundreds of years ago when there were still enough fields for the animals. Persuaded from their garish, gentle-aged clothes, they are blank swathes of white where once upon a time their last owner had patted down soft antique wallpaper of tangled yellow flowers over her three-scored year memories.

"They were his favourites, lad," Mrs Betty Highgate told me on the morning I came down for the viewing, and her trembling hands traced an invisible face into the pattern. "Grew them in the garden, too, every summer, back when we were allowed, of course. You won't remember. Every summer 'til his last."

In the bedroom, where Betty had lain younger and stronger with this man who brought forth such incredible bursts of life, where I would lie with Anna and strive to make our own, the damp had scowled through the swirls of yellow petal, reaching for the husband who was gone from the room and this earth for 22 years.

I thought Anna might want to keep the paper. She liked yellow. She took one look and began tearing it from the wall, bringing chunks of plaster crashing on to the floorboards. It took us days to remove the bandages from the walls. It was as though the cottage was being scraped bare of its skin, scabs, scars and all, and it would twist and turn from our hands until they were left nicked by the slip of the scraper and rubbed raw by sugar water.

"Sugar water's what you need, lad, if you mean to take off his flowers. That's the way we did it when I was a lass. But he loved his flowers, did Bill."

Anna finally poured the sugar water into the giant thorny tangle of overgrown roses and bought rolls of chemical peel. We sanitized the entire building in an hour.

Everything looks white and clean now. And quite startlingly empty.

****

IT is three weeks since we last spoke and a day after I last heard Anna's voice on my mail. It is the day after I find my lungs transplanted by two sheets of wet paper, the day after Anna has told me in one sentence our relationship has ended, the day after I learn from Charlie that she is already in New York and will be staying, and I wander the streets near Zero Station, past the Morning Parks and incidental shops, walking into winter with the cold already too deep inside of me.

I marvel that there are people all around with so few broken pieces inside of them, so whole that they can take the time to stop and debate the merits of direct debit charity with a drama student in her yellow vest of the day.

"Excuse me, do you have a minute for the orphans of Batavia?"

The girl is floating backwards in front of me on her buzzboard, her voice soothing and familiar but her body offending my senses. She stops suddenly, proffers a metal badge, no, pushes it instead into my coat pocket.

"Sorry, not today," I say to the thick veil of knotted yellow dreadlocks. "I'm not really shopping, you see, because my heart is drowning and I need to find a life jacket."

Actually, I say nothing, but sidestep her and enter the shop. An antique bell tinkles above my head as the door opens into the musky room. It is miraculous The Strand stands at all, an island in the midst of Parks, four one-storey walls that hide a tight, befuddled maze of shelves overflowing with anachronisms, paper-style books and plastic music discs.

When finally I find it, the life jacket's spine is cracked and the pages loose, but the cover is a surreal portrait of a beautiful young girl, her black hair combed into a shiny bob, a single tear running from one black-lashed eye down through the apple of a rouged cheek. It is a love story, I know, though I don't open the book, for the blurb on the back tells me of a man named Gatsby. I stare at the cover again and suddenly know what I have to do.

****

I DRAG a stool up to the bar of McNabb's, trying to ignore the throat-tightening aroma wafting from a nearby veal cafietere, and wonder how to begin.

I trace the lines of my new moleskin bound notepad, whose makers vow is modelled on the books that inspired writers of old to share their secrets, with my heart beating too fast in my fingers for there to be much sense in it at all.

Sense in what? Where do I begin?

I wonder is it okay to take the girl's tear-streamed face from my coat pocket or might I attract the attention of the hulking Abidar, so that he'll remove his black-sheened rump from the wall where he is wiping the insides of his nose on to the Vendor control panel. He thinks because he watches everyone that no-one can see him. The green light of his gun flashes in its holster and his mirrored sunglasses swivel the room towards me and I look away quickly.

I rummage around until my fingers pull out a hard button, the badge. Strange. Whatever face it once showed for the cause of Batavian orphans must have fallen off. All I see in the now bare metal are a pair of tiny eyes, tired and cold.

I stare into those eyes until I remember my dream, the one of the ancient city, where fire-haired love was stolen in a world of darkness and rain, where madness had erupted from the heart of a man and only the red edge of his sword could bring justice. Did someone tell me this story? Its voices seem beyond me.

I'm swirling the beginning of these thoughts into my second meatbeer when a man, ginger unshaven, potato-cheeked, dumps his shopping on the stool next to mine, but one hemp-woven bag falls on to the floor with a single, ominous crack.

The man stands bowlegged and shocked still, and he bends stiffly and peers into the bag and then turns his crimson face to the lady at the nearest table, who flicks her hair at him with her red nails.

The Abidar shuffles a few steps nearer, his huge glasses tilted towards the mirror on the ceiling.

So the man slowly lifts the bag. It rattles. He replaces it gently on top of his lumpy grocery carrier, pats down the edges, and takes his seat, and I'm thinking ha, ha, ha, anyway, so that's someone else in the world with broken bits.

Then I notice the man's hand is shaking as he stirs the blackness in his cup, round and round, again and again, round, and I spy the terrible cheapness of the tartan-strapped kid's phone on his thin wrist, the value tin of cloned peas peeking shyly from his bag, and when I sneak a glance up across the table, I'm shocked to see that he's standing on a cliff, about to fall in to tears, and when he becomes aware of me he touches his brow hurriedly and kneads the wet furrows with the back of his hand.

I see, quite suddenly, that he is an old man.

And I realise that in the bag is someone's birthday present, and he's travelled all the way into the heart of the city on the Mole, a special trip, and he was pleased as punch to get this gift, perhaps it's exactly what his wife would like, and then he got the week's shopping for her, to boot, and thought he'd have a nice sit-down cup as a reward, special too and, hang the cost, even if he already has her favourite Siren brew in the bag.

And now the gift is broken into bits. And her birthday will come too soon. And the Abidar is looking directly at him. The red light of his gun glows red. Maybe the old man has forgotten to take his ID card with him.

I want to reach out to touch his hand, still the tremors, and tell him it's okay, and maybe he can persuade the girl at shop to take back the gift, replace it, maybe I can distract the Abidar. All I have to do is spill my drink. He'll have to fine me.

I don't do any of this, of course. I get up with my own broken pieces and walk out of the bar. I leave the old man with his story unshared inside him because I'm embarrassed and a coward and I cannot stop the tears from my own eyes.

Even the clip-screen teenager hovers in silence and allows me to pass without a word, but in my head I scream at her because what can dreadlocks and direct debits do when the world allows such loneliness?

****

SAFELY inside Carmelwood, the only building for miles in what they now call the Old Parks, I breathe and I breathe, and when I am calm, I promise myself that I know what to do. I sit at the desk before the latticed window and stare at the rose heads, brown and misshapen and forgotten.

I take the fountain pen and ink jar from their wooden box, the last gift left me by my parents, and I write: *I knew a girl whose heart was always such secrets, yet whose smile told everyone she met that here was life alive.*

I stop and dip the pen.

If there is such a smile in your own mind right now, let it make your heart laugh for the rest of the days. If the laughter makes the rain feel warm on your face and the sound of the traffic become a medley of comic trumpets, remember. Because if such joy can come from these small tendernesses, then everything is going to be okay.

I read my words, try to imagine small tendernesses and realise I can't think of any and don't know what I'm talking about. This isn't my story. It certainly isn't Anna's. She doesn't need a book for a mirror. She sees enough of herself already. I try again.

In the beginning, I should have guessed that words are not the only liars; silences can speak falsely. If I had spoken out loud, when I still held her attention, I could have told her my story.

No, this is wrong too. A story must begin with heroes and heroines, characters who do not like to examine their own innards in company, and it must have villains, who would like nothing more, and, Anna, I promise you, it must have mystery.

Charlie Blake III is wrong to leave behind the soil and the roots and the branches and the growing. The rags and the bones make the magic.

Imagine rags and bones, Anna.

IMAGINE the graves below your thin window are not dead, that in their hearts they laugh and scream. You lie asleep in darkness dancing when the wind slides in, cups cold hands around your head, and fingers worm inside your dreams. How the earth begins to crawl, and now you hear the scraping stones sigh slipping over secret halls where silver veils are slowly bled; their voices are not far below, a thousand lives untelling all, burning in their shadows a thousand loves are wed amid the joyous rattlebag of bones.

See the broken hillside stained by the cloying wash of a December moon and naked air hisses through the trees, trying to silence the disembodied sounds of the ancient city far away below.

Hush! Listen to the graves!

Now the stones tremble like teeth in black gums touched by some giant hidden tongue, and the dry bones huddle terrified in their prisons just beneath. In their shrunken, hollow hearts they silent scream.

An unseen violence is surging upward, devouring the earth. A madness is bubbling, howling nearer, nearer, seeking escape.

Tonight, the fury bursts free.

See the deep erupts high into the night, a hatred blacker than the starless sky.

And it smells life.

Life, the juice of rags and bones, and it pours from the dark night of my nightmare, Anna, into this moleskin notebook. Whose life?

Down through the midnight streets, a screaming that pierces the bare soul, plunges through neon explosions, red, yellow, white, into the heat of the heart of the city, beating insanely with the force of a million lives, past astonished faces, laughing at fear in round hysterical eyes where innocence is burned black, and down, down through the maze of bedlam voices, on, and on, to the doors.

They shatter, cast aside by one thought in a thousand shards of fire.

Stop.

Silence.

A breath of heavy incense whispers out into the square and is lost in the cold night.

Enter here. Slowly.

Here, where the vastness of space is barely encompassed by the cathedral walls, heavens hang from the dome, candles burn a thousand thousand glinting eyes like suns far off in those melanic corners of other worlds.

Only the click of slow steps echo, a soft breathing.

Pause.

The high altar is touched by a single flame. A shadow slides across the red cloth, as a drip drops slow circles in black mirror depths of the font. Over there, below the furthest arch, in the deepest recess, stands a figure.

A pale hand reaches out, tentatively, is dipped into the water, testing.

At once the fat blackness of the air is torn, shriven by the silver throats of a hundred angels, and the figure turns.

Janu's young face, open curtained by brown curls, offers eyes full of blue. The touch of the holiness glistens on his brow, spreads darkly across the broad crimson silk of his chest, washes the golden wings of the King's eagle.

See now the cathedral swells with voiceless, shuffling people. Their taffeta colours spill around him, seeking proper places for the High Mass, merge finally into shades of brown and coarser cloth huddled together in their warm aroma of closeness, fearful and almost paralysed in the shaft of dust-hazed light between the doors.

Through all he sees Rosalia.

Softness of summer moving through the shadows. The gold braids spill from beneath the blue velvet, half-hiding her eyes. Her cloak is clasped at the white of her throat with the golden orb he once gave, so long ago, it seems now an ancient time. But she has passed and his skin waxes cold as these mortal ghosts coil so close.

He is kneeling invisible three rows behind and all through the litany his eyes burn through to the picture of her face, and the incomprehensible drone becomes lost in circles of circles of itself and sinks into the mute murmur of the throng.

He watches when she kneels at the rail and the blue folds fall around her shoulders and he is lost in flames. Does the Cardinal's hand tremble before the girl's upturned face? Beautiful fragility.

Is any of this real?

Perhaps it is as real as my head and heart will allow, for my tale of the swordsman and my life of a writer come close entwined now. No matter from what dusty dead end of The Strand's labyrinth or half-remembered dream I may have learned of his ancient city or heard whispered his name, I would like to believe Janu is more myself than I would waking admit.

Now I can almost feel the gentleness of Rosalia's whisper on my cheek, as if, Anna, you were here in this room, in the bare-walled cottage, standing behind me, letting your hair spill on my shoulders, here where there are no Hits, no hunting parties, no strangers or Abidar.

I feel happier, for I can see now that these walls are not at all bare but dappled cream and yellow by a sunshine that has touched far beyond my own ken, perhaps warmed more lives and lit deeper mysteries than this winter afternoon can know. I could have learned so much more from Mrs Betty Highgate, had I thought to ask.

The sun is in my eyes and I must squint at the words as I write.

The afternoon was blinding. Janu, stood with Giraud, aside of the steps, impatient, as the city poured gratefully through the cathedral doors, out in gurgled drops into the yellow air.

You do know how pathetic you look? Giraud wiped red wisps from his eyes and shifted his wide hat again. August's gaze burned his cheeks.

A fellow Guard bested by a girl!

But Janu smiled. Victory in love is complete surrender.

Victory in . . .? cried Giraud. Poetry now? Then what of duty? We have a duty to all the innocent women of this city. Truly, you should put aside this fascination with unrequited lust. No, I've seen you gape. But look now! You've missed her.

Rosalia had indeed passed and was already in the boiling of the square below. At once, the perfect circle of the Cardinal bubbled into focus, miraculously dilated amidst parasols and preening.

The girl and that ubiquitous Choufos woman curtsied before the bulging purple. Rosalia drew back the hood of her robe and touched her lips to the nuncio's fingers and Cardinal Marlov's swollen face curdled.

Foxed by a man in a frock! cried Giraud in delight.

Janu was already striding down the steps. He stopped in the Cardinal's shadow and stood, an imbecile's grin, facing the girl.

And with all these young questioning, do they say libertines, yes? No? Well we find it, I must say, most encouraging, most rewarding, yes, to see you, intoned Cardinal Marlov, as though reciting yet from his book, and Rosalia blushed as her eyes flitted to the figure behind. She coughed to cloak her smile, and the Cardinal turned slowly to Janu whose eyes were screwed in divine rapture, mouth open to the wide, welcoming heaven.

Tired, Monsieur?

Janu opened one eye.

Your Eminence.

He stumbled forward and bowed most extravagantly. Marlov raised his hand and Janu puckered his mouth to the fabulously fat fingers. And then he looked to the girl, said, Mademoiselle Rosalia de Graci. He took her slim hand to his lips and he held her fingers there.

Confused curls leaned suddenly up into the girl's shoulder, followed by a half-moon face, tilted absurdly beneath a lemon wig. A thin slug arched its wiry back across the powdered brow. Rosalia's hand fell gently to her side.

And the handsome Madame Choufos, breathed Janu, and Rosalia coughed violently. But of course the two most -

Monsieur! interrupted the Cardinal. A pleasure indeed, yes, I must say, but I would speak with the Mademoiselle! Yes?

Of course, my infinite pardon. The work of the church is everlasting.

Choufos' head wobbled forward on its stalk. And have the Guard no duties to attend?

My sword is ever sharp for such deeds, dear lady! But surely not on the Lord's day? Marlov breathed loudly into his kerchief and Rosalia half turned away.

But I see I must go. Until very soon, Your Eminence. My Lady.

Janu smiled once, bowed, and walked off to find Giraud. And Rosalia watched him until he was lost among the happy crowd and she squeezed tightly the warm scrap he had slipped under her fingers.

I wonder how you might feel, if tomorrow I caught one of those rare and fabulous aeroplanes and appeared without warning in your New York office. I'm sure it is perched high enough above any loitering memory of me.

I wonder, if I stood by your desk surrounded by your new colleagues with open mouths and twitching elbows, eager like a huddle of hunger-mawed chicks, what you might say?

What would happen if I smiled once only, just once, and slipped these scraps of thoughts beneath your fingers?

Might you be intrigued by a tale more abstract than screenmails, attracted by a romance less intrusive into the daily habit of your need to smile and sell laws, tempted by the promise of a lovemaking that allowed both of us to breathe?

What would you make of Janu, who, after all, has only to wait?

Alone on a low bridge, arms outstretched along the roughness of the wooden rail, and watching the sky fall below. His face was a wavering splash of white, crowned by the jagged leaves of the trees, wonderfully, hideously, hysterically transformed.

He was still smiling and it was more than the warm day, the quiet sound of laughter from far across the unkempt lawns; he was lost in the waiting, in the sense of expectation in this tightening of his chest whenever he knew she would soon be near. So suddenly entranced once more by this astonishment of loving.

Rosalia? Rosa. These strange moments were each waking from some dreamless sleep. To touch, to breathe, to know.

But of course it was worthy of risk. Though Giraud would never tire of trying to gorify the danger. If Captain Cindecis should discover? This girl of no family, s'truth, and linked to the Cardinal? Why, his skin would be used to cover books in the Palace library. If even Choufos should know the truth! He would be wise to seek hasty passage to lands unknown for fear of her shrieking and her scratching.

Janu cared not for such thoughts; obstacles best ignored to be overcome.

Turn now. To see Rosalia walk towards him through the waves. Chains and rings of gold tumble before her smile and eyes silver beyond blue, and the summer light through soft slipping folds of her dress caresses softer lines, and in her hands is a book.

Her treasured book, and he hears her whispering, half lisping the unfamiliar, sometimes stumbling, and her shy laughter whenever he sighs.

Good day, my lady!

She was surprised.

Why, sir, do I know you? You have the face of the same young man I saw mock his Eminence this day!

Not I! An impostor, surely?

Well, he had the same ill humour. Oh, and I see the very sword of which he jested, and she tugged at his scabbard.

Now it was his place to blush and he looked around, hastily whispering her name, taking her by the arm and leading her across the bridge, down the narrow stone steps to the river's edge.

Isn't the King's man a funny red?

In the quiet beyond the city afternoon they sat on a giant's skimming stone half-hidden among the bowing trees. For a long time simply watching the silver rushing by. And she reading to him. And the day softening into crimson.

Her head was bowed deep inside the pages and her hair fell forward, concealing her face. Only the silence sometimes sighed when her words were taken rudely by the breeze.

She had chosen a new tale for today, the fantasy of a warrior who searched for his stolen love across all the world, known and unknown, who wandered alone through alien lands, growing ever older, but always dreaming fulfilment of his heart was just beyond his reach, brushed inches from the tips of his fingers, until all he could speak of was the remembrance of a name, now known only by the careless winds, always beyond . . .

Rosalia's voice was a whisper. Always just beyond. But truly his courage could never die, and on, and on he travelled across the sea of fire, and beyond ... beyond ... and she stopped.

Janu touched her hand, but she did not move, did not lift her head, did not speak.

Rosa?

Was it a soft tremor that passed across her shoulders just now?

Rosalia, what is it?

She looked up then. She met his gaze for only one last instant and he could see the hurt in the blue glistening.

The story, she said, quickly turning away, just that.

Rosa, please. Look at me.

She did so, but her eyes were closed upon beads of silver.

Janu, we cannot live forever in storybooks. She hesitated. Promise me you would not waste your life seeking the impossible, not like some foolish poet, not lost in some fanciful writer's dream.

Rosa? He held her to him, for the longest time, touched his lips to the softness of her own, held her until they were wholly closed one into the other. He whispered then, I would follow you beyond the sun.

He felt the firmness of her breasts rise.

And the water chuckled nervously to itself, having shivered under the bridge and emerged safe, only to be surprised by the figures of two lovers. Perhaps the sun would be forgotten and its dangerous life washed into these ripples. Perhaps only the cloth formed of invisible bonds would be warmth enough tonight.

Rosa, why do you never speak of your own? I still ... I don't understand. Why can't you simply leave Choufos?

Broken, her whole body, it seemed suddenly, with her head against his chest, cradled by his hands, her being staring into the river as she spoke.

You know she is my family. She has been with me for so long. Since . . .

Rosalia freed herself from his arms. But it is so late, Janu! I must go. I'm so sorry, sorry for all of this.

Sorry?

She stood up at once, pressing flat the front of her dress, and she passed the back of her hand across her face, as if more annoyed with herself.

Anyway, you really must stop me getting in a state over words in a book! All this? This is a fantasy, no more.

And he knew she would not thank him to inquire further. So much still hidden from him. A girl whose heart was such secrets.

As they walked the long path through the trees to the gates his hand sought hers and she squeezed his fingers in reply. But they did not speak and the evening grew old and grey and draped crooked arms around their shoulders. Rosalia was lost in her own thoughts and he walked outside, feeling her disquiet but unable to look for her beyond this subtle touch of skin.

Suddenly her hand fell from his and she broke from him, walking with head bowed to the stutter of her tiny steps.

Janu almost called out but spied the figure shrivelled on the path ahead, and, though her thin, pointed head was indistinct in the jaded light, he knew beyond doubt it was Madame Choufos.

He stepped quickly aside into the deeper shadows of the trees and watched, and he believed he spied her face split as she greeted Rosalia. She had been watching them all this time? All this day?

When Rosalia reached her the woman turned and scuttled away through the gates. Rosalia followed at once. And she did not look back.

Just as I know now that you did not look back the day you walked away from me into the Mole Hole, Anna, your gaze burrowing down into the long corridor that would end in never returning.

****

Chapter Three

Walking On

I HOPED with every step of my own that I must surely think of you less, but every step brings you back to mind. Today I tried to lose you in a curving corridor of crimson light, but it was clotted by hermetically sealed entrances, each metal sphincter flanked by two black-uniformed Abidar, their gun lights red as they scanned our IDs. One by one the gateways opened and our straggled party marched deeper underground.

Room 102 evidently was a very long way beneath the City's biggest Siren Supermarket.

"Hit-proof, fresh produce, no delivery costs," explained The Manager. He was 12 years old at most and, no doubt, one of the new fast-track sci-students from Siren's University, where you told me you had finished your first thesis, Anna.

"But where are the products brought in?" I asked, trudging behind him. "I mean the food?"

"The animals? They are here already, Mr Blue," said The Manager in an adolescent whistle.

"Live animals? Here? Don't they need stuff? Water? Daylight? I mean the air, it's so hot."

I tugged at the seam of my enormous anti-contamination suit, which was sticking to my thighs. The Manager turned his back on my questions and led our disjointed caterpillar of bloated, white bodies through another gateway, and on and down we went.

The other members of the ten-strong corps, pluggers mostly, looked immensely bored. One stroked and pinched an eyebrow until a black glove suddenly covered his face. We'd been warned there would be no recording. The wide-eyed offender crumpled as he was swung from the ground between two Abidar and hauled away unconscious. Not a word had been spoken.

His departure did not trouble his companions. One complained he had missed lunch because he thought there would be a tasting.

Another gateway dilated into a pink-walled tube that narrowed to a red plastic portal. It puckered before us with a soft sucking sound and, one by one, we clambered into an enormous chamber.

So thick was the lemon-white light, every movement, already encumbered by the suits, was laboured and slow. The room itself was massive, almost a subterranean Park, but instead of trees there were thousands of glass cylinders rising from the ground. Every tube was a different size, the smallest barely knee high and a foot across, the tallest the height of a man and the width of a buzzcar, but from each came the same eldritch illumination.

All around us pastoral scenes came alive on the walls, oceans of green grass, constantly changing, morphing into acres of wildflowers, and spreading into the blue skies and white clouds of the vaulted ceiling.

We had landed on the surface of a miniature planet.

"Welcome to Room 102, the City's first integrated Food Lab, ladies and gentlemen," said The Manager.

"But where are we?" asked a plugger.

"What is this place?" asked another.

"This, ladies and gentlemen, is the delivery room."

"But the animals? Where do they come in?" I asked, peering into the nearest cylinder.

"Mr Blue evidently chose not to read the InfoDat," The Manager reported to the assembly. "If you look more closely, Mr Blue?"

He tapped a large, chest-high cylinder. I stepped forward and stared into its milky interior and, slowly, horrifyingly, began to suspect there was a shape inside, the outline of a body, the semblance of something pulsating, alive. And then it was there, solid, floating before me. The foetus of a small cow.

"The beginning of your steak, Mr Blue, the origin of your meatbeer, the template for the sofa in your apartment. All of these cylinders contain similarly fresh products."

The foetus blurred before me. I could not think what to say, so I said, "Do they have names?"

The boy looked up at me, his thin smile tipped by a moustache of pimples, and said, "Names are unnecessary."

He stroked the side of the cylinder and the body inside trembled.

"There can be no waste," he told us. "Every product is grown in its own womb. Some are small, others large, each one designed specifically for texture and taste. And this is where the food stays until the day of delivery when, plop, it falls into a funnel below for processing, then, whoosh, it's straight up to the shelves upstairs."

There was a pounding inside of me now, rising not just into my chest, but my head and along my arms to my fingers, rolling into my eyes, making the surface of the planet Room 102 pulsate.

Perhaps the others felt this way, too, for all had stopped their inspections and turned in slow motion to look at The Manager.

"Ah, you feel the Drum," he said, "It helps production. We can't say why. Not yet, at least. We will. The produce can't see, of course, but put pretty pictures on the ceiling and they grow faster. They can't hear. Fill the air with the ultrasonic beat of the Drum and they calm down."

"Calm down?" I asked. "You mean they can get violent? How can they possibly get violent?"

"Mr Blue?" came a sigh from behind me. I turned to find a young girl standing before me in a hip-hugging white skirt and precariously low blouse. There was a paper hat on her head decorated with a red cross. "Perhaps you would like to sample one of our new products?"

The nurse was carrying a tray of glass vials filled with a clear liquid.

"No, no thank you," I said. "I need to…I'll just look around."

She smiled and moved to the others and The Manager gripped my arm.

"Perhaps, then, you would like to see Mother?"

"Mother?"

The child led me in a slow, heavy-legged stroll through the gardens of cylinders until we reached the largest tube, set apart from all the others.

"Meet Mother," he said, "Mother, this is Mr Blue."

He turned to me as if I might proffer the glass tube a hand to shake, shrugged, said, "She's spliced from the original coma candidate. Cloned again and again, of course, to make all these beautiful babies."

I stepped closer until my nose was against the glass and squinted into the creamy fluid. The indistinct form floated in there, held by a slender tube. Here was a hoof, now the thickening of the thigh, and the long bovine body, slowly rotating in the liquid, until from the ether came the neck and a head, the face, the nose and mouth of a human, formed and quite distinct, with heavily-lidded, closed eyes. Suddenly, the eyes opened, stared straight into me, wide and angry and terrified."

"A woman!" I cried. "A human woman. She's looking at me."

"Impossible, Mr Blue," tutted The Manager, turning me, pushing the small of my back, ushering me back to the others. "They never grow to full gestation. Not even Mother. That way they're fresh."

"But the head was human," I insisted

Several of the pluggers turned to me, laughing and shaking their heads.

"Read your InfoDat next time," said one.

The nurse began handing out another round of vials, this time brimming with chocolate-coloured fluid.

"It's fresh," she smiled at me.

"Excuse me, the rest room?"

Inside my cubicle I turned both taps and the sink swirled with water and chlorine. I splashed the mix on my face until my eyes streamed and my skin tingled and looked pink in the mirror.

Before emerging from Room 102, another InfoDat was handed to each of us. I knew that when I slotted it into my computer it would reformat itself and be ready, styled for the page broadcasts.

When I reached the office, however, I did something strange. I slid the InfoDat into the shredder slot and began typing my own account of our journey underground. I had no idea why. It felt right.

Home now in the cottage, I sip whisky from the bottle I found hidden, long ago, in the attic of Carmelwood Cottage. Not from Siren, illegal, perhaps Bill Highgate's secret, it makes my throat burn but it feels right too.

Although I think of you, you do not phone.

Finally, I fall asleep but do not dream of you, Anna, or of Janu. I dream of green fields and blue skies and a world that pulsates to the beat of a giant Mother heart, at whose centre is trapped the face of a young woman, who stares at me all night with angry, frightened eyes.

****

SERENITY comes often in my sleep now, even though I find myself in the dark city streets of my dreams. But it does not last. I think sometimes I see your face before I see the morning light. Even now, hanging among Batavia's blue skies in the Mole, you appear unannounced in my thoughts, to begin conversations we finished months ago.

I begin to find it strange, now that I'm alone again, that I could have lived so long apart from a stranger who would have such an impact upon my ability to breath properly.

Imagine so many hours in days when lives are lived without even the knowledge of another's existence. How many of these Mole riders know their neighbours in the next apartment? We cannot even look each other in the eye as we travel to work. Why should it surprise or concern me then that no-one ever speaks of those who are lost on Holy Night?

I don't know if I myself care.

Truth be told, rarely now do I recall with confidence or enthusiasm moments or thoughts of worth that do not hold you by my side. Not the first night my father let me stay awake on Holy Night and told me the distant thuds were the hooves of a lost tribe of monstrous horsemen. Not the graduation day when I scandalised peers and mentors with a stuttering speech about the need to rediscover books and their forgotten trothes. Not Bernie, the first real girlfriend, from Cashelan, not even my first story published by Charlie Blake III, nothing.

Slowly, I realise that from the moment I allowed the thought of you to be dipped into my heart, it had been there forever, as tangible and real and important as the beat. Any personal battle hard fought was now without purpose, every professional plan made but knocks on a door I no longer wanted to open.

My only focus now had become this masterplan of an imaginary life. Janu's.

> *HIS hands were clasped behind his back and the point danced and cavorted so teasingly, tracing coquettish circles before his eyes, sliced into his forehead.*
>
> *Janu reached up with one finger as heat trickled down across his the bridge of his nose. He grimaced, lifted his right knee and kicked hard. Immediately his attacker's slab-toothed smile chomped on a curse as he crumpled to the ground, clutching himself, and his sword clattered heavily onto the flagstones.*
>
> *Another man leapt forward, cried out wildly as he made to strike, but Janu had recovered his balance and deflected the first raw blow on the flat of his blade. Sweat and blood stung his vision, screwing his eyes, but a wide grin opened his face, and he lunged forward, plunging as though straight for the chest before him.*
>
> *The man stumbled, losing one foot in the moaning pile of limbs below, and with a grunt fell backwards and down.*
>
> *Janu whirled to catch the third blade almost in his curls, and with both white fists around his hilt, flung the offending weapon in an arc, baring his attacker's silk. At once his steel was against a throat's white bobbing and black seized the eyes of the man before him.*

Janu? Janu! Stop playing with the infants and come up here! The Captain wants to see you.

A triumphant flurry of red hair was followed by Giraud's face on the balcony above. But that face was unusually grey with ill humour.

Janu let the tip slide slowly and nodded.

Henri, but all good things . . .

The man sniggered, nervously, saw Janu's smile, laughed. Time to see the master, Janu! Maybe Cindecis wants golden boy to lunch?

With luck he wants his head for lunch. The limbs on the ground behind them untangled amid much grunting of curses and Calan heaved himself onto his feet. Then these so-called practice sessions could end.

Just master your swords, my friends, and you can end them yourselves.

Janu strode from the courtyard and vaulted the marble of the grand staircase.

Hurry yourself! said Giraud. He's in a filth-ridden mood.

When they reached the door Giraud clasped his arm.

Remember, don't be rash! His temper is quick but today it's also heavy.

Always! Always you worry! The fire in your hair has singed your brain, my friend. Wait for me in Porio's. Your full tankard for my lurid tale.

And the door was open and closed and Janu gone.

Captain Cindecis' back denied light from the window even though his lion's head was bowed to the courtyard. Janu stood in the silence.

Do come in, said Cindecis. I've always found your social graces match your sword manners.

Thank you. Truly my sword is my guide in all - Mother of! Cindecis turned. Already I have heard enough. These schoolboy banalities . . . such ill-conceived humour is the reason you're here before me.

The Captain's silver beard only put a firmer edge on his jaw, his eyes were dirty ice, yet now he hesitated.

I watched how you toyed with those men - hah, those boys - below. Yes, now I see also the cut above your eye. Just sometimes, Janu, you are good, but it seems always you must play the fool for the world.

He shook his head. Why must you live so recklessly?

Janu shrugged. Life? You told me yourself, Captain. It takes courage to enjoy it.

Cindecis may have smiled, said, I was younger then. And you were a boy. But your courage . . . That is why I am about to give you the chance to prove to others what I know already.

He stepped forward.

The time for play is over, Janu. Some days ago the Cardinal thought fit to write to me. In his inflated, pompous way he mentioned a girl, a certain de Graci, who is, shall we say, in his care. He also asked . . .

And now Cindecis could barely cool the sudden anger that flushed in his face. He inhaled sharply.

No, no Marlov demanded that I give you leave to attend him. The church, no less, will play hostess in order that you answer certain questions concerning this girl.

Then did his anger surge free, pumping into the creases above his eyes.

S'truth! Demanded of me, Captain of the King's Guard! Demanded, mark you?

He stepped back, a fist fastened to staunch a wound in his side, and Janu's eyes sought the unswept flagstones. So it was a matter of pride only.

It has taken me some time to think this through. Already I've left this too long but at last I must make my decision. I hope you appreciate I act in all of this first for you and for your good name, the name of your father's family. And of course for the good name of the Guards, your Brothers.

When Janu did not speak Cindecis stepped closer. Janu raised his head and they beheld a mask whose eyes would not meet his own.

I will ask once. Is your love for the King or for the priest's girl?

Now did fear burst inside Janu, a malignant bloom that wound tight around his throat, squeezed thoughts, and suddenly everything was inside this moment, this was the future he had dared to challenge. Of course, there were no words. No thoughts for words.

Cindecis' hand was on his shoulder.

You know you must choose. Such affairs could taint us all.

But they are both my life!

Your life? Cindecis flung his arm behind him to the Royal Insignia on the wall. This is life, your duty! Do you not love your King more?

On my honour, Captain, I love them both more than life!

No! barked Cindecis. No! You risk the honour of all my men. Already this rash liaison has brought too much shame.

Shame? I don't understand.

Cindecis' fury was wild but it choked on fear and a terrible loss. Apologetically, feebly, he thumped the eagle on the young man's chest.

Here! he sighed. Surely, tell me now, Janu, this is where your heart is and then let your head follow. Faith, no, do not throw your life away on the madness of young lust.

Janu stared at the wall, at the wings bled with the finest golden thread into the royal banner, but she stood there before him and he could look only into her face, her love, her inexplicable sadness as she walked away from him that day, their last.

The King has my sword, let her have my heart.

The back of Cindecis' hand smashed against his cheek but Janu did not react, turned once more to face his captain who stood in disbelief at his own action.

Janu, forgive me. Do not make me do this.

Slowly, numbly, Janu unbuckled the scabbard and placed it in Cindecis' hands. The captain stood, frozen to the sheathed blade, as it shook violently in his hands. Finally, he spoke in a broken-backed whisper.

Your dishonour is bitter. It leaves me sick.

He lifted his eyes and his tongue from between slumped shoulders.

Leave us! Go! Hide well in the petticoats of the fat man's whore! Ha, so you are angry now! Go! Go, before I break this sword over your fool's head.

My captain.

Janu bowed once.

The walk was the longest walk and every step anger and the very next despair for all was beyond belief. He must keep walking. He must step out of this cruelty.

But as he marched through the echoes, down the staircase and out through the sudden silence in the courtyard, the faces of his companions looked upon him in confusion until a voice crashed down upon them from above.

This man is an outcast! Mark him! All of you mark him and know him for he lives in our homeland no more! He lives no more.

This Cindecis can put a man in his place. Janu has lost everything. But was I not prepared to risk when first I sought you?

Charlie Blake III almost leapt on me as I emerged from the research pod.

"Caught!" he cried. "Checkin' up on your lass?"

"No. Well, yes."

He sniggered and wiped the bottom of his canister on a batch of first prints.

"Tut, tut, my dear boy. Illicit use of the City directory. And certainly for immoral purposes."

"No, it's not like that."

"So what do you want, Blue? It can't be her, a law broker? Unbelievably pretty, yes. Unbelievably perfect, I doubt it, no woman is, not even in bed. Unbelievably unavailable? Beyond all reasonable doubt. You missed your window."

"My window?"

"She," and Charlie nodded once to emphasise this was juice, the irrefutable essence of fact, we were dealing with, "says you missed your window when you spilled drinks on her last night. I must say, she does have a point."

"I...How would... you were playing Russian Roulette with oxytubes. Anyway, she hardly stopped to talk and, well, there was a crowd. I mean, we touched, she walked before I could open my mouth."

"Well, she must have kept on walking because she walked all the way back to her ex-lover. Moved him in to her big old tenement apartment."

"Well, right then."

"And get this!"

"It gets worse?"

"The ex, he's a bloody big Abidar. Seven feet of thuggery with a gun that'll glow red if you as much as go near her again with a glass of meatbeer."

Charlie splutters coffee down his shirtfront and hugs me hard around the arms, the wrinkled crown of his bald head banging on my chest.

"You still want her stats?"

His tiny eyes peer up at me, blue-black and red-rimmed, challenging me, and I knew he would not accept anything less than yes for an answer.

I did not realise then that, wherever I thought I might be going, the way ahead was anything but clear.

THROUGH nowhere streets Janu's mind was accosted by colourless shades. The night was unbearably heavy for a deadness had crawled unseen towards him in the mists snaking from the docks and his breath came in short, swollen gasps for the air was rancid and choking the world.

Fat white faces loomed closer through the veils and as they grew near bulbous eyes looked up into his own, and they were laughing at him. Such hideous laughter. Every step took him further away. An awful emptiness had begun to seep into the cracks of his brain. Every step brought him nearer to the abominable priest.

He could not count how many days, how many weeks since he had been able to see her. How could he have clothed reality in petty deceits? Why should he have waited? When would he see her? How could he tell her? When?

Inside the private offices his wraiths clung to the room, menaced the weak candle flames and threw tortured figures upon the naked whitewash. Stale incense loitered in the corners, twirling itself into thin nervous wisps.

A brooding fear seized him with some half-remembrance of that smell. His eyelids fell and at once his mind was touched by an image, a burning cross. Calling? Someone was calling out his name. Arms open, reaching out from the fire.

He was shocked back into the empty room. His gaze was pulled to the crucifix on the wall before him.

Nothing. Nothing at all. No-one.

Rosa?

He heard footsteps shuffled on marble and the door clicked behind him. He turned.

Ah, my dear, dear Monsieur!

Marlov floated miraculously into the room.

I must say, I was so glad when I was told you had come. I'm sure you know Madame Choufos?

She spidered out from behind him, all garish red powder blotched on to pumice skin. Her insect eyes darted to Janu and, for a moment, they faltered, flung themselves away. She followed them to a chair next to the Cardinal's desk.

Janu stood until Marlov ushered him with a sweeping hand to be seated. In the chair before the desk. Janu stared. Long at the tortured figure of the crucifix.

With a long, contented groan, Marlov settled opposite.

Well, this is just all too, too tragic, Monsieur. Really, I must say, too awful for words, and the Cardinal's fingers were wrung in the helplessness of it all.

Janu did not speak.

Marlov leaned forward on his chins and lowered his voice.

No, no, you see you cannot blame yourself, my son. You could not know. Certainly, you could not foresee how it would all end. Such tragedy.

Silence.

The Cardinal sat back into the creak of leather, turning his ring, feeling the import of its seal, watching Janu's face. Madame Choufos shifted uncomfortably, her gaze quivering on the walls. Marlov coughed.

You see, when we first realised the young girl was missing we were very concerned, obviously. You were our last hope, but, ah . . . of course, it is all . . .

Missing? The word was a barb wrenched from Janu's throat. Rosalia is missing?

Marlov's glanced involuntarily at the woman by his side.

But, Monsieur, he gasped, *you were not informed of this in my letter? For almost two weeks she was not to be found. But of course that is why I demanded your own very dear Captain send you along at once! At once, I told him!*

The black, suffocating horror was swelling too fast inside Janu's head. Suddenly, he felt nauseous.

Ah, my son, cried the Cardinal, *then you are free from all blame indeed. Please believe, if . . .*

Janu could not hear properly, his thoughts were suffocating and the blackness was already gnawing at the edge of his vision.

Where is Rosalia?

The Cardinal screwed his own eyes in deepest pain and Madame Choufos buried herself in a knuckle-roofed church and began to sob there, the points of her white linen shoulders bobbing together.

Janu smiled, and shook his head slowly, and stared at the Cardinal.

Where is Rosalia?

My son, she is gone. They found her . . . that is, they found her poor body in the river this morning. Why, this is just too awful.

Janu smiled, he might even laugh now, at any moment, and he shook his head against the violent, all-powerful blackness.

Where is Rosa?

Marlov half-stood, reached out and held his hands against Janu's shoulders.

You are hurting of course, Monsieur. Have courage in your faith. Alas, the girl had lost her own religion. We believe when she discovered you must know her awful truth she chose instead to take her own life.

Her truth? Her what, her truth? spat Janu, in agony, and he struggled to his feet, searching wildly, hunted, he swayed, clutching for the edge of the desk, for the edge of the world.

Where is Rosalia? Tell me!

God's truth, my son, you must see. She was still fleeing the ghosts of her past; her less than virtuous past.

Janu's hand clawed at his side for his sword, could find no hold, and the Cardinal clambered up, fell back with a horrible thud against the wall.

Oh, as the Lord is my love, we all, and Marlov nodded to Madame Choufos, who was prodding fingers into her clenched face, we all tried to help her, we tried. I'm afraid she was not destined to be by His side.

Suddenly Janu was breathing into round, pink blotched skin, but he did not recognise the Cardinal as he held him by the flaccid folds of his throat to the wall. He stared into the man's horrified eyes and saw nothing, listened to the hysterical screams of the woman and heard nothing., squeezed the feeble gurgle from Marlov's heart and felt nothing.

Nothing.

Only the blackness, tight, blackness, tighter.
You're killing him! someone shrieked.
The body slid from his hands, gasping, quivering, jerking within its vestments on the floor.
Rosa, whispered Janu, and then he was seized from behind, cold steel pulled against his throat, and his legs were kicked from under his body.
The soldiers dragged him through the long halls out into an alleyway where they wrestled manically for turns to beat him with a metal bar until he could no longer raise the shards of his arms. A boot stomped down into his face and someone cried out, Well aimed, Cranor! Purple pulsed from his head and he could not breathe for the burning, and there was no shelter for the fire was inside him, but he cried out not once.
When they laughed that his whore was rotting in hell he tried to stand, but they kicked him back down, and the same shrill voice cried out, Run, soldier, run!
Silence then.
Two black boots appeared in the drowning beside his face. A white glove grasped his hair, wrenched his head from the puddle of his life, and a row of shark's teeth spat in his face.
Go save your harlot now, unbeliever! Go steal her from Satan's bed!
And then Janu was alone, his broken body oozing between the cobble stones.
Rosa? And his breath trickled red. Rosa?
Nothing.

Nothing? I've done nothing to stop this, but I did not see it coming. Perhaps, this is not the way it should have been. But this is my book of a dream and this is what has happened and now there is nothing. Without love there can be nothing. And love is dead.

How far we have come from its birth. In those earliest days, despite the re-emergence of your Abidar lover, I lived in the illusion of love's free breath, slapped fresh from my back.

That's because the mind is like the heart, I told myself. It detests an anchor. It wants to sail away on low sighs and high seas.

In the next moment I would tell myself, no, I don't need kites for my heart. It isn't safe. Give me my anchor. After all, you had yours, all seven feet, uniformed, stamping his authority into your precious laws.

But Charlie needed juice, if not for the points then for his own amusement. He caught my elbow as we crossed the skybridge to the office. You had dropped the Abidar.

"The giant is no longer in the princess's tower," said Charlie, "and Sam has her stats."

Sam was trying to splice the two halves of a broken laserpen using his teeth.

"Nah, nah, not a kite, a sponge," he said, between loud suckles.

"Right."

"Nah, you dunk it, don't you, in the bucket of life, soak up all that soap, all that good, hot stuff, and you slap it all over your girl just like she was your new buzzcar. And what happens?"

He looked at me sagely through the empty sockets of his antique spectacles, worn because he thought they made him look foppish.

"She gets cleaned?" I asked.

"Sweet!" he cried and his padpen lasered my eyes.

I blinked hard against the red light and sank further into the seat and felt the thing half swivel away.

"And what happens when she's left all nice and shiny?" asked Sam.

I gritted my teeth. "Listen, if you could …"

"Well, your heart's left all squeezed out, isn't it, and so you have to keep dunking, slapping, squeezing, and one day, before you know it, with all that slapping and squeezing, she's sitting in your hoverport, gleaming, just like she was brand new, but your sponge, it's gone all kind of hard in the centre."

I stared at Sam. He said, "You want her stats, don't you?"

I typed the address. I read the screenmail. Re-wrote. Reread. I typed. Read it one last time. Again. The message stared back, daring me.

Anna,

It's Jimmy Blue from the Siren party. You know, the one you showered with cocktails? Or maybe it was me. I wondered whether you might like a drink? In a glass this time.

Sent.

Nothing. Minutes into hours and the next day. But every time I plucked up the courage my hands fell to my knees. When I picked up the phone courage fell into my stomach. Finally, they met somewhere in the middle, and I was speaking to someone called Jude.

Any message?

"Heh, no, I mean yes. Well, you know, if you could just say Jimmy, that's Jimmy Blue called. Well, thank you very much."

Then suddenly your voice. I can't remember how you got so quickly inside my head, if I'd redialled or you called me back. All I remember is thinking why does this girl sound so confused?

"Your message? Yes, Jude told me you'd called?"

I could see you both exchanging shrugs.

"No, no not that message. Did you get the screenmail? Yes, I guess it is, old-fashioned, I mean. Well it was yesterday, actually. Ah, right. Well, this is kind of . . . you see, the mail was . . ."

On the other side of the empty office Sam's padpen was tracing a word on the ceiling: "Sponge."

"Well, basically, you know, I, ah, wondered . . . no, it's not. Actually it's Jimmy from the Siren party. With Charlie Blake. Yes the Third. . . wondered if you might like to . . . just whenever, maybe today, tomorrow, some time?"

"A drink? Uh, huh, yeah, that sounds good, Jimmy Blue. But Laws, you know. Really busy. In fact, I'll not get out of here at all. Maybe later, yes?"

"Yes. Great."

"Okay, bye."

Somewhere across the office a phone rang. And was answered. It took me much longer to lift my heart out of the bucket. It was wet but soft.

The first wringing happened two weeks later when I passed you at the corner of The Strand. I stopped but my body walked on right out of myself. My head at least turned. I thought I saw genuine embarrassment on your face or maybe it was a mischief in your eyes that told me you know that I know what you're thinking, Blue, so you'd better start fighting for me.

I think that's how I saw it.

Or maybe it was the smile you threw over your shoulder that felt like a hand gripping me and holding on, tugging at me, making me turn three times more to watch you until you were lost to me among the noon day crowd. Did you know that I watched you disappear?

What I know for sure is that once upon a time I almost met a girl and it felt good to be alone because it was a dreaming loneliness that liked to sit long hours making midnight-coloured plans.

****

Chapter Four

The Silence of Yellow Roses

I'M HUNGOVER and afraid of the silence of the ocean, of the little death in the circles of the sea that can swallow you whole if only you open your eyes for one second too long. Never lose your head inside those slow swirls, for you will feel the great enormity of depths crash down inside you, the wild waves rising to overwhelm your senses, and every frontier of your body will be drowning in a great roar of nothingness.

Two months have passed and I sit on the wall of the Old Harbour and shiver in my threadbare red duffel coat, the one at which you had thrown one short, sideways glance, so I felt like I'd just shrugged on a hand-me-down from a meatbeer-swilling uncle.

I watch a seagull wrestle a plastic shopping bag from its grave among the dunes.

I almost laugh to see it sneeze and snort, its beak clamped by the bag. But the cries of the gulls above us, once the loneliest and loveliest of sounds, are raucous and uncouth this morning and embarrass the moment, until the gull goes hop-a-lolloping off into the long yellow grasses and, aware of myself once more, I get up from the cold concrete and walk on.

For once the throaty obscenities of a buzzrod does not fill the seaside, the engine's roar bouncing off the high-rise buildings that jostle for space nearest the flood water, pushed ever further from the heart of the city by the Parks. The silence is not out of respect for the lone walker but the fact the communal chariot sits on its haunches on the waterfront, the innards of its jets spilling out on to the ground. The kids crowd around the open bonnet, with the reverse peaks of a dozen caps beseeching the grey sky, looking for a signal.

Today a quiet calm has come to town.

Here on the strand, I can hear the real silence, the nothingness that calls from way out there in the hollows between the waves. I search the skies for another aeroplane but, of course, there is none. And it is a long way to New York.

There is a whisper among the dunes and it is then I remember the silence of yellow roses. The silence that whispered in my ear on the morning I sent you flowers.

At first it had been subtle, almost unheard.

"Your weekend misfit money? All of it?"

"I guess so," I confessed. "But don't tell Charlie. He'll never leave it alone."

"What if she didn't get them?" asked Sam. "I mean, what am I saying? Why would she want them? Didn't they use to give flowers at funerals?"

"And for romance."

Sam shook his head and puzzled at a spot on his chin.

"So, that's it then. The boy Blue meets his match."

Charlie found out, of course, but there was no room left for sympathy in his shrinking head.

"Flowers? Are you trying to set a plague on us, Blue? Did you get clearance from Health, shite for brains? I tell you, Blue, you really do get some downright kinky notions. Flowers?"

For Charlie romance was something that kept him awake at night only because it was brought forth from the imagination of a plugger whose literary carnival cavorted sweatily in the square of Mrs Blake's bedside holoscreen. With every flicker, he would moan inwardly, Mrs Blake would sigh outwardly and pat the ample, freckled flesh at the top of her nightgown until he must wince and burrow his face in the pillows, praying tonight would not be the night to feel fingers of love reaching for him under the duvet.

I knew this only because he once felt the need to tell me why he slept so often on his office couch.

"She'll get the bullet, too, one day, you mark my words."

No-one ever marked his words. No-one ever got the bullet.

"That Anna girl's got you marked down, my lad! She'll be calling her big-balled Abidar and he'll red light you and you'll be off on the long holiday."

"But they were yellow."

"What?"

"The flowers, yellow, her favourite. I think they are. It said so in her Stats. Anyway, I just thought she'd have been in touch."

It was a day of regression into adolescent nightmare, being made to sit through the kind of dream that once could grab me on the darkest nights and pull me from sleep by the shoulders and shake me awake with dread: a thief has taken my breath and locked it in a glass jar and is running off down the road with it, away into tomorrow or the next day or the next, maybe never to return.

A scratching makes me turn. My friend has returned. He offers me the plastic bag and I unhook it and he clacks his bill and pecks at my shoe.

They say the gulls were once afraid of humans. That must have been before we brokered the deal and gave them the refuse mountains.

We stay here together, best friends, me feeling the wind slide cold, wet fingers through the huge buttonholes of my antique coat, he looking out to sea, unblinking, the breeze ruffling a single, kiltered feather.

You know, I would have given you yellow roses every day.

What am I thinking? Your garden is already overgrown with lives and dreams fresher than mine. Tom Patterson is reaping armfuls right now in your penthouse.

Perhaps I should be glad. Perhaps I simply fell into a dream of you, was swallowed in a gulp by the great expanse of your secret ways and smiles, and now I'm climbing out, waking up. Perhaps I should not be surprised now that when I rewind the fading frames of our love affair they already seem like the crackled images of a vintage movie.

One image stays, though, caught in the bright glare of the bulb, when, finally, at precisely 5pm, after a day's wait, you strode up to me in the Mole Hole and slapped me on the cheek, and lectured me, loudly and without detour, on social decorum, especially pertaining to an office of law, and why private lives were simply that, for ourselves only, and just who was I, a stranger who could not even hold his drink without spilling it, to think different and send roses?

You took away the silence completely and filled me instead with confusion and a stinging cheek. But you weren't finished. Entering the Mole, just before the doors cut us in two, you said, "By the way, Blue. Thank you. Yellow roses. How did you know?"

Sometimes, just sometimes, when we're gasping and the silence is almost overwhelming, coming up for air is the moment we learn what being alive is all about.

After a while the seagull leaves me, too, flapping off into the grey to join his co-workers at the tumbledown mountains of trash. I stand for a few minutes longer then lift the sticky bag and wedge it in a bin-burner, glance over at the buzzrod gang, still peering into the innards of their vehicle, straight at a black and round bulb among their caps.

I hurry, slowed by my preposterous coat, to reach the car park gate and clamber under the barrier, not really knowing why or what I will say, but when I stand straight again the bowler hat and its wearer are gone.

"Stupid!" I tell myself, "stupid!"

I walk up to the group, breathless and red-faced.

"Dno," mutters the tallest lad in txt speak. "Hd look. Sd zero. Wnt way."

Fingers point down an empty street, where only a lone gull sits staring back at us. He is sitting upon a small, black mound.

I have escaped the circles of the sea. I am home. But I am sitting alone on the shores of silence because I know tonight the phone will not ring.

And I know that if love is dead, some part of me must have died, too. Perhaps it is time to leave that part in the slough, and climb out of this place altogether.

The Morning Parks

I write a single word on the wall screen. I have not found a record of it anywhere. Instead, I spin the bowler hat on my clenched fist, like a globe. It is smooth, shiny and slightly scuffed on the inside brim and, inside the crown, written in fresh blue ink on a faded label that once said only Made in Batavia is the word: Eilidon.

I spin the hat round and round. Something is about to give and I think I know what it is.

ONLY the damned can truly laugh. They scream and they crow with the blackfire wildness that boils in their blood; such is their abandonment, a final grasping comfort to face eternity with a horrible, mad glee.

Janu moaned his own delight, and the truth of damnation played upon his lips. All through the twisting snarl of streets he shuffled his lame dance, below the leering gargoyle heaven, amid the hideous side-scuttling lives in all their ignorant content, fearfully avoiding the blind madman.

It would not be right to speak of purpose, but his ranting steps could not fail. Soon he was within the obelisk gateposts of the park and around him the night was hung with the dirty rags dregged lifeless and dripping shame from the swollen waters of the river.

He stumbled on, cascading between the terrifying giants who rose from the earth around him to claw at his face with a thousand tearing fingers.

But when finally he came to that place the darkness was lifted from his battered eyes. Beside the running of the moonlight he knelt and placed his brow on the cool wet grass and knew he would not leave this place, this secret garden where they had last touched, a lifetime ago.

Everything had become so simple now that he felt and thought as a child. Even the steel seemed soft and warm and comforting as it slipped up through his guiding hand and opened the prison of his soul.

Rosa filled his mind, and in this eternal now he sank back into the earth, with no pain, and his life flowed red into the black and silver of the river and was lost in the silent, swirling everness of sleep.

****

Chapter Five

Girl In A Fish Tank

I HAVE killed Rosa and now Janu has killed himself and I cannot sleep. Instead I lie in the darkness reaching for my next move. I know I have to walk out of here because even the act itself can make things happen. I like to think that every step speaks of purpose, even if I lack direction. And so, aimless, I make strides.

Lately, Anna, I have taken to walking in the Old Parks around Carmelwood.

They do not seem very much like Parks at all, in truth, for there are no paths and little or no order. The lawns were long ago conquered by chest-high grasses and acid-skinned weeds and below the highest clumps await unseen humps and holes so that the miles are perilous to walk. Too often an ambush of branches and thorns rears up, blocking the way entirely.

How anyone travelled though here, let alone old Mrs Betty Highgate, seems incomprehensible.

I've read, thank goodness for The Strand, that once upon a time, almost long forgotten ago, our forefathers wandered their way all over the world. Even if there were no hedges, they could not know then what lay ahead, and so with every foot forward they sang into being the rivers and the forests, the salt pans and the dunes, even the edges of the endless, unfathomable oceans.

Wherever their tracks led they left a trail of music. The wonder of wander, it sang, the wander of wonder. I'd like, just once, to hear this music.

Even as I realise this, that it is time to leave, I steal a glimpse behind. Sure enough, loitering in my background thoughts, is the beginning of our night, the first together.

"We've done it!"

"Congratulations! Done what?"

"Won!" shouted Sam down the phone.

We met in the Sky Bar, above the mile markers and therefore the only public venue allowing team colours to be shown outside arenas. Another of your new laws.

So there we sat, gathered in green and yellow hoops, reverentially staring into the holoscreen, re-running the victory, bludgeoning one another's sensibilities with bare innuendo, blowing as much froth from our brains as meatbeers.

"What do Siren put in these chasers? Katara?"

"Ka what?"

"Here we go," said Paulo, "Jimmy's about to take us on a journey down the Zambezi."

"The Amazon," I said. "It's a sauce made from ants. Their jaws..."

"Get out more!" cried Wes. "Here, Xena! How about another round for the champions? What are you on about, Sam?"

"I was telling Blue hearts are like sponges."

Paulo asked, "Weren't you supposed to use a stick and vinegar with a sponge? It was medical, for wounds in the Last War."

"The machines still use supersize sponges to mop up all the guts and stuff after a Hit."

I splayed my fingers over the holoscreen, ignored the instant uproar.

"How do you know, Wes?" I asked. "When did you see a Hit up close? Anyone? The last time? Ever?"

"Aw, leave it, Blue," said Wes.

"C'mon Jimmy!" said Sam.

Paulo pulled me back down on to my seat, but I shouted, "Does anyone here know anyone who's ever been Hit?"

"I do."

The conversation fell and lay dead on the table. The holoscreen fizzled, crackled and powered down.

Xena stood with her huge hands flat on the table top. Her blouse, unhinged at a blue-veined navel, was worn atop a pair of lemon jodhpurs, and the bust and blue eyes of Tizzy Carmen, on whom Xena had remodelled herself when she left the Abidar and manhood, were thrust into our group.

"Okay, Xena, no harm meant," said Wes.

"He's just a bit excited," said Sam, "What with the fact we won and he's still never watched a game."

Sam locked my head in the nook of his arm and I inhaled hot sweat as I gazed up at Xena.

"Yes, sorry, Xena," I mumbled. "More chasers. Take one yourself."

I watched our host stomp off on thighs that looked grafted from a horse, nod briefly at the Abidar by the door, who laughed.

My head was ringing. My phone.

"Are you coming to wish me happy birthday or are you just playing hard to get now?"

"What?" I stood up. "Of course I am."

"Well listen up, Blue, I'm in the Madara so bring a torch and a net."

Anna. Maybe I should just, I could. It took too many minutes to flag down a buzzcab. It took longer to persuade Sam to get in.

"Look, Sam, it's in the Interior, you know I won't get in alone, it's past curfew for singles. And there's going to be lots and lots of women there. You know? Women. Remember them?"

The buzzcab door clicked above our heads.

"Onward driver," Sam shouted at the screen, "Men on a mission. With sponges!"

I'd never been to the Madara. The screwdriver staircase was so strong it threatened to pull the soles from my shoes and the slow spinning emptied my head. When the doors opened the only sense of direction came from the blue arrows on the corridor floor. It was incredibly dark, even for a meatbeer cellar. Another door swished aside and we shuffled through the clamour of Saturday night revellers until we met the barrier.

Sam stared into the blue-lit wall of water. He pointed to the inhabitants, the giant, swollen clown faces the size of buzzcar wheels, staring back at us, fanning their bulbous black eyes with yellow frilled fins. They must have cost a fortune to make. It was the first time either of us had seen fish.

But I was staring at the girl in the fish tank. Your image was perfectly mirrored in the glass, the long flames of your hair setting fire to the water.

As I approached, you were half turned from me, and my eyes were allowed to follow the cascade of blonde all the way down your back, down, and unable to stop, the length of your naked legs, then rise again, around those curves, across the twin dimples of your lower back and . . .

"Hey, Blue!"

Your body turned to follow your face and I thanked the dimness of the cellar for throwing a veil of charity over my own because my eyes had stuck on your naked midriff, the glint of silver in your navel, those soft yet distinct circles of bare breasts below your cropped shirt.

"Anna."

The introductions were quick and informal. Anna, Sam. Sam, Anna. Tabby, Blue. Blue, Tabby. . .

"Anna?"

The girl called Tabby had pulled my fingers into her mouth and was sucking slowly on each tip, her large eyes fixed close to my belt buckle. I looked around. You were laughing.

"Don't worry, Blue, she likes you."

"Hi, Mr Blue!" purred Tabby. Her feline corneas glowed green in the light from the tank until the lids of her eyes rolled shut and mine opened on a wonderfully unbalanced night. Perhaps it was the meatbeer and the heat of the cellar. Perhaps it was the effect of the shots of indigo flamethrow with which you kept the party in chest-burningly constant supply.

"Aaah, more Firestarters! There you go. Come on, boys!"

Just your smile would send the clowns flapping to the back of the tank. No-one in their right heart could argue with you that night. No, it wasn't the meatbeer nor the Firestarters, I am sure it was the infectious mania radiating from you that warmed the night.

My mood was a paper bag, empty and fluttering in the rise and fall of your friends' conversation, suddenly full and swollen, hyperventilating every time you spoke directly to me. That night your let's-be-having-you humour turned the floor of the bar into a trampoline, a place where it was not wise to stand still if you wanted to keep your feet, where I stood, stumbled, where, finally, I laughed at myself and the impossibilities of trying to look serious.

I let go. I surrendered. This was the first lesson: if you didn't have the whitewater courage, you shouldn't be riding rapids, because you'll find yourself washed up on the rocks, coughing on insecurities, as the party raft races on into a future, Anna at the helm.

I grabbed my oar, I was on the river, and right then, right there, I was happy to drown for the very trying.

How and when we crawled up from the Madara I cannot recall. The facts that were then are not now, long lost in the blur, the whirl of a fast-forward night, and the slow-motion replay will only pause now at sudden points of impact, such as here.

The kiss.

Not extraordinary, but so unexpected I almost laughed aloud into your mouth. Standing in the queue for the Cookie Club you turned and pressed your lips not on to mine but around them and the moment became taste, texture, and movement.

The beginning of our first night together.

Much later, as I plunged into sleep, I dreamed of a place where there were leaves so broad and thick you could wear them as a raincoat. Around me were a thousand insects that must be from worlds beyond the stars for they had kaleidoscopes for eyes, some had no heads to be seen, some crawled like miniature trains then spread umbrellas and lifted off the ground.

There was a frog the size of my thumbnail hiding in the cusp of a flower. There was a girl, too, standing in the midnight before me, but I could not see her face for mine was hidden in the surge of her hair. When she kissed my cheek she began falling and, though her arms were around my shoulders, gripping, beseeching, I could not hold her, for my hands were red and wet and so I tried calling out her name but the thought of it would not come.

I scared myself awake and, as suddenly as I found myself in your embrace, you disengaged yourself with a short sigh and turned away. The end of our first night.

I am truly awake now, holding nothing but this wall. It is dark and hailstones rattle against the cottage window. I sink into the covers and seek out deeper, darker places.

IN the sprawling bones of the building inhabited by the Sisters of Hopeful Redemption, at the furthest end of a long forgotten hollow, was a door to another cell. Unlike the others, this door was always locked, and even Mother Symna herself was barred entrance. It was whispered at prayers, beneath conspiratorial veils, that only the Cardinal himself held the key and only he knew the secret of that room.

But tonight the old Mother had ordered the torches lit, and, greedy after such long slumber, they spluttered in excitement and licked the wet walls. The passage seemed naked and surprised. It reeked of stale, wet straw and sulphur.

Now voices echoed up from the stairwell. Closer, closer, and finally from the gloom emerged the face of Mother Symna herself, a tiny wrinkled white disc at the centre of a squat black apparition that billowed like a ball of angry smoke.

In her wake came Cardinal Marlov, wheezing, with one fat fist around the silver cross on his chest and the other grabbing for the wall.

Hellfire!

She gasped in horror at his ejaculation.

A moment, he cooed. My dear Sister, give me one moment.

She stopped but did not turn. Her back was more impenetrable than any wall and Marlov waved a hand irritably at his vacant side, until a small, thin woman appeared.

Go before us, he croaked.

Madame Choufos scurried herself forward at once, of course, edging around the vastness of Mother Symna, and she took down a torch and ruffled forth a key from within her parakeet clothes. The door opened inwards. She took a breath and entered.

You may leave us now, Sister.

The ball of black smoke did not move.

We have God's work to perform here, my dear, delightful Symna.

His words hung dripping between them.

Finally, the cloud swirled and she had passed, the anger in her toothless old head hidden deep beneath her veil, taken to the wooden kneeler in her own unlit cell.

The Cardinal waddled to the door. Hastily, he placed the cross to his lips, muttered a contrition, and entered. The room was small, windowless, with vile breath seeping from the cracks in its rib cage, semi-liquids plopping through the holes in its stone ceiling. The fingers of disgusted light clawed for a shape in the far corner, but Madame Choufos stood just inside the door, unwilling to go further. He took the torch from her and stepped forward to a small shape huddled beneath a grey blanket. He stood taller in the excited flame.

You have a visitor, said Madame Choufos, and her shrill voice belied her twittering heart. Will you not greet him?

The bundle did not move. Closer stepped Marlov, closer, he took hold of the damp rag, snatched it away.

Rosalia de Graci blinked into the uncertain focus. Her skin was translucent and she held deep in her eyes the innocence of a child watching events from far away in another world. Her delicate hands were locked tightly before her.

The Cardinal glanced at the woman by the door, who shrugged quickly.

She has not changed.

For a long time nothing happened. No noise. No movement. Perhaps the earth had stopped spinning entirely. Not for Marlov. His breathing slumped deep into his chest, a flash of sweat clutched amorously at the back of his neck, sinking him clumsily onto his knees. His face was inches from the girl's. She did not back away. Madam Choufos' hand came to her mouth for she found herself almost whimpering.

When the Cardinal spoke he was a father to his prodigal returned.

Sweet child, dear daughter, my Rosalia, do you not recognise me?

His voice was swollen, thick in the barrel of his throat, it squeezed all breath, but he pushed hard to be heard.

Yes, yes, I am the one who will redeem you. I am chosen, you see. A higher place awaits. You see, yes, I will bless you now.

His hand came up to her face and his nails traced a slow circle on her cheek. She was glass, hard, cool, so fragile.

Marlov's eyes closed and he exhaled long and deep and his fingers rested at last. The tiny woman behind him was muttering, twittering, slapping her palms about her temples so that clouds of white talcum billowed from her wig and veiled her face.

And then Rosalia turned her face until her lips touched the Cardinal's fingers and he opened his goggle eyes and almost laughed in delight as she held her softest lips there and began to suckle his fingertip and then she turned and she spat full in his face and was still once more. Her eyes were unmoved from his.

His hand came swiftly to her throat and squeezed and squeezed and squeezed and his fist left marks like wildflowers on her, again and again and again, and with his other hand he sought his own redemption, and all the while the tiny woman cried out in ecstasy for the girl's forgiveness so they all three knew it was for her soul and for rightness.

His will be done! Again and again.

Finally he had shuddered, and lifted himself too quickly, too painfully to his feet and stumbled to the door and the woman had followed at once and then all light and the cell had been left mercifully blind after the key scraped in the lock and their footsteps were lost.

Alone, the girl stares into her private universe and giggles quietly and clutches herself tightly to a small golden trinket embedded deep into the soft flesh of her hands.

****

AN explosion from Charlie Blake III unceremoniously uprooted my maudlin mood and threw it from me into the corner of the room. My Room 102 story had somehow caused an alarming dip in the points.

"What were you thinking, Blue? I mean what were you trying to begin to bloody achieve here? What were you even doing delving into the hell pits of Siren? You got the InfoDat, wasn't that enough?"

"I was looking for the truth."

"Oh, don't make me weep tears, soft lad, the truth? There are no points in the truth. Spin makes the world go round, spin."

Charlie's face was having one of its swollen days, bobbing like a huge raspberry on the end of a giblet.

"Stop the spin," he wheezed, "and we'll float off into the stratosphere and be sucking truth through our ass for a drop of air until we burn up in that great big ball of burning brightness some of us down here like to call the sun."

"I call it the sun. I called that laboratory as I saw it. She, the thing, it looked at me."

Charlie clawed at the papers on his desk screen, rummaged through the flashing pages, found the offending words, "Beating hearts of infants were afloat in test tubes? Bloody hell, Blue, are folks supposed to read this over their breakfast?"

I thought about the girl's face in the cylinder, her eyes fixing themselves upon me, and said nothing.

"Look, Blue, you're going to have to change your prescription, because the pluggers all saw something different. We lost three points in one night!"

Charlie sprung to his feet, began pacing the floor, flicking sharp glances at me.

"Is it the lass?" he asked. "Are you pining, is that it? Sure would explain all that crap I found in your computer. What's with the notes on the musketeers? Can you not write poetry like every other lovelorn bugger?"

"It's personal," I began to say, caught Charlie's eyes, added, "It's an historical novel."

"It's historical bloody bullshit wrapped up in poetic rat's piss, is what it is. Why are you writing about the past, no, not even about the past, about fairytales of the past? No-one wants to know."

"That's exactly why," I said.

Charlie sat down again, placed his hands on top of his head in a bid to stop the swelling.

"Is it truth, Jimmy, because I don't think it is?"

"No, it's a story, Charlie. But that's not what I am, you know it's not. It's not what I do for this newspaper. Am I the only one who wants to look beyond things? To find the origins?"

"Jimmy, Jimmy, you think the public reading that their breakfast comes from a monster baby in a glass tube is sharing the truth? Hybrid embryos? They knew this shit once already, then got tired of it. They don't need to relearn it every new day. Facts aren't point winners."

"I'm not looking for points."

"No, Jimmy Blue, that's your trouble and so it's my trouble. You're looking for a world without maps. Listen here, sonny, this is a wake-up call – there be no dragons. The earth was InfoDatted a long, long time ago."

"It's all madness," I said. "Bombs, Morning Gardens, faces in our food…"

"No, it's not madness, not when we spin it! Sticking to the spin is what keeps us sane, keeps us grounded on this lump of shit."

We sat perched in an ungainly silence, each teetering on the edge of saying something, not knowing what might tip us over.

"Right, your choice," said Charlie, finally, and he held up the bullet before placing it on the desk. "Take this. Or just go away for a while. Get out of the City, Jimmy Blue, for your own good. There have been too many people asking questions about you."

He held up his hand to stop me.

"No, no more stories. Go somewhere clean and tidy without anything to trip you up."

****

Chapter Six

A World Without Maps

THE displaced and the dispossessed will often describe their journey as a fragment of hell. Not knowing where they are bound, all hope is yoked to memories of the home they will never see again. The nomad, however, is only ever truly content when his heart is lost in the beautiful song of motion. He will tell you that, just as one cannot take the beginning out of air, so no end will be found in the rock beneath his feet. Whatever flower has opened herself here and availed his senses of her golden treasure, there is in his nostrils the promise of oases just beyond this morning's newborn burning.

The ancient sailor, too, will recall often, between swirls of spiced forgetfulness, once was the day he could not fight that tremendous lifting of the heart with weighing of the anchor, or stem the swelling inside himself when the sheets ballooned and snapped into life. The weight of these winds, the whoosh of this bow wave, the wheel of those white birds above, all were a symphony that could transport the soul as easily as it could a cargo of rock salt.

There are books that tell me this.

This tangible sense of journey is something we have lost in our new and safe existence. The cocoon of modernity, spun so finely by Siren's best young minds, despite its functionality, can feel like a straitjacket of the senses.

Not for me will the early morning mist rise around a low murmur of heavily swaddled tribesmen, a calm broken only by the short clamour of pots and poles and bedding as they are loaded once more atop the impatient snorting of huge beasts.

Not for me the swollen tide and sudden, salt-laden air, the creaking of eager timbers straining to be far from the bedlam and bustle of late trade at the quayside, the frantic roll of carts' wheels on the wharf.

Perhaps I have spent too long lost in the maze of other worlds in The Strand, travelling through yellowed paper pages, but sitting in this airport, I do not feel the heightened buzz before embarkation. My body is not girding itself to welcome travail ahead, my limbs not stretching for the freedom of each new step, nor my eyes widening with the promise of a freshly painted canvas. Instead I feel a cloying sense around me, almost as of claustrophobia.

Very soon I shall be ushered into my stall inside an ageing steel bird, distracted from the terrifying absurdity of sitting in a chair at 40,000ft by a holoflick on my tray, before being plonked into my destination with all the satisfaction of a hard day spent riding the Sky Bar's elevator.

I thought I would have been more excited about the aeroplane. I would never have been able to afford the taxes for the flight had not Charlie, quite out of character, arranged the tickets himself, and yet now I feel only the empty stomach of anti-climax.

I am in the Speak Easy and my eyes have sunk into the bottom of a half-empty meatbeer glass.

In the spider eyes above the Vendors there are images of a smoke-filled piazza, each screen offering a different angle on death. A dozen citizens have been shot by unidentified snipers. How shocking, I think, that the diggers have not yet removed all of the bodies.

The central eye cuts to Dan, man on the scene, and despite the flak jacket and his look of steely determination, all I can focus on is the ability of his sideburns to remain perfectly still despite the gnashing of his jaw. Perhaps this is something one learns at the Siren News Academy.

Wouldn't it be wonderful if I grew sideburns that could be beamed bold and immobile from a frontline straight into your New York living room?

"Unshaven. Unflappable. Unrequited. This is Jimmy Blue for Siren TV. Now back to you in the studio, Todd."

One screen cuts to a grieving relative. The sound is turned off but no-one in the Easy is watching and, anyway, the old lady is not saying anything. She simply stares into the camera as behind her two Abidar swing the broken bodies of her son and husband on to the back of an open buzztruck. The caption adds that the bodies were taken away for a full examination.

I swirl the last of the brown liquid until it is froth in the bottom of my glass. Stung by my conscience, I shuffle the morning newspapers for a few minutes until the plastic screens crease and distort in my warm fingers.

I even consider taking out my notebook and picking up the tale of poor Janu.

Instead, I order another meatbeer. It tastes of everything and nothing.

Perhaps I'm empty because I thought I would feel like a child about to embark on his holiday. I can recall my first trip away was to the Cashelan, in fact only a few Mole Holes from the city. In fact it was there, my father told me, was the finest pint of meatbeer a man could ever drink, served in Mickey's Kitchen, a scrum of different pubs, with two small cafes nailed on like bookends to add a little bit of stand-up respectability to the place.

Wasn't it there also that I not only discovered Siren alcohol but answered the call of first love? Of course, I probably never told you about this, about Bernie McSharry.

I spied her as she thumped a hover ball against the back wall of the Kitchen. And on that blazing hot Saturday afternoon, while my family sat inside, I loitered on the wall, pretending to watch the world go by. The world being an old man in his ancient buzzcar.

Bernie McSharry was a slip of a lass in shorts and a top way too tight, but then I was a skelf of a lad myself, with almost as many curls bobbing in my smile as on my head.

"Ah, Jeanie Mac!" she cried, throwing the hover ball at me before even a look. "Well, see if you can't show us what a City boy can do!"

That afternoon her strangely accented voice worked a magic on me and before the end of the week we sat wrapped in our own four arms on the one wall, and on the day of my leaving scrawled addresses on our phones.

Inevitably there were the mails, the holopics, and even for a while the prospect of trying for the same university. And then, of course, the longer silences, which grew through the university years, when we were too busy pretending to be serious and grown-up for romance, and finally the days of trying to find work, when we were too busy trying to be anything but serious and grown-up but everything suddenly was and the one thing that could have saved us we'd turned our backs on.

Two years later I was in a bar in Harrow Road when I heard the voice.

"Jeanie Mac, is that you, Jimmy Blue?"

I turned and there she was, gold ringlets and a cleavage as big and deep as her laugh, sitting in a cubby hole, shoehorned betwixt two other girls who nudged her ribs in a twin-elbowed vice.

"Jimmy!" she cried. "Ah, Jesus, Jimmy!"

And she jumped up and reached across the table with her bangled arms, pulling me down by the neck, intent on breaking it.

Celebrating ?

"That I am. Finally off to see the world. I needed to breathe again, Jimmy, breathe in all of it, the wide, wide, widest world!"

Her chest threatened to burst forth in joy and I'm sure it would have filled the pub with her wanderlust and sucked us all back in there too, and I dare say we'd all have been perfectly happy.

That weekend would last six months, what we called our second chance, and see us cross the world together, all within a few blocks of the City. I wrote my reviews, some of which were published, Bernie worked bars, some of which kept her on more than one night. We were each never far from being shown the door but happier for it.

We were young, we were in the City, and we were tremendously drunk at a sun-bleached table outside Malone's. Charlie Blake III had finally offered me a full-time job, while Bernie would have to get up to the Interior for an interview with a government firm. Shipping, I think she said. We'd celebrated the end of our second chance by branding ourselves with matching tattoos: an entanglement of lion and eagle on our right shoulders, which Bernie said was an ancient Cashelan love symbol, though she maybe she stole it from a beer mat. This was our last day but one.

"Jimmy, have you ever been so desperate for someone," Bernie whispered, her head on my chest, her words vibrating through her dimpled chin, "so entirely consumed by the thought of them, you can't wake up in the morning without their name on your lips and their face fading, like, just falling away from you, so fast, back into the blackness of it all, except it's you the one who's drowning?"

"Mmm," I sighed. A cocktail of sunshine and meatbeer had made me sleepy.

"No listen," she sighed and slipped slim fingers through mine, "have you ever been so hooked on someone that you have to make sure, you gotta know, know beyond everything else, beyond every little doubt, before you leave, they're going to be happy? You know, even if that means they're, well, sharing time with someone else while you get on? 'Cause only when they're safe and happy can you let them go, do what you have to do?"

I remember that I watched a blond walk by. He was dressed in a pink tutu and black biker's boots and carried a parasol. Malones, even at midday, was always surprisingly surreal.

Bernie was still talking.

"Are you listening, Jimmy? There's no way you could do what you have to do if you didn't know. How could you, how could you walk away and live without knowing?"

She stopped and plucked at the chest of my damp t-shirt. Suddenly, I could feel her waiting.

"Mmm, of course."

Silence, then she said.

"Well, that's enough, enough in your heart anyway."

Strange that I can remember this now, after all this time, yet I cannot remember any such conversations with you, Anna. Why can't I remember them?

Yes, but I remember Bernie had laughed. Of course, she laughed. She was always laughing, especially when I called her my angel in a mini-kilt. Then she punched me in the belly, which hurt, because

I'd been drinking meatbeer for three weeks, and the moment was broken. I remember now, too, that I was grateful because both of us must have been tired of being filled with emotion.

Suddenly the idea of sitting outside Malones and getting drunk together forever seemed like the only thing in the world to do.

"Twelve confirmed dead," said Dan.

I knew I was getting drunk. Someone had turned up the volume and Dan's voice had grown insistent but I wanted to think about Bernie. When had I seen her last?

Not when I last was in Cashelan. No, not for years. When did I last hear of her then? I was passing through on my way to cover a Siren science congress, before InfoDats took away the need for trips, and didn't I bump into Mrs Mac in the Kitchen? She had the same laughing eyes and dimples as I remembered on her daughter, but her old face was latticed by the fresher inroads of worldly worry.

"Ah, well if she isn't still somewhere in India or Africa or some planet or other. Sure Paraic has an address, I think. Ach, you know our Bernadette. Comin' and goin'. She's trawlin' the filthiest bars, God forgive me, did I say bars, bazaars I meant, for the clothes and the jewellery, you know the things you can't get in the City any more, not in Siren least ways, but you'd not believe till ya see the stuff she brings back from her trips. Heaven bless, treasures they are. Treasures! And you know she sells them all and doesn't keep a penny. Not one. S'for the trees, she says, and to save the poor wee baby animals in the forest!"

And Mrs Mac bellowed her laughter.

"Aye," said Colm the barman to me later, "She was home a good few summers ago. Ach, built like a man she was! And dressed like a barn in a bin liner. Said she was selling all this ethnic shite at a stall. Actually, come to think of it, I don't remember where. At least I never saw it. Anyway, she said she'd be heading home in a month or so. Cashelan, says I. No, my spiritual home, says she. Right ye are, says I, and I'll be off now to the Kitchen because there's a few spirits waiting there for me."

I laughed along, but now I recall I immediately felt guilty. I was no longer with Bernie, but I was not free to laugh at her or let go of memories. Do you laugh at ours, Anna? With Tom?

The Morning Parks

Anyway, Bernie, how had Bernie come into my mind? Yes the meatbeer, the best pint. Yes, another, why not? Press the bar. You know I think this one tastes even better than that last.

I was sober last night. Must have been. I was packing my case when I glanced up at your miserable clutch of yellow petals, floating in the holoflask, and I knew the silent, sad mood for wanderlust that had fallen upon me was the most natural and logical thing in the world. Only movement could free me from my thoughts.

But even as I think of that holoflask the glass cracks and melts and the yellow fragments are the wildflowers you picked from below a window of Carmelwood Cottage after that first viewing.

The house, just a jumble of whitewashed bricks, no more, a fossil in the Old Parks, seems like heaven this day. And, if I'm honest, it is so only because of how we are: I think I will always remember. You are so beautiful, more than I can ever remember. Your smile says you have not a care in the world, so nor do I, with no-one here but the two of us and Mrs Highgate fussing inside over cups of real tea.

I remember now what you said, having forgotten so long.

"So this is your famous countryside? You know, I'll miss you if you ever move too far away."

"Will you, Anna?"

There was a silence, not uncomfortable, but needing to be filled. We'd spent the perfect day together, after all.

You said quietly, so quietly I almost missed it, "You know, I've read there is only one true north for everyone."

I was so happy that the next morning I put in my purchase offer for the cottage. Moving here would never be too far from the City or you. Not if you knew your true north.

A number? Was that the flight being called? Not yet.

You have been called, though, far away. And have you found your true north there? While here I am moving, too, yet going nowhere. Hadn't I better finish at least something in my life?

Let's see here if Janu knows what it feels like to let go?

DEATH is every contradiction. Shatter of his million particles and their liquid union. Asunder and created whole. Nothing matters any more and everything is to be held, achingly, forever. Submerged in the familiar colours of reality and adrift in the invisible unknowing, untouched, empty of self.

And yet Janu knew his life entirely, every essence held in a single intangible thought. Far away, truth was in his reach.

Movement, journey, yearning, reaching out.

He knew a gold surpassing all imagination, swimming reflection of vast alien sun. An ocean held childlike, cupped in a hollow atop the furthest mountain. Shimmering, the water trembling, lest she spill her tears, slipping against warm flushed skin. Climbing breathlessly, then he dives into the agony of golden depths, tearful blind and wild with sweet sadness.

Silence stops in stillness. Forever.

Inside himself. In the centre is the light unborn. Smiling ancient eyes. A tiny hand reaches out and holds him and the fragile touch is truth. Holding eternity in one word.

Why?

A question so alien, unwanted. Yes, yes, alien but searching, seeking him, a burning which is knowledge, the taste of human betrayal, the unwelcome clasp of a hand which rips him forth, drags him out, screaming, blind, helpless, naked, engulfed once more by the pain. Born.

The bond is broken.

Suddenly Janu breathes again, and it is the stench of his own death, which fills his lungs. He tries to scream, but his mouth fills with earth which is life.

My head, full of my tongue, is stuck to the inside of my stomach. I hardly recall boarding this aeroplane, but I remember Dan calling out to me, he wanted to tell me something before I left. It's the dead, he says. They are in Batavia.

Batavia? But that's where I'm going, I tell my hostess. She smiles sympathetically, as if she had known all along, and buckles a belt across my lap.

As the jet took off I was already sinking into sleep, my thoughts a circus of Gothic tombs, a grieving widow with Dan-style sideburns and my own hand reaching out, clutching for a necklace of petals that fly from me into the sky like the true wildflowers they always were.

****

Chapter Seven

The Memory of Incense

IT'S freezing, Jimmy. You're letting in all the cold. Come in and close the door, for goodness sake. No, Anna. No, the cold is already inside us. Goodness is gone, flown away, left these small birds on the step. Frozen dead they are, cupped together in each other's wings. It isn't the winter. Lack of love's what killed them. Can't you feel it yet? Sssh, listen! That crack isn't the ice. It must be the aeroplane, these things shouldn't still be flying. Look out, Bernie, the wings have fallen off! Tell the pilot. We're on the ground? Okay, Dan, that must be the guns then, the guns are louder now aren't they? Can you tell us anything about this latest development, Jimmy Blue? Well, all I can say at this moment in time is a bunch of really bad men over there are getting nearer to here where I'm standing inside your spider eyes. I don't know if you can hear this in the studio? I think they're humming some kind of traditional human battle song. Quite fascinating and strangely arousing.

Bang!

I woke.

Above my head the air-conditioning unit sparked again and settled back into a phlegm-rattling thrum. When I could thole the noise no longer I reached up and pulled the flex from the wall.

My chest had frozen into a solid slab of meat but the night heat had tangled my lower half into a merman's tail of slick skin and soaked linen. I kicked out, disentangled myself, stiff-leg stilted into the bathroom.

The shower nozzle drizzled brown, stopped. Squinting through suds, I fumbled for my watch. 07:00. My first day in Batavia.

At least there was water for the basin. I fumbled in my toilet bag for a lazor, began shaving in the blue light of the beam, stared at the floor as it became slick with brown water, oozing from the crack in the sink, what hadn't disappeared into a slow, sucking whirlpool.

I knew it wasn't just the heat making me feel dizzy.

I turned off the taps and sank back on to the bed and stared at the flesh-mottled ceiling for a long time. Thousands of miles from myself. Still got to get away. Get out of here.

In the lobby of the hotel a man in a slumped black suit waited on the distended lump of cushions. He blinked once and his eyes narrowed. Cheap, slow corneas. His face, cratered and greasy, dripped around a bone white smile.

"Morning! I mean Buenos," I nodded.

The smile remained and five fingers raked the slick of black hair.

I stepped outside and was immediately attacked, the heat attempting to kidnap me, wrapping an arm around my shoulders while slapping a hot, suffocating towel around my face.

It was already 08:00 but the streets were empty. A holiday? Perhaps everything was closed because of the shootings in the piazza? I didn't even know where the piazza was, whether it was even in this city.

Here, in the shadows of the sprawled business district, with its hollow skyscrapers and metal sheds filled only with stale, hot air, the streets were a recumbent jumble of 60-storey, no-star, no-guest hotels and shuttered hole-in-the-wall stores. Where there were pavements, the litter had gathered itself into neat little steaming volcanoes. On every available hoarding space were patchwork posters of El Presidente, Senor Chavez, an avuncular fellow with a round brown face and bouffant moustache and the ink-black eyes of a man who could happily strangle the newborn.

The Morning Parks

Batavia's capital was quite unlike any other city I had ever been. True, as in every other city anywhere in the world, there were the four key elements of human existence: the signs advertising Siren, the indeterminate smell of something burning, a for-hire buzzcab that would never stop, and, yes, there he is, the drunk never seen before yet who greets me as a long-lost intimate.

But here there were no Morning Parks. There was no sign of manicured lawns or tailored trees. Where buildings had been destroyed, fragments of empty, blackened shells remained, with twisted metal bones protruding from the brick and concrete.

I stomped my way past the decaying piles through the heat into the heart of city, my new companion in tow, a long beard and overcoat on flappity, grey legs leading an invisible oompah band with his beer bottle baton.

I soon gave up all hope of an accidental cafe. The heat was too much even this early. I should turn back. Instead I turned a corner into a suddenly burst bubble of noise and movement, a cobbled piazza framed by huge arched walkways, chequered with round tables set under white parasols, where red waistcoated waiters scurried amid the hundreds of patrons with baskets of bread and pots of steaming, aromatic coffee.

Tight groups of swell-bellied old men huddled in dark suits over cards and glasses of meatrum. In one corner there were stalls heaped with huge, nubile fruits and earth-caked boulders, in the other was a trestle with plastic figurines of the Madonna, lined up in battle formation, and a clothes horse draped with outrageous, rainbow-coloured shirts.

I felt my dejected companion shuffle on the edge of this new sanctuary, an invisible boundary barring entry. The drunk cursed and wheeled away. Unapologetically, I made for a table in the heart of the others.

Now here am I in the shade, sipping real orange juice, forking a greasy omelette, with my notebook open in front of me, scrawling in the slim margins where Janu does not live.

Maybe today could get better.

The morning grows longer, I have scribbled. My body has certainly grown heavier with the shock of real bread and devilled eggs and far too many coffees that do not come with a crunch, but my mood is lighter, buoyed by the unintelligible chatter of those around me.

It is half past ten but all of the seats have filled with families, babies to grandparents, all waving excitedly at the waiters, at each other, talking at one another, so loudly, so animatedly, so bravely, I think, since the word Chavez punctures their conversation repeatedly like a fire cracker. Or a rifle shot.

I could not have imagined such a scene. Where are the Abidar?

For a moment I, too, cannot help but feel part of this, a scene from some colourful, antique holoflick.

I eye the empty cup and wave at the harumph of a waiter. He has tried to clear my table twice already.

I sink further into my chair and smell the unmistakable scent of oranges. No, there is apple here, too, bitter yet crisply sweet. Now something else, something entirely new to me, cinnamon, vanilla?

I raise my head slowly, inhaling. I want to sit here forever in yellow light, enjoy the alien aromas. I wave again, order my coffee, and read my notes as the new scent settles happily on my shoulders.

THE roan was difficult to spy within the greyblack columns. Until she stamped one foreleg and blew white breath. The rider leaned forward and slapped her gently across the solid muscle of her neck. It is only the wind playing her fingers across the bones of the branches.

Ahead, the boundary of the graveyard was watered indistinct by the early morning, and there nothing moved amid the forgotten tumble of time-broken stones.

But here, below their huddled skeletons, the ragged clothes of tarnished gold would swirl, chase themselves across the hard ground, and cluster nervously around the solitary wooden cross.

The rider nudged forward, coaxing without voice. He threw the hood back from his face and bowed his head and now he could see the words etched too boldly into the soft wood.

So this is your victory, Janu? Exiled, even in death.

Giraud dismounted, crouched before the name, and the wind clawed like a shrieking mourner at his back.

He felt nothing. Even the emptiness had left him.

Thoughts are stones, he sighed. Muscle and tissue and flesh and earth, latticed with the bones once called friend. Such strange happiness we seek to end as this. A bittersweet taste after all.

Must I think you chose well, Janu? Can I believe the living wise to adorn themselves with the mantle of grief, or stain your cold courage with envy for your warm life? Yes, still I am jealous of your sweet breath.

The trees rattle their sabres. The world is walking slowly into winter and cares not that she is dying. I pray such cool embrace could steel my arteries, crystallise my blood. For none shall speak your name. In every sinew I will breath hatred for what you called love. The heart is weakness that bleeds us dry. My heart beds with you, oblivious in the womb that awaits us all.

A sound? People approach on the road below. The wretched moan of a dead man's refugees.

Giraud half rose to leave, but on impulse reached out. The name was rough beneath his fingers, lost beyond even touch. Yet at once his hand was grabbed, his whole body dragged forward, and he cried out and the world disappeared, reality exploded into void, then he was back on the ground, kneeling before the cross, every shredded breath rasping through his body.

And the world was new. He could feel the fear in the drumming breast of every creature, the terror in every frantic pulse. And he smiled with knowing and his eyes were hatred indeed.

He rose then and rode his horse from that place and when he met the road the ragged funeral procession stopped and stared up, their faces covered against the rich legacy of their loved one, all but their rabbit eyes, and he smiled at their plaintive moans and he spoke.

Whom do you curse?

Sir? A half-naked boy who was shivering.
The rider pointed to the makeshift box.
Sir, 'tis my father.
Giraud leaned down then whispered. Bury him deep, boy. Outside are the dogs and they fear not the smell of death.
And he rode on into the heart of the city.

I lay down my pen and wave, ignoring how the empty tray is gripped like armour with crossed forearms to the waiter's chest, and order a tall glass of ice-cold water. Giraud's anger has solidified inside me. It feels empowering.

And at the very heart, in its temple, Marlov could feel the lump at his back, kneeling in silent stupid adoration, so perfectly oblivious to every word. Dear God, always their crassness disgusted him. How the ignorant feared burning.

He was unbearably bored inside himself and tried to throw amusement into the pit by filling his jumbled litany with references to this day to come, to his own lust. He could almost taste the freshness as his mind touched the treasure hidden for him, hidden not so deep, slow writhing, chained in her trembling cell, her perfect skin, the sweep of his hand across that hot silk, warm wetness that clung.

A hot breath touched his cheek, incense filled his nostrils. He faltered in his sentence. Why has it grown so perversely hot beneath these vestments? The coarse weight of faces was leering hard and dead upon his shoulders.

He sneered. If only they would all follow that fool Janu. Poor demented brave warrior Janu. He should say a prayer for the repose of his soul? Yes, oh, yes, pray for the damned! Delicious. The thought of the young guard giving his life left him breathless.

He knelt with a slow thud before the altar, half raised his hands in supplication and resumed his mumbled homage. Ah, when did this kneeler become such sharp rock beneath his swollen knees. He sways uncomfortably and still the clammy heat clumsily massages the nape of his neck.

Somewhere someone is muttering. Muttering? Yes, calling his name. He turns. The heads are all bowed. Obeisance.

He clasped his hands, stared hard into the grey folds of the white cloth, when a ghastly pain seized his head. No, not pain. Surely, this is not a whisper.

I am coming.

Slowly his gaze is dragged above, to the figure nailed in agony.

He has never noticed the pain, not until now. Real human pain screaming for release in every contortion of the wood. That pathetic face, crowned red with the spikes of every sin, transfixed in eternal torment. Those betrayed eyes pleading to the domed heaven. So real now. So real they move, they move, they roll down, they look upon him, and they know. My God, they know!

I am coming!

Marlov's hands fall, grab, clutch his stiff vestments to his throat. No, no, this cannot be, but those eyes will not release him, he can feel them scoop inside his mind, searching, ploughing through his life, churning every thought and every deed. Racing nearer, nearer, to the dark place.

He tried to clamber to his feet, stumbled backwards, his mitre tumbling from his huge shaven head. There were gasps now, a wave of shock rushing through the congregation, and Madame Choufos in the front pew fell into a dead faint.

See! The crucifix is blood. Flames dance from within the wood, they leap out in a fury of colour, crushed madness, scorching his eyes, screaming into his brain.

I am coming!

The figure on the cross is holding out his right arm from the flames, his long splintered finger is pointing into Marlov's soul.

I am coming!

A hand grabs Marlov's elbow, he whirls, Are you well, Eminence? Eminence? The priest, his worried young face, his wide eyes, his alarm, stare into the Cardinal. Please!

Marlov tries to speak, turns, lifts his eyes to the cross. No, it was nothing. Nothing.
   Dead wood.

Not wood, not dead anyway, but the aromatic notes of bark and sap. The smell has become so real.
   A girl is walking towards me. Her hair, scooped back by a single blue ribbon, is braided thick and black, like a ship's rope, wet and weighted to the small of her back so that it draws up her face, proudly, and the peak of her small chin sails effortlessly around the tables.
   Now I can see in the loop of her slim brown arm is a polished steel bucket, filled not with flowers but colourfully wrapped incense sticks.
   I look up at her as she nears but the sun swells around her head until her face is dark, and when she moves closer still to my side it hides everything from my view but the slow smile, shy and unsure.
   Can someone really be so happy selling incense, this pretty girl here in the heat of this city?
   "Life goes on, senor, whether you are happy or not."
   "Sorry? I mean, perdon?"
   "Your face, senor. You were thinking so much sadness."
   "No, I was . . . no."
   I point to the bucket, ask, "Which is the one I can smell most right now?"
   The smile crinkles her eyes and reveals the tips of her teeth, which are small and white and perfectly square and bite her bottom lip.
   She says, "Tolu. It is from Eilidon."
   The word slaps my face and suddenly I am fully awake, alert, but in the same instant the steel bucket is nudged into my side.
   "Yes," I say, "of course, I'll take this."
   I grasp for the stick, too quickly, for I feel it snap in my grip, but say nothing and slip it under my notebook and delve into the side pocket of my cargo pants for coins.
   "Eilidon," I begin and in that same moment I see the lion and the eagle staring at me from a circle of flesh on the far side of the piazza.

I wheel awkwardly in my seat, my hand stuck in the pocket, and watch a head of short blonde spikes and sweat-stained white vest lost immediately in the passers-by, too quickly swallowed by the clamour.

I stand and the incense seller takes fright for she steps back into the sunshine and immediately vanishes into the light.

Bewildered I take two steps from the table and the harumph scuttles up to me, fearful I will leave without paying. But I have seen it. I'm sure I have. The unique blue-black image of love in a circle of swirls, the stamp of lion and eagle entwined, embraced and entranced, tattooed on a bare shoulder.

I turn to the girl to tell her but the incense seller is gone.

****

Chapter Eight

The Circus House

STATIC wrinkles Sam's face. I slap the screen.

"Hello? Hello, have you got me?"

"Now, Jimmy, yes. How's the sabbatical? You look like shit, you know."

"Weird, Sam, no really, really weird. It's like I'm living in a scene from my own history channel. Bizarre. I think they put more than beans in the coffee. It's not Siren's, you know, I think it's fresh."

"Yeah, right. And the climate? Hot? More shootings?"

"No. But I got your mail. What's happening?"

"Listen, it's Blake. Screaming blue murder. We're down in the points again, of course. He wants you do something from there."

"Here from Batavia? No, it seems quiet now. Pleasant in fact, if altogether weird for me."

"Well, best see if you can get your hands on a deck of unpleasant InfoDats and mail them yesterday. Maybe best you call Blake, too, Jimmy. Don't think he realised he was sending off his only real points winner, even if you did mess him up with that Siren stuff. You know he's already calling you the Exile."

Sam's face bounced once then the screen blacked entirely.

"Hello? Sam?"

Static, a flicker then he was back.

"Yeah, yeah, I'm here. Lousy link you're in there, Jimmy. By the way, there's a screenshot came in for you, branded from New York, coded though. Doesn't she know where you are?"

There is a scream and I turn. Forty yards from my link, on the opposite side of the street, half a dozen men in army fatigues, guns slung over shoulders, have surrounded a woman. Her head is covered by a black shawl. She stoops closer to the ground. There is a scuffle, someone falls to the pavement, another scream erupts and, involuntarily, I take a step forward, then freeze.

Everyone is shocked still, now everyone is running, now I watch from the link as two of the soldiers emerge from the chaos of fleeing bodies dragging another man between them. This man must be unconscious for his head lolls back on a neck that is too long and his feet drag so that his shoes and socks come off and his heels leave two slicks of gloss red paint on the road.

His body is folded into the back of a buzzvan and all of the soldiers clamber into the front. The buzzvan jets around and passes the link and I feel the hot air brush my legs as the last soldier looks through the windscreen straight at me and smiles. I look at the ground.

The woman is still screaming and I know she is stumbling after them.

"Jimmy? Jimmy, what's happening? Get out the way, I can't see."

I turn back into the link and my legs feel weak as I crouch closer to the screen.

"I'm here. Listen, things are, it's getting a bit wild, right here, now. Anna, you said Anna…"

"That's what I'm saying, Jimmy, can you hear me? I've lost your cam again."

"What? What about Anna, Sam?"

Another burst of static then nothing. I thumb the screen. Nothing. The link is dead.

I stand up and turn and watch the woman wrestled by her family back inside the building. A horrible, breath-stealing quiet descends on the street and I realise I am entirely alone.

I begin walking. Walking, I hope, in the direction of the hotel. My feet are heavy and slow. I cannot get what happened to fall behind me

The Morning Parks

quickly enough. I see the image of raw flesh. It is peeling like butter from the man's heels.

****

"TRANSPORT, Senor?"

The atmosphere is a choking mix of bullet rain and bayonet red mud. Sometimes it's pouring so hard it's difficult to tell which way is up, for it seems the mud is falling from the sky and the rain leaping from the ground.

Moving out into this alien landscape is dangerous. Batavians move fast. Often it seems the lower halves of their bodies are made up of tiny engines and two wheels, as they trundle across the mudflats at amazing speeds, often directly into my path.

I seek refuge in a closed doorway, squinting out through the bullets, glimpse hundreds upon hundreds of grey apparitions, buzzscooting in every other direction, while here I breathe in mosquitoes in the hot shadows amid an incessant buzz that no flurry of palms can dispel.

"Hey, Senor! Cerveza? Transport? Massage, Senor?"

It is my fifth day in Batavia and I have learned that everyone from the shopkeeper to masseuse touts for business like a toddler demands his Siren milk; with loud, long repetition, and a high-pitched urgency in their voice, close to tears.

Despite the seeming abundance of fresh food, many of these people are desperate. Here in the city that is the Gateway to Dreams, poverty is a constant nightmare.

Today is a market day. Around my hotel the streets have sprouted clumps of plastiboard. On the stalls hang clear plastic bags filled with water and floating bricks. Only when I get closer do I realise the contents are cloned fish, fat with googly eyes, unblinking, staring back at me forlornly. Perhaps they are dreaming of rivers they have never seen.

The one-way avenues, river rapids of three-to-the-saddle buzzscoots and hammer-headed white-bellied buzzcabs, are edged with freshly churned, ditches that bubble with water.

"Putting in drains after the floods," says a voice from the shadow of a doorway. "But they forget to buy the pipes. You want me to get buzzcab, Senor?"

Despite the speedway I witness only one close encounter. A huge man in a beige suit opens his cab door and is instantly belly-impaled on the handlebars of an ancient buzzscoot.

"You bloody bitch!" he bellows, wiping the wide curve of his shirt. The girl in a flimsy white dress bows her head and reverses quickly away, turns her beautiful doe-eyes to me, then to the road ahead, and hovers on, leaving a wake of white mist.

Finally, the rain pauses and the steam rises from the earth, bringing with it an unimaginable stink. I seek refuge in the rooftop pool of the hotel where I float on my back, even here trying to ignore the acrid stench of warm chlorine, admiring the single cloud in the blue skies beyond my lily-white belly, just like the marshmallow in the Mole advert, wandering again why I am here, where is the incense seller, for she has not returned to the piazza, and where is the wearer of my tattoo?

Eilidon. Can I be sure the girl said Eilidon?

Later I search for supper along a deserted canal front. A tiny black creature, the size of a hover ball with a pink tail, has the same notion and scurries between my feet to cupped palm-plates of rice and cut flowers. The brown-bellied boy in ragged shorts, who tries to sell me fruit-flavoured candy every morning, explains these plates are offerings left every morning to placate the devils that come on Holy Night. I buy a handful of banana chews from him, but they stick to my teeth and fizz until I have to spit them out and the boy runs away, laughing.

In the Monkey Bar, the concrete walls are decorated with fragile pink paper lanterns and garlands of white flowers. I choose a table overlooking the street and watch the world go by in all its bedlam: happily unravelled strings of families, tightly knotted couples, the same bewildered, pinballing tourist in his beige suit, searching for his Dream, looking for company, growling at anyone close enough.

The mountain of white rice has a rich seam of yellow. They are called pepper, says the girl. I smile at her and begin to dig.

"Fantastico!" I say to the bemused waitress, "Yes, I mean, very good."

Buoyed by the taste of more fresh food, I wander the night streets until I come to a bar where a band play in bare feet and dinner jackets for me, the barman and half a dozen porcelain skinned dolls in red hotpants. When the girls begin to make their fly-bys, I know it's time to drink up and leave them to circle the band instead.

But next morning I wake from a surreal dream of mosquito-headed vendors and man-eating holes. I think there was even a doll in hotpants on a bicycle chasing me, begging me to have a massage. My body is not used to food. But the pain of my hangover is nothing to the discomfort I'm feeling as night falls.

I'm in a windowless room in a suburb of skyports in the north of the city, trying to make a deck of holocards come into focus. Not for the first time I ask myself how I have come to be here. Of all the things I've tried for points this is probably the most stupid. Charlie would be squeezing his head in his hands, if he could see me now. Perhaps he will never see me again.

"Eeargh! Where your money, you silly boy?" shrieks the man opposite and bangs his gold-ringed fingers on the blue felt and sticks his tiny, yellow marble eyes inches from mine, his jowls waggling like an angry wattle. "Where?"

He'd been far more amiable when flouncing into the circular room, carrying a metal box. He'd pressed both thumbs onto it and it dispensed a wad of credits the size of a brick.

"Mr Lee," our croupier Uncle Aree had said to him, "so sorry. No dominoes today. China men, they no make it."

"Why you no link meeee?" gasped Mr Lee, placing one gold signet in his mouth and making a gun shape to Uncle Aree's head with his other hand.

"You very naughty man. But who this lovely boy?"

I shake Mr Lee's gun hand and a huge girl squeezes on to the bench beside me, blocking the only doorway. She giggles like a schoolgirl and nudges my ribs. I smile miserably at Senorita Cee.

"This is Mr Jimmy Blue. He is a Blackjack man. Will you play?"

Before I can think to protest Mr Lee nods and Uncle is dealing.

This had begun a lot better. I have to tell myself it did, it must have.

The link is dead, and the next, and another. So I'm sitting in a café, stirring my sore head into more thick coffee, when Senorita Cee introduces herself.

I've only enough time to see she is an enormous Batavian girl, perhaps aged twenty, perhaps forty, shoehorned into bulging denims and a Chavez Rocks t-shirt, before she has settled heavily next to me and is telling me she is staying with Uncle, who lives with Mama, who has a bad heart, and she came to the city with her sister, who is going to enrol in the Siren outreach programme, and who should meet me because I could help her in the city, and here's her own number for me to call and what do I do for my job, with those fancy clothes, and maybe I could also give advice to Uncle Aree, he's a croupier at the casino, yes here in the city?

Miss Cee belongs to one of Batavia's extortion gangs. I'd read the InfoDats before flying. But there is no harm in talking. I should get something for Charlie, earn some points and my way back in. No-one has been shot lately. I persuade myself I can walk away with enough juice if the situation gets uncomfortable.

A 30-minute drive in a buzzcab takes us to the white mushroom, hundreds of feet above the streets of a suburb south of the airport. They must have made these buildings before the Hits began.

"Ah," cries Senorita Cee as the portal opens, "I forget but Mama and my sister will be at the hospital."

"Yes, Mama got bad legs," says Uncle, who appears from a back room and is a chocolate brown man in his sixties with warning red wires for hair. His eyes are lost in the crinkles of his cheeks, as he reveals two remaining front teeth. He does not seem the kind of man who might spend his afternoons kidnapping tourists.

"Bad legs?"

"From the bad heart," says Senorita Cee, quickly announcing we will eat. She fills the table before my armchair with dishes until I'm the centrepiece of an alien smorgasbord of whole, bug-eyed fish and chunks of pale-fleshed mammal.

"Real, all real Batavian food, no Siren!" she cries.

I pick at some rice, queasily aware they could be trying to poison me.

Between spells of chewing and staring at the blank, windowless walls, I listen to Uncle's sporadic attempts at conversation.

"Alone?" he asks, incredulous. "Your wife does not like Batavia?"

"Yes, I mean, no, I have no wife."

"Ah... well then it is best she is not here."

I skip Senorita Cee's offer of coffee and suggest perhaps I should be going.

"Oh, no! First we talk?"

Uncle warms his voice. He earns so little at the casino. Fortunately, for both of us he has a system for winning at Blackjack. If only he had a friend like me to help him, for only a rich foreigner like me would be allowed at the table.

I smile. I'm to be groomed as his accomplice? The rub will come soon after when I'm asked to grease his agile fingers. Simple. Well, that's that.

"Well, Uncle Aree, I hope it works out for you, I really do, but I must be going."

Senorita Cee is crestfallen. But Mama and Sister! They will be here in only ten very small minutes.

"Yes," cries Uncle, his eyes suddenly appearing in the middle of his face. He produces a pack of holocards. "Ten minutes. You watch."

I watch and, while we wait small minutes, he shows me how to cheat at Blackjack, his slim brown fingers and thumbs, fanning out, curling, tapping the table, revealing the next card in the air before him and the next and even the banker's with a variety of shapes and codes. The air crackles and the holocards blur with the speed of his fingers.

"Bueno!" he announces, when I win another hand, surely both of us knowing full well a casino's com-spy could never miss such fumbling.

"I've really got to go now."

"You try in casino?" Uncle gasps.

"No, no money."

"Well," he says, "a senor, he win 40,000 in this room. Yesterday. In this room, you understand? Here, yesterday. Dominoes. Bad man. Give me no commission!"

"Oh, too bad," I say.

"He's, you know, big man. Greedy. They all greedy. Hey, you practise him, Senor Blue? Get my money? I give you 200, no charge. You win, we win. You lose, no problem."

"No, no, I really must go."

Enter stage right big, bad man.

I'm already on my feet, but Senorita Cee's air-cushioned hips have me cornered and the China man has produced his magic box of credits and in a rush and a haze and a flurry of words and holocards, Uncle is already dealing.

"Okay, okay!" says Mr Lee. "Let's go here, let's go!"

The air in front of me is filled with rectangles of colour and before I can even focus on them, the first hand is won, easily, of course, though Uncle has had to repeat his signs. That's about 800 from the first deal.

I win the next hand. I think that's 2000. I look at my watch.

"Well, you know, it's that time," I venture.

Uncle nods slightly. Is he agreeing I should go? Is he saying I have to stay?

"So this hand you feel lucky, lovely boy?" cries Mr Lee, clicking his fat fingers in my face.

"Maybe, maybe. It's my last hand!"

"Last? Oh, but how can I win my money? You bet so strong, lovely boy! Okay, okay, last. Let's go!"

I'll lose my winnings, Uncle's 200, everything. Or I'll win and leave the credits here with him. Either way, I'm out of here.

I haven't banked on Mr Lee. Another brick slides out from his box.

Uncle counts.

The bet is 37,000 credits.

"What you do now, lovely boy?" asks Mr Lee.

He knows. He must do. I don't have credits. Can I fold? Is it allowed? I stare at the cards floating before me, glance at Uncle.

"You need the house credit, Senor?" Uncle Aree asks me, showing me the next card with three fingers. It is an ace. I know Mr Lee's sitting on 20. The black back of his cards hover inches from my nose. I have 10. I'll win everything

Uncle is kicking me under the table. Senorita Cee is hammering my ribs with the giant pad of her elbow.

If I take Uncle's credit and win what if Mr Lee discovers we're cheating? I picture his gun-shaped hand. If I take credit and lose? What's to stop Uncle cheating me now and producing the wrong card? Mr Lee must be paid.

Can I fold? If I fold won't Uncle believe I've just thrown his share?

Right now I realize I'm not very good at playing undercover and the cards blur and I can see Charlie Blake III's face turning purple and Mr Lee cries: "Eeargh! Where your money, you silly boy?"

Uncle points excitedly to his screen, says the house covers and decides I've already agreed by pushing the next card at me. It floats there, veiled, waiting for me to touch the image.

But Mr Lee isn't satisfied. He wants at least a credit card produced.

"You don't trust me? Then the game is void!" I declare.

Both men look shocked. Senorita Cee is shocked. I am shocked. I don't know if can do this .

"No, no. S'ok. We finish," says Uncle, cowed. He hasn't expected my tack?

"Mr Lee just need insurance," he says, "Maybe you have a card, Senor Jimmy Blue?"

So this is it. But I have neither card nor credits with me and empty my pockets to prove it. Everyone looks flummoxed, until Senorita Cee, with a sudden, grim authority announces we shall postpone turning the cards for two hours. They are frozen, retina-locked, and the 37,000 credits disappear into a drawer hidden below the blue felt table.

On cue, Mr Lee exits stage right, out into the night.

Senorita Cee turns to me. I will get credits to match the stake then we can all win, she tells me, quite matter of factly.

"My credit card is not working properly in Batavia," I say. "The links are dead."

Someone bumps heavily into furniture in the adjoining room. There is a loud cough.

"Yes, of course," I say. "But if you take me back to the city. I'll contact my bank."

I'm ushered back into the buzzcar. There are two men already inside, but only one turns to me. It is dark, I am tired and on edge, and I cannot be sure it is the man from the hotel lobby. But when he smiles at me, it is the same smile, and I stare at him, say nothing, cannot even squirm as my right leg is pinned under the weight of Senorita Cee's thigh.

I try to see the link on the windscreen but the second man hides it with his shoulder.

"It's a pity I didn't get to meet Mama and your sister," I say.

Senorita Cee's little girl laugh has disappeared. She wants to know what hotel I'm staying in. I cannot remember the name properly.

"Bata something."

The man from the lobby says nothing. We drive in silence. The men stare ahead and Senorita Cee hums softly.

"Ah, we can stop here," I say. "I can check everything here, just here the link is good. They will port the credits."

This pleases Senorita Cee immensely. She rediscovers her laugh.

"Oh, yes, you must try this, Senor Blue. Much better. We can wait."

"No, Senorita, you are so kind already. Come back for me here in just ten minutes. Banks are so slow."

The man from the lobby with the skeleton smile turns slowly and looks at me, nods once, and Senorita Cee opens the door.

I stand in the doorway of the link and watch them drive off then stop and hover at the corner. At once I run across the road, through the neon-sparkled rain, up an alleyway, down another, through the crowded streets.

Only once do I stop, when a young soldier appears at a corner before me, his rifle already swinging from his shoulder. But he seems more shocked than I, lets the weapon fall and backs against the wall, and so I walk on, breathless, confused, waiting for a shout that does not come.

An hour later I'm here in my hotel room with the chair jammed against the door handle.

****

Next day I did not leave my hotel room until noon. I'd swigged from a bottle of meatrum and counted the cockroaches on the headboard because I could not sleep but now the sun was baking my brain. I could not bear to spend another minute in this concrete cell.

The couch in the lobby was empty.

I wandered until I reached the empty piazza. It was late and fat shadows stretched back and lay down in the corners. There was no sign of the incense seller. Down through the raggedy streets, into the deeper quiet of downtown apartment blocks, I wandered to where siestas whispered from between half-closed window shutters, from bedrooms where I imagined lazy fans breathed erotic daydreams on to heavy eyelids and naked limbs.

I had a sudden longing to feel the slow rustle of cool sheets. The meatrum had been too much. The sun was too high. I imagined your long legs, Anna, curled around mine, and those breasts bathed in the citrus light of the City afternoon through your window.

I sought shade under the laundry lines of the drunken back streets, blundering once into a line of flimsy curtains or towels, until I found a narrow way where the smell of carbolic and cotton lay like a fire blanket on top of the garbage fumes.

I turned at the sound of leather scuffing the cobblestones, the squeak of a step, stopped short. Shadows crowded the entrance to the alleyway, when I turned, yet he was unmistakable in his slunken suit against the wall. I don't know how long the man with the skeleton smile had been following me. How close, then, were the others?

I ducked under the white flags of a low-strung line and came face to wood with a doorway. It had fallen backwards into the wall in fright. There was no handle, just as there were no windows to puncture the brickwork on either side, but a metal sign tacked to the lintel said in handpainted red letters: The Circus House.

A quick scraping of wood on stone and then a black curtain of cold slapped against my cheeks and chest and thighs. I stood blinking, pinned, until I could see my next few steps. The inside of the room was a chilled crypt, its corners not shadows, simply not there, as though the edges of this entire canvas had been rubbed too often by greasy fingers.

I stumbled forward. Even as I stood at the glass-topped bar a bottle was pushed before me, but not from a Vendor. Without a word, a tiny barman climbed back onboard his stool, his head bowed, his nose buried in his burned-black beard, his round, wrinkled eyes upon me.

I turned to the door, but I had not been followed inside. This is too much, I told myself. Too much. But, of course, I took a long swig before his bottle foamed itself empty. Immediately the barman climbed down from his stool and produced another meatbeer.

As I sipped and watched, a hole would open in his whiskers, but no words appeared. Mine host was content to glance up occasionally with his huge, shocked-fish eyes. And slowly return to his reverie. I stood for a long while, sipping and waiting for the door to open until, finally, inevitably, I returned to my own.

Anna? I checked but my phone was still dead. It seemed no privs worked in Batavia. I should get to a link. What if they were waiting outside?

Enough. I pushed the bottle away but another appeared. When I looked up the barman was already clambering back on to his stool.

As the third went down, swallowed quickly so that I could not taste its warmth, so did my anger, my fear, and I tried to think not of strangers, of Blackjack, Blake's points, of the incense seller, the memory of Tolu, even of a tattoo on a bare shoulder. What strangeness, that there should be such a mark on someone else's shoulder.

Anna. What do you want? All I want is to read your message from New York.

"Cervezas, senor?"

Strangely heavy, my head swung first left then right. A tiny doll had appeared at each shoulder, faces messed with rouge and lipstick, as though their mistresses had begun playing at make-up but were called away too soon. Despite the cold in this meat freezer, each girl wore a thong and their tiny breasts were cling-wrapped in clear bikini tops. Both, I noticed, stood barefoot on the chill concrete.

"Cerveza! Cerveza!" they cried, giggling, plucking at my elbows.

I considered pleading poverty, could not think of the words, when the barman appeared and the girls were already clasping huge beer bottles, tightly so that they left wet marks against their chests, had begun chatting to one another, as though I were no longer here, their high-pitched conversation flitting to and fro like a fretful butterfly across my lap.

A butterfly? I had seen a butterfly once. Where?

I stood bewildered, felt myself sway slightly, my tongue dried by mouthfuls of the girls' overwhelming perfume and raw sweat. Should I excuse myself or stand here until they got bored and moved away? Silence seemed more polite. The air was too heavy to talk anyway.

Finally, I think it may have been before I finished the third beer, or the fourth, the girls retreated, giggling, to a corner of the room, where they vanished instantly into a dark smudge.

I finished this bottle quickly. I, too, had best disappear.

I tired to lift my hand to wave, but this time the barman's eyes did not appear.

"Your credits!"

I didn't turn because my ears refused to acknowledge the menace in the voice behind me. It was only when a claw dug under my collar bone and swung me round did I meet the giant who was about to punch me. It wasn't a man. It was a black bear, flat-nosed with dark wool from belly to brow, dressed comically in a man's jeans and leather waistcoat. The bear was growling.

"Credits!"

I glanced sideways. The barman's eyes had disappeared entirely inside his beard.

"Credits!" growled the bear.

I stumped fingers into my trouser pocket and found nothing. My satchel? Here it is. Still on my shoulder of all places. You see? Don't you worry, Mr Bear, it's in here, surely, that the wallet is.

"Credits!"

I shook my head, grinned stupidly, even though from inside my stomach my head was screaming up at me: don't smile, idiot boy, run!

I did not feel the first punch in the gut nor the second on the cheek, not even the third which snapped my head backwards and left me squirming and twitching on the floor, but quite shortly afterwards I felt the sudden impact of all three at once, followed by the piledrive of a boot smashing repeatedly into the back wall of my stomach, right up into my chest.

A shadow passed near my head, a shoe with a squeak of leather, and the air was punched by a shaft of warm light as a figure disappeared out into the street.

At last the bear stopped kicking me and slunked away. With the lasting, final image of the tiny, bearded barman, suddenly so tall, approaching my face with his barstool raised preposterously above his head, I felt nothing.

****

Chapter Nine

Going Underground

DEAD wood. My head. I'm trying to find the softness, but voices get in the way and feel for me with sharp nails and would drag me back up into the hard place.

I'm slipping again. Soft and wet and I want to stay down here, even if I drown, because here the hardness cannot touch me.

The voices insist. I try to think of a girl's name but she is too far away and lost from me. I try to see her face but when I almost imagine a smile and long golden hair she is always turned from me and I feel suddenly afraid because I know she cannot hear me call. Nor is the girl Rosa here. I think she is gone for now, though she was with me in the darkness for a while, breathing in my ears, whispering secrets. Not Bernie, for she was a dream from long ago. None of these.

I see instead the face of an old woman in a black shawl, lit against the ribs of a hungry church, a hollowness that swallows us both whole. Now a cell where there is only hard sleep.

Dead wood against dead stones lost in the dead sleep of heavy lids and a vision of one hundred immaculate angels robed in black, singing waterfalls and fountains of exquisite harmony to their mother, and she would bow, meekly, gracefully accepting benediction. Do you see such grace?

This radiation of love, around her the halo of ageless purity shining for all the poor and unfortunate to behold, a beacon to the whole world, a meek genuflection of maternal comfort to sinful and small leprous children. She their cure. She could be. Everybody knows she could.

The silence in the room snapped her reverie. Mother Symna shrunk even deeper into herself, a spittle of sour self-disgust trying to find her dry gums. She fingered the smooth-worn wooden beads between her claws, moaned in short, stifled iambic inhalations.

Her mantram was her weapon. She could block out the sickness, use the prayer to barricade her soul with thorns. Nails dug skin from her paper-crumpled palms. No, not pride, give me pain, give me pain, give me pain.

Lost in the words, fastened to the prayer.

A baby is crying.

It is the wind.

No, no, beyond. Almost forgotten now.

A baby is crying.

What? No. Closer! Somewhere below. Whining like a lost dog. Maybe.

Sleep almost came.

A baby is crying.

She took up the candle and scuffled along the corridors to rouse the doorkeeper. The coughing man was not pleased to be rolled from soft dreams into the midnight, but feared the old woman more. He led her out into the freezing air, followed the faint outlines of the gravel path, and unlocked the gate into the Sisters' walled garden.

Not a sound. Not a whiff. S'dead stillness, s'all. His lantern winked at him.

Perhaps, well, maybe a mewing?

Aint only the cat, s'all, Mother, he'll be caught see, chokin' on one of my snares, dead by light o' mornin', let's get back then, eh? Whassat?

She held up a hooked hand. The pathetic sound had stopped. But she felt revulsion, she was horribly aware of being watched. Something in the more serious night of the far wall. She snatched the lantern from him and thrust it forward. It shook on her weak arm and the light spilled and splashed and the shadows remained.

Then a heavy shuffling sound.

Mother, can't we go back inside now? Eh?

The doorkeeper was already stepping back, his round face a quivering, but the black robes hobbled slowly forward from him, drawn, the lantern sweeping the path.

First the sound of laboured gurgled gasping. Now the grating shuffle of a dragged weight, trailing and crunching the fine stones.

Nearer.

Stop.

The whimpering of pain.

Mother Symna lowered the lantern a little, took one more step forward, just a little step.

A child's face squinted up from the dark, thin and beautiful, and streaked with tears. Such blue beyond blue eyes and matted locks of soiled gold. Her own love. Blue lips will try to speak, mewing, will try to make the words for mama.

Help. Help me. O, my child! My own! Come to me! Mama! Mama!

At once the old nun started forward and at once the light bounced off the wall revealing not the child's body but terror and abomination, a wolf's mutilated carcass. The child burst into a wild crying, it tried to drag itself forward, it shuffled, it crawled and bled towards the horrified old woman.

Help me, mama! Help me!

Mother Symna woke screaming in her cell, fumbled for the cross around her neck. Somewhere outside a dog was howling.

The howling is the moan in my own throat, unable to escape because my teeth are clenched. I am aware the hardness against my back has disappeared and I panic in short, sharp breaths because I am falling from the sky, until I realise I have been lifted, I am being carried by the voices, for it is they who are soft now, carrying me in whispers.

A hand on my brow and that, too, is soft and cool, and so I care not the wind is clawing at my bare back and wet splashes the skin as we move on through the sky.

> *Howling winter days turned to nights and nowhere could escape the voices of the wind, riding insane circles through the city, laughing through the narrow streets, keening beneath doors, battering on windows with icy fists.*
>
> *Hail sliced like knives across the open spaces and no-one would dare leave home, the hiding places; huddled beneath prayers and hollow talk, staring into embers that cowered in the grate.*
>
> *The mutterings by the hearth were of apparitions, of the girl who cried out her lover's name, unseen by the river, of the packs of rabid dogs that hunted now on the hills above the city, of the nuns who had barricaded themselves inside their convent, of the Cardinal cloistered in his chambers, ill with fever and hallucinations, they say, those who know, dare whisper.*
>
> *The old ones have never seen such a winter, and some speak of a time of judgement and the coming of death. The young ones, for once, listen. And are silent.*

I don't want to listen, but I feel someone is near. I don't want to rise. Come close. Closer. Not close enough to know who you are.

An angel's face surprised in a flicker of candlelight, with skin brown and eyes as black in mine own, then nothing again, a smell of something rich and tree-like, burning, no, only this night of dreams where ghosts of dreams are writing themselves into my head.

> *City midnight. Now. Close to the metal roar and chemical flash of our lives. But here, through the heavy iron lattice, which hangs drunk and oblivious on hinges twisted almost from the stone, a staircase down into deeper darkness past.*

Blind, follow the fall of each juddering step. Cold, wrap yourself in prayers. Numb, don't reach out. Walls move.

Not enough air now to fight the stench. Kick soft scuttles crawling at your feet.

Shock into thigh-deep thick-clinging wetness. The stairs have ended? Thin slats of pale yellow neon sluice down from the streets, and sliced by the grill show the slow shiny channel slithering and swithering half-headed away into the tunnel.

Walking beneath the city.

Stop. Climb drip shivering into the hole above the waterline, through a passageway clawed in desperation from the rock. Fingernails have marked these walls. Up close. Gouged. On your knees now.

Finally, opening, widening into long lighted halls, golden catacombs, where in every skull in every hole in every wall a candle grins.

On and on between the endless rows of eternal maniacs and their blazing sockets to this last chamber, black but for the flame which burns at the feet of the figure seated before you.

Enthroned silhouette.

Come closer. Closer. Look upon the white face. Is it pure bone white, white scarred, bold in its bald nakedness? But you are not close enough. Closer still. Closer! Whose eyes open ebony mirrors? Who do you see?

Janu! Not dead? No take him back. Janu died, not me. Where are you going, Giraud? Come back, I'm not dead. Tell him, Anna! Anna?

"She is not here, Senor."

I wake to the memory of incense.

My face feels thick, the skin numb, not my own, and it is difficult to let the world in through my eyes. At last, they open to a sky of leprous green and red wallpaper, turn down, along the twisted sinews of yellow bedclothes, against whose embrace I kick involuntarily, feebly. Their grip is too lusty, my legs weak.

I twist my head, hear inside my head the throat grind against its own dryness, and the bed drifts into the room and under me, as dark banks fan on either side, until we come to rest with a stomach-churning jolt.

Above me hangs the dirty white rectangle of a battery lamp. On a wicker seat beside me is my watch, the metal clasp of the strap twisted but the minute light flick-flicking.

I try to focus beyond.

There is a girl standing in the corner of this room with no windows

"Who?"

My voice cracks in its dryness.

"Who are you? I don't. I don't believe in angels."

I think the angel smiles, even though I cannot see her face.

"I was in a bar? There was someone."

"You cannot walk into such a place alone, Senor, and walk back out."

Her voice, velvet wrapped around my head, feels familiar.

"It was… The Circus? The sign said… I mean, the girls."

"You almost paid for them with your life. Claro, Senor Blue?"

"You know me?"

My head is battling against my words, forcing me to choke on them. Even the hum of the battery on the ceiling is enough to cause the room to pulsate horribly.

"Si, si, I know you. Sleep now."

"No, please, who are you? Where am I?"

Closer to the bed she steps, closer to my face bends, yet her face is hidden still by the dark mane swept from around her shoulder.

"You are lucky, Senor Jimmy Blue, that we tried to watch you every day. You did not make it easy. The cards and then the Circus House."

"Why? Were am I?"

I try to sit up but cannot find my arms. I'm aghast for they are gone, disappeared completely. No, no the blood moves into them painfully. On the bed she sits so light I can hardly feel the weight of her, until she sweeps back her hair, reveals her face, and I look into her brown eyes and she smiles as she takes my fingers and gently rubs..

The incense seller.

"You have so many questions, Senor Blue."

"You, from the piazza, it's you. Yes, I, my stuff! My satchel?"

"Yes, your notebook? Safe, should you need it again."

"If I need it? I need to get back to my hotel."

I am thinking more clearly, that I must send a message, I must make contact with the real world.

"There is nothing at the hotel now. We found nothing. Only the man who has been following you."

"Nothing? There are, no, the man, what man?"

"You like the forest, the rivers, yes?"

"The forest, yes. Yes, I suppose, of course. What man?"

"So you wanted adventure here? You thought the girl was breaking your heart?"

I say nothing but stare out from the hollow of my pillow, feeling like a little child visited by his mother after a nightmare.

The girl waves her hand and a holopic charges the air above the wicker chair. I stare into the face. It is Anna. I remember. When was it taken?

"How?" I begin, "How? Who are you, senorita?"

"I am the girl who will give you the story you were seeking, one where hearts and people grow whole again."

She stands quickly and steps away from the bed, suddenly angry with movement.

"My name is Maria. Sleep. Tomorrow you will be stronger. It has been four days now and by light we must be gone from the city."

"Four days! Four? Where am I?"

Before I can say more she is pressing a glass to my lips and the draught is bitter on my tongue but wet in my throat, and I am grateful to feel myself sink once more, for already I am aware there are no voices. I dream not of the red room, nor of the black heart of the ancient city, but move through warm, white mists, buoyed on the ripples of an emerald stream.

****

Chapter Ten

The Tree Of Life

BACA, the captain of the bongo told me a tale. The others were asleep, their bodies looped between mounds of baggage and strange, outlandish equipment, and so the old man spoke from beneath his cap in a croak almost outcoughed by the puttputtputt of the ancient, petrol-fuelled outboard.

"Only the coochi coochi knows where to find her, listen, but he smart, smart fella," said Baca. "He keeps secret. Not 'cause he wicked. No, no, he the tickle monkey, how can laughter harm anyones? He keeps secret 'cause he knows she precious, fragile, big treasure. She the mother tree, course. Listen to me, mister. Her fruits gifts. Gifts falls on every person, big, small, all colours. They falls all over the whole world.

"First the tapir follow the small fella but he get lost. His nose too big. Too close to the ground to see coochi coochi swing aways. Sniff, sniff, tapir scurry home, no problem. The cawcaw bird try. He get lost, dizzy in head, 'cause he make such bloody horrible squawkin'. Hey, he smokes too, you know. No joke. Mister, it easy for the coochi coochi mono to hide from that bloody stupid bird. Squawkin', squawkin', cawcaw fly home.

"Others try. Oh, many, many. All get lost. They get nothin'. They empty bellied, grumblin' all time every day. See they know they must wait for gifts to fall in good time.

"But the squirrel, he run after coochi coochi. The squirrel run crafty, mister, no lies. He pretend big he no interested in coochi coochi or any tree. Me's only looking for nuts, he says. But all the time his eyes on coochi coochi. And so, one day, he get come where mother, the tree of life touch this earth."

I didn't know any of these strange creatures but said nothing and Captain Baca took off his baseball cap and scratched a proud tar-black tuft. His other hand rested lightly on the tiller, his red-rimmed eyes on the river. He replaced the cap, twisted the peak to the back of his head.

"The squirrel run back, chatter, chatter," said Baca, nodding. "Small squirrel, big mouth. He want boast the whole world. Big, big hero. All the animals follow him and they gets so work up. All in a dance to get gifts but they can't climb, mister, so they bitin' and clawin', first the tree, then each other, and they burrowin' and they diggin' until, all of a sudden, listen mister. Can you hear her, mister? The tree is screamin', she is swayin', and the mother she is crashin' down on top of them all, every one of them, her children.

"And the earth starts cryin', huge earthquake now and boulders is fallin' from the sky everywheres and the animals all dyin'. The whole world dyin', mister. Cos the gifts is gone and the tree dead, killed her own."

Baca turned away and spat into the slow boil of water. For the first time he took his eyes from the river and looked at me.

"Nothin' change," he said.

For a long time we stole upriver until on both banks the slick brown soil was overwhelmed by a gladness of green and gold. If the tree of life were dead, its children were still at play in these fields. They lined the banks to greet us, their eager arms entwined and heavy with rainbow-coloured alms, so delighted by their own images, that they dipped eagerly into the mirror, forming tunnels that invited my eyes into deeper, unknown places.

But in the heat of the afternoon nothing stirred out here on the river. The water ahead was sluggish. Our wake lapped at the banks but once and died. The morning clouds had tired and lay prone on the horizon. Under the boat's canopy the air grew thick. The body of the boat opened its pores and I could smell its damp insides, the earth-formed hardness of wood.

Later I sat in the hollow of the prow with a towel draped around my head, breathing in the close sweetness of water, feeling the dizzy vastness of this new place. The bruises on me were healing quickly now. My thoughts were content to watch the river bend forever into the south.

Only the tree's children would know we had come this way.

"That dragonfly," said Baca.

The creature by my hand sat like a fragile glass ornament, its wings glistening like melting ice, its huge purple eyes floating before its body. My friend, you could fly anywhere. Anywhere.

It was different for the butterflies in my City, I thought. It is different for me.

Leaving Batavia's favelas would have been impossible without Maria's inability to recognise the word no from anyone. She possessed a power to motivate action where refusal was not only impossible but churlish.

I simply did as told when shaken from oblivion. A bundle was thrust on to my chest.

I could not see in those first few seconds but I think she must have stood, perhaps stared. I was completely naked and blind, unable to speak

"Come when you are ready," she said finally. Her face began to materialise as the centre of a pulsating halo. Then she was gone from the red room and the door clicked shut.

At first I could not understand who she was. When I remembered I could not understand her words. And when I remembered the bundle and felt its contents I could not understand why I must wear these unfamiliar clothes. Everything was happening outside of my head.

I sat on the edge of the bed until the room settled into the hum of the battery lamp. When I touched my face it felt like wet bubble-wrap and the pain that popped and crackled across my skin jarred me awake.

Where? How long? What now?

The cargo pants and vest were loose, but at least I found my own boots by the chair. I could not tie them, my fingers were not yet my own, so I shuffled nervously to the door, a 12-year-old who had slept in for school.

I climbed an uneven wooden staircase, panting and light-headed.

I was in a storeroom lit by a single naked bulb. The shelves were stacked with food tins, every one wrapped in a different label so that the confusion of colours hurt my eyes. Barrel-sized plastic water containers towered precariously in a corner. In another a drum of kerosene, propped on two lengths of wood, was leaking at a badly soldered seam. The fumes choked the air.

It took me a few seconds to realise the outer door was concealed by a sheet of black plastic, but before I could move to them they flew apart and Maria entered.

Your face, I thought suddenly, is so beautiful.

She frowned, shook her head, and I realised I had spoken aloud. Embarrassed, I avoided her eyes as she pushed a hot towel into my hands.

"Eat," she whispered. "I will come back for you."

She disappeared back through the doorway.

I unwrapped the parcel to find a small empanada and, even as I followed to the doorway, ate, alive to my hunger. Before I could raise the plastic curtain I was stopped, this time by Maria's voice.

"He is strong enough now."

"Strong? said a tight-jawed baritone. "He barely got out of a card game then could not stand up for himself when they reached him in the brothel, Maria. What will he do in the real world?"

"He does not need to stand, only see us do it."

"Ach," said the second voice, disgusted. "You've read his notebook. This man-child cannot see beyond his own bleating. Lost loves? Horror dreams and men with swords!"

"Marcus!"

Laughter. Maria was laughing. The sound was light. I knew the man called Marcus must be smiling, too, for the grin was wide on my own face as I chewed the empanada and surely it was her laugh and not the kerosene making me feel giggle-headed as the tins began to jostle for space around my head, crowding all around me nearer the door to listen in. So light. Laughter so light I could think no more of links and hotels and newspapers than my own two feet.

Dancing feet, way down there, in those silly big man boots. Got to tie them, reach them as the floor rushes towards my face.

Even as I lay on the concrete, the empanada stuck under my cheek, Maria and Marcus talked and talked and their words made no sense and I was happy to listen to their music. So warm now.

I was cocooned in warmth. Against my cheek was a silk softness. I could smell Tolu. And I could smell kerosene. For a moment, light came through the letterbox of one eye. There against my feet was the leaky drum, still on its planks, but now it was in the back of a buzztruck. It jolted once and my cheek bumped deeper into the warm silk and I knew instinctively that through the thin material was the softness of Maria's thighs.

The buzz truck rumbled on into the lasting night. I remember only Tolu warmth and the deeper softness of sleep that held me for much of the journey. Our arrival at the airfield was lost in machine-gun fire rain, which pinged off the hard-packed earth, rebounding into bowed faces. I staggered towards the tiny flier, held up by arms and fingers unseen and unknown.

My face was pressed against glass until my body was vibrating perfectly with the jets, and we rose, bounced once and hauled ourselves into the dark skies until amid the drone and vibrations sleep came again, this time with the nightmare.

An enthroned silhouette. Come closer. Closer. Look upon the white face. Pure bone white, white scarred, bold in its bald nakedness. Come closer! Whose eyes open? Who do you see?

I opened my eyes to escape Janu.

I was propped up between two fleshy bulks, heavy-set men, both dressed in black combats and vests. Both were asleep for their breathing was raucous even above the noise of this open-backed petrol truck. In the cabin, through the grime on the glass partition, I could see a misshapen sponge of blonde spikes, also asleep, boomeranging in slow arcs against gravity. The back of the driver's cap read Henrietta's Bar: Siren's Finest Teas.

Opposite me, on the other side of mounds and sacks and boxes, Maria lay the full length of the bench, her head on the crook of an arm. She was awake and looking at me.

"We aren't going to the hotel are we?" I said.

Maria continued to stare.

"You're not an incense seller are you?"

She smiled and put a finger to her lips.

Just then the driver tapped with his knuckles on the glass. The man on my left came to with a snort, torpedoing my ribs with his elbow, Maria clambered up from the bench, and we all stared ahead through the glass.

A barrier of thick branches had been placed across the dirt track. A red and yellow flag fluttered nearby above a small tin shack. Abidar.

Maria climbed down from the truck and disappeared inside the shack. The man on my left, his unshaven blond jaw a grimace beneath sweat-beaded crew cut, pushed his huge frame up off the bench and stood with his hands on the edge of the rolled-back canopy. No-one else left the truck. No-one spoke.

A group of Abidar sat staring at us through their dust goggles from the shade of a tree. Before them, tethered to the trunk by a length of plastic twine, was a tiny black and yellow animal, round-faced, huge-pawed.

"Tigre mariposa."

I turned to the whisperer on my right, little more than a boy, ruby lips in a brown leather face, beneath a mop of black curls.

"They catch him, senor, very rare, for to make the clone. His mother no."

He shook his head and shrugged.

The animal pounced on the long grass, chasing an invisible prey, and one of the Abidar tugged on the twine and the ball of fur somersaulted backwards on itself and began to mew. The Abidar ignored it, their goggle-eyes never left us, but when the crying of the cub grew louder one reached out with a boot and swiped at the creature.

"Enough!" cried the giant above us.

The Abidar were on their feet at once, red-lit rifles in their hands, and the man above us had both hands on the side of the van, ready to leap down, but the boy beside me grabbed his wrist.

"No, Marcus!" he hissed. "No!"

Maria reappeared and without a word Marcus slumped back into his seat as she climbed aboard. They looked at one another briefly, Maria angrily, as the van restarted and we trundled on through the checkpoint.

I looked back but the Abidar and their tiny pet had been swallowed by the trees.

No-one spoke again and I felt too groggy to try. I closed my eyes, tried to swallow the bile rising in my throat, and the world reeled from me while my stomach jolted on.

Some time later we arrived by a river's edge where there waited a long, shallow boat, hollowed from a single, enormous tree, with a canopy of tarpaulin and broad leaves.

"This my bongo," said, Baca, the truck driver, as he helped me down, proudly twisting his Siren cap. But I was tired and irritable and could not find the strength to rouse myself or question Maria. I sat on a crate, nursing a new bruise in my side, as the others transferred crates and sacks into the boat.

"Come," said Maria, when all was ready, and I boarded and sank at once into the pile of sacks in the bow. The rope was untied and we moved slowly out into the current.

As sleep struggled to overtake me again, I still didn't know where we were going, but the farther the boat carried me from the pain inside, the happier I would be.

****

Chapter Eleven

Ghosts

FOR two days we motored upriver and no-one spoke more than their need. Each had an allotted task: Maria to prepare food, myself and Pedro, the young Brazilian, to set up a web of hammocks and mosquito nets, tied to the mainstays of the boat's canopy for camp was made aboard. Teri, the pug-nosed, blonde-spiked girl from the front of the truck, was in her late teens and, to spite her prettiness, neither smiled nor spoke as she washed the day's meal dishes. At all other times she would sit, muscular arms folded, and stare back downriver.

Only Marcus avoided any duties, choosing to spend his time when not asleep casting a line and gut for triangle-toothed fish. He pulled them orange and blue and silver and beautiful from the river before pounding their spines gleefully with his huge fists.

"Yes, real fish. Piranha!" he laughed when he saw me stare.

Aside from his story of the tree, Baca chose to engage only the river, his mouth clamped tight upon a black root, eyes hidden in the shadow of his cap.

Once Pedro broke this unacknowledged communal vow of silence, chattering to me about the trees we passed and the strange animals in their branches, but mostly about the girls who lay on the beaches near his village, laughing and nudging me until Marcus chastised him for scaring his fish.

Maria would acknowledge me with a nod or a smile, but mostly she was impatient, eager to get further upriver, anxious perhaps that I might begin asking questions before we reached our destination.

I, however, had no questions to ask. I looked forward to many things but they were simple things: a cup of hot, strong coffee, made from real beans, seeing what lay beyond the next bend in the river, watching fantastically decorated birds erupt from the treetops.

I thought rarely of the Circus House or my lost belongings, of Batavia or Charlie Blake III and unfiled newspaper reports. I did think of you, Anna, but when I did it made me feel at once desperate and helpless. I told myself that, if I only knew you were okay, it would make all of this bearable.

"You must not worry about those other things," said Maria.

The hammocks had been strung up, the others were already asleep, but we sat by the flame of the single lamp.

"Do not worry for the things you have no control over, Jimmy Blue."

Silence again, then she sighed and looked away, said, "When the rains fall the waters here rise and this labyrinth, all this maze of rivers, will change its pattern. It happens so suddenly even Baca will take off his cap and scratch his head. Such is the nature of our river. Here nothing will ever stay the same, only the giants. You know our giants, the tepuis?"

She looked at me so I shook my head.

"The mountains. Solitary, they rise far above the trees. Like giants."

"Yes, I think maybe I saw one," I said, finally. "In a picture. It seems a long time ago."

"Of course, the Gateway."

I could see Maria's smile in the glow.

"They watch us through the clouds, Jimmy Blue, the giants. Baca says they sleep over the veins that run through the earth, have watched over us since before there was time. Baca says they were old before even the tree of life itself knew the beyondness of all things."

"Baca knows many things," I said. "Does he know where he is leading us?"

Silence, then, "He knows this river. He has learned it is like our country, our people. Chavez was once ousted by his own generals, did you know, thrown out of power and imprisoned? A new day came with the businessmen, who showed their faces only in television commercials, who promised the people we would prosper. And now, they say, no Chavez is back on his throne, and the men with the figures and the briefcases and the promises are the ones who are in prison. This is not true, of course, no-one has seen a prison wall but the people of Batavia themselves."

I could feel Maria's eyes flit upon me often in the darkness, as though to check I was still here, that I was truly listening.

"Yes," she said, "yes the rains come and the waters rise and everything changes all over again. Only now the giants grow tired and have turned their backs to look away from the forest. This is the way things are."

"If this is the way things are, if you say I must not worry about things I cannot change, why do you sound afraid?"

The girl leaned forward, turned the wick until the orange light shone fuller on her face.

"I said do not worry for the things you have no control over."

I did not know what to say, so I said, "Okay, but I can hear sadness in your voice. Am I right?"

"You hear yourself, everything you have brought with you is still in your heart. Are you not the writer who has created a world of despair and death?"

She had not raised her voice and yet I felt stung, immediately guilty, as though by bringing my story to the forest I had sneaked something vile and unholy into the sanctuary of a church.

She put out her hand. "But please. May I see?"

Bemused by her interest, I dug into the satchel and handed her my notebook. She plucked at the pages, found the marker, read.

I'm sorry, but his grief has made him useless to the Guard. He's lost his own mind in Janu's grave and Cindecis himself knows it.

"Have you lost your mind, Jimmy Blue? In whose grave?"

"It's a character," I mumbled. "My imagination, no more."

Maria did not smile and I felt in that moment that somehow I'd betrayed something, someone, Janu? All that hurt so lightly dismissed? My own?

Maria read on, though soon her voice dropped almost into the bottom of the boat, and I was thankful because for the first time someone was reading my work and the only thing I could feel in myself was an unnatural discomfort.

They walked on, footfalls heavy on the tundra of this moonlit square, but finally Henri shook his head and his words ballooned white around his face.

No. No, he just needs more time. If I had fallen on my own sword, wouldn't you be taken aback?

I would, said Calan, 'Tis more usual your wife bellyflops onto that prize.

Henri stopped. That's no prize. It's given freely. Well, freely if not quite willingly. He shook his head briskly and they resumed walking, Calan sniffing in deep the silver, Henri peering intently down into the cracked mirrors.

Stopped. And my lady does not bellyflop, even if her ankles seem hidden since the day we spliced.

A few steps more, now Calan turned. Still, all said and done, I can think of nothing more fearsome than your wife descending from heaven onto my unsheathed sword. Any man would be praying for oblivion in the shock of her exploding.

Look, cried Henri, if I didn't know her better, I should take great offence at such, these fleshly larcenies, and be forced to slice you myself. S'truth, you're a bachelor! What do you know of the sacred bonds?

Sacred . . . ? Bonds are for people who want their hearts in chains, said Calan in an offended wheeze. And anyway, he pronounced, you can't trust love.

What?

Common nature. Look at that spider?

Where? What spider?

That one from foreign lands, hot jungles somewhere, south, north. The one who does the business then, before he gets to the warm eight-legged embrace, ends up as croissant.

"It's true, some, they will kill their lovers," said Maria. "Always the female, of course."

Even in the darkness I knew she was smiling again.

"She knows to kill is best for both, because it is good for the young."

She reached out and patted my leg, lay on her back so that the lamp lit the softness of her face and neck and threw her curves into relief. I found myself relaxing a little.

Henri shook his head sadly.

Yes, insisted Calan. It's true. But you just don't know what's going to happen, do you? That's the nature of it, the way of the beast. You just never know.

They plodded on.

I know you'd better get your mind off beasts and my wife's nightdress and back on the job of finding Giraud.

They reached the end of a narrow side street where a doorway had fallen into the wall of dishevelled bricks. A moment of blindness and the scraping of obstinate wood, and they were engulfed by a wave of orange heat, sucked by its backdraught into the tavern.

A mutter of drinkers huddled before the hearth turned to them at once, twice as quick fell back to urgent mugs and tight silence. The room was too small, framed by low wooden beams, stained by smoke.

Calan approached first and a huge bear rose from its stool by the fire and came round. The landlord wore his soiled sop-sodden shirt wide but his face was closed in the thick wires of his huge beard, blackened by the flames. A hole appeared in his singed whiskers to reveal two long brown tubes.

Yugh?

Yugh s'right! Calan, smiling.

We're looking for a Guard. Henri, not. We believe he may have taken a room here in your ... hostelry?

The landlord stared at the counter for a long time before the hole shut tight, sucked, and reopened to launch phlegm onto the floor between them. The head shook from side to side, painfully slow.

Yugh? Calan, shaking his own head.

Red eyes glanced only at Calan's chin and the hole opened towards Henri. A madman upstairs, is all, it gurgled. A Guard gone missin' in these days 'at are nights is worth much too much to know, I reckon? Yugh?

Calan, shrugging. Henri, who nodded once.

Calan pointed and the landlord looked to the beams as a gloved fist hammered once onto his upturned nose, caught him by the hair as he slumped. Henri leaned his back, watching the flicker of eyes at the hearth and the head moaned a vivid pool onto the counter, until Calan shook it by the grease.

Up . . . upstairs, fourth room, the hole spewed and an elbow pointed abstractly aloft.

Calan let the hair slide through until an inscrutable face thudded into its own liquid and a muffled whine.

Upstairs the building's insides heaved and sweated, defying the cold with its own fever. Dark patches glistened in the weak light. Hacking laughter came from below, was stifled, cut short by the landlord's garble. Here the air choked on dampness and stale vomit.

Reminds me of a charming house, a decrepit chateau of yet some renown where my first girl lived, beamed Calan. Ah, young and in lust!

"The Circus House? You had a premonition!" Anna laughed and I looked up as she turned the page. I lay propped on my elbow, happy now to watch her as she read.

Henri took the sleeve from his nose. Let's just take him from this hell hole. He needs to be among his own.

The two men stopped at the fourth door, paused.

This one?

Henri took off one glove, rapped the wood.

Giraud?

Nothing.

Calan shrugged, beat the door with his gloved fist.

An indistinct whisper from within, metallic, a sword unsheathed.

Calan grabbed the handle, pushed his way inside. Flames, tiny flames, everywhere, a room floored by thousands of flames, a carpet of wagging tongues, soft yellow spikes, all around but for a circle in the centre, for there sat Giraud, imperial on the room's single chair, shrouded in his black cloak, sword laid across his lap.

He lifted but a little his head and nodded. Quietly, calmly, said, Go. Leave now.

But Giraud, cried Henri, pushing in past Calan who stood bewildered. It's your rescue party. Come now, what a welcome is this?

Giraud rose and his sword was to the door.

No! You will go. Go while you can.

Calan grimaced and shook his head but Henri ventured further, stepping clumsily between the candles, hopping on a curse as he singed one foot.

Now calm yourself, he said, pursing his lips to cool the pain in his heel. We'll be gone soon enough. But you must be calm, my friend. Put that offensive wire back in its bed. You might cut someone. No? Well let me.

Henri held out his hands and Calan said, Give him the sword, Giraud.

But Giraud's eyes closed and his head flicked to one side.

Shh! Listen.

Henri turned to Calan who raised his eyes, was shocked by the swirl of lights reflected on the ceiling, a thousand insect eyes glinting down on them. The wind rattled in half-hearted drama against the window pane.

He's coming now, said Giraud.

Yes, that's right, who's coming? said Calan. *Are all these candles lit for someone special?*

Oh, for God's sake, just put down your sword and we'll all of us leave, said Henri. *Is that all right?* He felt pricked into anger, at the pain, at Giraud, at Calan, at himself, for maybe he was becoming unnerved by Giraud's talk and the strange room that had been overrun by their uneasy shadows.

Come, let us leave! This place steals my breath. It smells of death.

Yes, you know, whispers Giraud, and his eyes burn with the thousand flames. *Can you feel it now?*

And yes, perhaps, slowly the air is being crushed, now that the candles gasp for life, now that to each Guard the only sound has become the immense thud of blood within his own chest.

He is coming.

The sword slid from Giraud's fingers and slammed onto the boards. And far away across the city, beneath the streets, something stirs, breathing itself into life, kicking, crawling, scraping its way from the abominable deep, and the breathing bates, and the beating begins, and the slow sigh of exhalation swoons through the catacombs until it swells and screams.

Run! Run from the coming!

But the passageway is overwhelmed, the profanity drowns everything, and still it comes, faster, faster, bubbling hot through brick-lined arteries, insanity howling leaps upon the night and sinks its fangs and eats the sky in a single gulp, so that mountains of concrete and silver shiver on their feet and the years ahead shuffle and stampede and feel ashamed when the horror has passed and raced far away, far across the rooftops.

Here is no place to hide.

The air is sucked whole from the room, candle flames die in the nothingness, and the three men stare at the window, stare as they fall helpless into their own images which rush toward them and explode into a million stars, stare as the newborn galaxy of noise implodes into a sudden stop, stare into this silence inside their heads, stare as into the void steps a fourth figure.

"Fire!" cried Teri, her first sound, and Anna dropped the notebook and the hammocks exploded and swung so violently that I feared the boat might capsize.

"Inflama! Inflama!" cried Baca and we peered where he pointed downriver. Miles away or more, I could not tell, above the treeline of the far bank a glow was forming, a surreal midnight sunrise of orange tongues.

"The loggers' camp," said Marcus. "Tara."

"But that is half a day's walk from the river," said Pedro. "It would take all the fire in hell to light the sky like that."

"Then Tara has brought hell to them," said Maria.

We sat for more than an hour, staring out across the flat water at the enormous halo, listening to what might be a distant crackle, a muffled thud, smelling the hot blackness finally reach us in the night air. Then, almost as suddenly as it had appeared, the light began to flicker, to fade, was gone, and we were left blind.

"Now, let us hope, not so many are grabbing for the tree, Baca?" said Teri.

Maria retrieved the notebook, thrust into my surprised hands, said, "Think carefully about what you dream for, Senor Writer."

She turned away and gathered a shawl around her in the hollow of the boat. From there I heard her say, "We need heroes, not ghosts."

This is the dream. The figure is silhouetted within the perfect virgin of the moon. The hem of his cloak moves but slightly as cold serpents slip through the shattered window and crawl towards them across the floor. He himself is perfectly still. The room silent.

Giraud was first to clamber to his feet and his boots crunched glass. He swayed, grasped the mantelpiece. Henri crawled to the door where Calan sat with his back to the wood, intent only on his breathless chest.

Come, my friends, do you not know me?

The voice is warm and close, but strange, more memory than sound.

Giraud stepped nearer.

Janu?

The figure held out one hand.

Giraud.

Giraud fell to his knees, covered himself with childish hands. Until the figure approached and touched a shoulder. Giraud began to sob, his forearms held against his eyes. And the figure leaned lower until Giraud reached up and pushed back the cloth of the hood and a tumble of dark hair curled around his hands as he placed his fingers upon what was hidden.

And then terror turns to face the two. From among the coils, twin embers scorch their hearts, madness peers at them from within its lair, with life that crackles and would spit death.

Do not be afraid. You look upon your friend.

The words struck them as the figure rose and he would come forward but Calan scrambled for his feet, slid on the floor, scattered spent candles and crystal shards, and his hands flailed wildly for the door.

Henri cried, No! Come no closer!

Giraud, too, had risen and he held forth his blade.

Hold! he cried, and his voice scorned. But do you not know him? Janu has come back to us.

Janu? This is not Janu, seethed Henri, it is a demon, and he struck fiercely with his own sword but a fist shot out and grabbed his edge, held tight until pain coursed through Henri's arm up into his breast and he must release his hold just as black reality threatens to kill all sense. The sword clattered to the floor and Henri staggered back, clutching at his chest.

A demon, yes. And you would see me bleed but still not believe.

The voice was distant now, fragmented.

Am I so changed?

I see only you, cried Giraud. 'Tis these two have changed in their love. None would believe me. Still they do not see the truth.

The figure turned to Giraud alone and the two soldiers were left forgotten by the door, spectators, strangers in this vagary.

Free her, Giraud.

The apparition turned to the window's hole, stared out into the vastness of the sleepless city, across restless stones, to the obstinate fastness of Hopeful Redemption, and spoke with his back to them.

From that darkness I heard her call.

His voice was hushed and they heard a terrible rattling emptiness that filled the room with the desperate borrowing of life.

I hear her now.

He turned and was hidden once more in silhouette.

Yet I cannot go.

His voice was distorted, unfocused, it bled without sound inside their heads with the dull rhythm of a terrible regret.

Henri, I am your demon. My breath is stolen.

He looked one last time to Henri and then to Calan and it seemed they saw a flash of Janu's face beneath the cowl and imagined in this dream he had smiled at them, and said, There is work for demons and morning comes too soon.

To Giraud he did, in truth, whisper, Only if she asks, tell her I am sorry. Tell her I followed beyond the sun.

For this last word the jealous moon fled. Leaving only darkness and disbelief.

The darkness was complete. I sat at the prow but I was not alone. I knew Teri was awake. I could feel her cold, immovable presence at the end of the boat. Like me, she was staring out into the night.

****

Chapter Twelve

Fire And Water

"22.15. Alert. Explosion at 221. Major structural damage. Production affected 65%. Casualties. Suspect insurgent activity. Immediate action required. Advise."

When Wardlaw received the message in his office he was not surprised by what he read. He already knew there had been trouble upriver. Shortly after being arrested for attempting to smuggle a leopard cub to a cloning factory, just before he could no longer speak, a buzzhop pilot had reported flying over the mouth of an inferno, near the Rio Sipapo's cocked leg.

For a moment Wardlaw stood scratching one huge ginger sideburn.

"221!"

A moment's pause then a face appeared in the foggy screen, removed its goggles to reveal nightvision red eyes that snapped to black.

"It's true," growled 221's captain, "they got in and blew half the compound away. It's taken us four hours just to get the fire under control. And no sign of them. We need more bodies here. We might have to get some people in."

Wardlaw checked his watch again. 22.25. He cursed, snapped shut the link to 221.

To add to his woes the journalist seemed to have disappeared entirely. His contact at the hotel had left the fool squirming on the floor of the Circus House, then nothing, not even a body.

Wardlaw's sideburns began to itch again.

****

I knew nothing of this, of course, when woken in darkness by Marcus, thigh deep in the black water, hauling in the ropes from the bank, slapping the hull near my head.

"Up, up!" he cried. "Up! Time to move."

He insisted we would travel immediately.

"That camp is a day away," said Maria.

"And they are a night nearer to us," he said, and the engine coughed into life.

Groggy, irritated by the alarm, I rolled the hammock into its sheath and said nothing. As for everything else in this madness, I was certain asking would tell me little.

Teri, almost animated for the first time, her hands on her slim hips, stood by Pedro in the prow as he probed the water with a lamp. By the time the air was growing grey we were already half way across the river and Marcus told Pedro to kill the light. Baca slowed the engine until the puttputt was a slow, soft clap. Maria moved to the back of the boat.

Scanning the water for the rolling hulks of drifting trees, Baca slid the bongo forward, closer and closer to the bank until Pedro grabbed Marcus' arm, whispered, "There!"

Six figures had stepped from the treeline, were wading out into the water towards us. Behind each trailed a long kayak.

Baca cut the motor. I turned but his face was inscrutable below his cap. We drifted slowly downstream with the sun rising in our eyes, and each newcomer clambered into a kayak and paddled with a single oar, silently, silhouetted against the rising ball of fire.

Six figures, their long, alien shadows stretching towards us, reaching out from the water.

The air was changed, something more than the new day was being charged. Marcus was breathing hard through his days' old beard and I feared he was about to leap into the water. Instead his eyes scanned the far bank, as he though he saw more apparitions in the deeper darkness of those trees.

When the strangers were close, yet too far to identify, Teri threw out a line to the first kayak and secured it to the stern. The rope was passed along and attached to each kayak and its inhabitant immediately huddled down and covered themselves in a blanket.

Baca restarted the motor, throttled up, and we lurched sickeningly back against the current, heading upstream and for the far bank. Not a word had been spoken. As one, the others faced upstream. Finally, I lay back down in my own huddle in the prow and almost at once fell back into sleep.

When I awoke I thought it had grown dark again. A blanket had been thrown across the bow to protect me from the sun. I shrugged it off. The far off drone of an aeroplane drew my gaze to the sky but it was a vast blue empty canvas. For the first day since my arrival in Batavia it did not rain. The heat was almost unbearable. Water bottles were floated to the kayaks on a line. But we did not stop.

Even as the afternoon grew heavy, Marcus grew more and more animated, talking quickly, often in German. He clapped me on the back, and I grimaced at the smack on my bruised shoulders.

"We go home now!" he bellowed, and grabbed my shoulders and shook me and laughed as he went back to casting his line in a wide arc out beyond the shadow of the bongo. Even Teri smiled as she trailed the lunch plates in our wake.

In dark contrast, Maria was silent. She had not moved from her seat beside Baca, her own hand almost on his on the tiller, the sinews of her thin brown arms urging the engine faster, her eyes constantly ranging upriver.

Pedro giggled conspiratorially, his happy eyes half closed but his teeth flashing at me.

"Oh, man, they've gone done it now," he said. "Fireworks? Yes, Senor Blue, gonna be fireworks."

****

"12.05. Camp 221. Insurgents not found. Three crew dead. Spotter reports traffic minimal. Require immediate security update. Advise."

The report flickered in a corner of Chris Warldlaw's windscreen. He knew 221 would keep filing these dispatches but the last thing the captain of the outpost wanted was for anyone to be sent upriver. That the river traffic was minimal was not information but a warning it should be kept that way so the Abidar could do their job.

He could ignore 221, leave them to their work. What he couldn't ignore was the growing fear the journalist might now be involved. If his source was right, his best chance of finding Blue was by heading to the Sipapo himself.

"It'll be easier finding a bloody anaconda's elbow," he thought and urged the buzzcar faster through the midnight favelas.

****

Chapter Thirteen

Eilidon

WITH the longest day weakening at last under the weight of night, we motored into a tributary, a channel barely wider than the bongo, until finally Baca cut the motor and lifted the propeller clear of roots, which had begun to grasp greedily for the blades. He ordered Pedro forward to measure depths with the pole, and we pulled our way forward by hauling from overhanging branches and pushing against tree trunks.

When the mud of the riverbed was scraping the hull and the way ahead more forest than waterway, we halted.

The kayakers untied themselves and passed around and ahead. A boy of eighteen or nineteen, sun-burned with blond hair, smiled up at me as he pulled alongside and I offered my hand to help him aboard.

"Salut," he said. "I am Johan."

"Salut, Johan," came a soft voice from behind him and I was startled to see a grey-faced man in muddied army fatigues just yards from us on a tree root. He was flanked by two young men, then more came, and young girls, their camouflage combats and khaki t-shirts blending with the foliage, until a dozen or more strangers had surrounded us.

"Salut, Gol!"

Marcus crashed by me, almost knocking Johan back into the water, and landed on the root, grasping the stranger in a bear hug.

I turned to see that even Maria was smiling at this welcome party, her face relaxed finally in relief. Two girls had splashed their way to the side of the boat and she leaned over the side and was pulled down into their arms.

Without torches, the walk should have been a raucous, crashing affair with bodies stumbling into the undergrowth, and yet with low voices and sure-footedness we moved in quick, quiet file, along a narrow trail for several miles. All I could see was the huge expanse of Marcus's dirty-vested back and more than once my nose or cheek bumped into hard-knotted muscle, inhaled rank sweat.

Finally, the trees thinned and a light grew and I realised we had come into a small clearing. On the far side small, grass-roofed huts squatted together, almost invisible, but before us was the entrance to a larger, round building and we filed through its low doorway.

A fire had been lit in the centre and already was encircled by young people, sitting or lying on palms fronds and matted grasses, slow-clapping our entrance. Wooden cups of an acrid, throat-burning liquid were thrust into hands, voices grew louder, braver.

"Welcome ," said Maria, at my side. "We call this place home."

She led me to a place before the fire. Everyone was seated, perhaps forty faces in all. I scanned the circle. All were young, from their late teens to their early thirties, a generous mix of races.

The man Marcus had called Gol was by far the oldest, perhaps fifty, his head shaved smooth, his face mossed by fresh, grey stubble. His eyes turned into my gaze, he smiled, raised a hand and the room fell silent.

Gol produced a round black shape from behind his back and with a flourish placed a bowler hat on his head. Immediately there was a great roar of cheers and laughter.

"Welcome, Jimmy Blue," said Gol. "Welcome to Eilidon."

"Eilidon!" came the chorus.

"Jeanie Mac!" cried the fire.

I watched as an apparition walked towards me from the open doorway, around the flames, blond hair spikes and bare shoulders gilded in the glowing.

Bernie McSharry.

****

Chapter Fourteen

The Treachery of Images

SHE danced around the fire, her white legs kicking defiantly against its orange, and I clambered ungainly to my feet, feeling every eye on us as Bernie wrapped me in breasts and bone, and I breathed in the suddenly familiar scent of her warm flesh, felt nipples pressed hard against my chest.

"Jimmy Blue," she whispered as laughter and conversation chased the silence from around us.

I smiled shock into the face and the grin of the girl who had aged but with the sun, not against it, and the spattered freckles rose higher on her cheeks as she looked hard at me.

"And what, I ask, are ye doin' here?"

"If I knew I'd tell you. But I could ask the same. I saw you before, you know, in the piazza."

"Ah, nonsense, Blue!" she interrupted, "have you been chasin' ghosts half way round the world?"

"Family!" Gol beckoned silence. He looked to me again, said, "Jimmy Blue we have almost met many times. Now I am glad you have finally followed the images and come home."

Maria stood to join Gol in the circle of light, Bernie dragged me back down on to damp palm fronds, squashed my face between her palms.

"I just can't get rid of you, can I?" she whispered into the top of my head.

"Gol has welcomed our new friend," said Maria, and Bernie relaxed her grip so now I could look up, "and so I introduce him to his home and to our family. This is the Writer."

Applause slapped its way around the circle, stopped at me. I felt I should stand and acknowledge the curious stares but Bernie clung to my arm.

"But who is he?" said a voice on my left.

"Tell us! Why has he been brought?" asked another, and I spied Johan's now sullen face flickering on the far side of the flames.

More voices rose, fell by Gol's hand.

I turned to Bernie but she did not take her eyes from Maria, who spoke again.

"It is true he knows little of our work or even of Batavia. And yes, Johan," she turned to the boy, "many here believe those not with us in action must be against us. But Gol already knows much of the Writer. And now his being here with us is testament enough to his intentions."

"What intentions?" a girl called out.

Beside me Bernie was shaking her head but Gol was nodding.

He said, "He will be our voice."

"Madness," said a shaven-headed youth, one of the kayakers. His accent was American. "Bringing a stranger. It's insane."

"You, too, were once a stranger here, Guy," said Gol.

"True, that's true, but even if he's not with the Company, how do you know he'll tell the truth. How can any of us be sure?"

There were nods. A voice cried, "Send him back downriver!"

"Without the bongo," cried another, and there was laughter.

Bernie's thigh tensed against my own. I could feel her take a deep, measured breath before she rose. She stood waiting until there was complete silence.

"This man was my friend," she said. She looked down at me and offered me to the group with her open palm. "Let me tell you, Eilidon, that I know his world, and he is fresh from a world that has neither care nor conscience. All others have turned their backs on us. We are forgotten. We need soldiers not witnesses. We need actors not an audience."

There were shouts of agreement. I was more bewildered by Bernie's words than Maria's announcement.

Gol raised his hand again, said, "Maria has agreed to welcome the Writer because she believes he will do the right thing."

"I have no doubt he will do the right thing," cried Bernie, moving closer to the fire, slowly turning to address every one of the group. "I have no doubt he is still the same good person I knew. But will he do the right thing for us? Will he break the pipelines with words? Will he stop chainsaws with headlines?"

"You must learn to trust," said Maria directly to Bernie, "especially your friends, Tara."

There was a flash of anger in Bernie's eyes as she met Maria's. I recognised that temper well. But she said nothing.

I looked at her as she dropped back to the ground beside me.

"Tara? You're called Tara now?" I asked, but she did not respond.

"Gol is right! Maria is right!"

Marcus threw his words into the circle as though casting for his piranha and his eyes scanned the room for anyone who might bite. No-one.

"Without help the Company will find us," he bellowed. "They always find us. They are like dogs on a smell and they will come as they have come so many times before and everything we have won will be destroyed under the blades of their balldozer."

"Bulldozer," cried Johan and the laughter seemed to snap the tension.

"Yah, yah, the bulldozer," said Marcus, laughing too, "and their hired little helpers will be laughing at us again down the barrels of guns. I do not want them laughing at me again."

"They will not laugh," said Bernie, "if we give them something more than jokes."

Silence returned and she turned and looked at me once, quickly, without expression, then rose from my side, left the grand meeting hut. She was followed immediately by six others from the party of kayakers, among them Johan and Guy. None looked my way as they marched in single file out into the darkness.

"As Tara knows, everyone is free in Eilidon to think and say as they please," announced Gol, "but in action we are a family not a democracy."

He addressed me directly. "I have spoken. You are home now."

"Yah!" cried Marcus, "And so now we drink!"

He raised his cup and others followed.

Maria returned to my side said, "Come, you are tired but we can talk."

And then she too left the hut and I followed, away from the warmth and light, the twangs of a badly tuned guitar, the slosh of a huge flask passed around the circle, out into the night.

"I did not know you knew Tara," said Maria.

"I don't," I replied, "I know Bernie McSharry. From a long time ago. We were kids. It seems we've both changed much since then."

Maria looked at me, puzzled.

"I never knew this name. It is true?"

"It seems you are not the only one with secrets, Maria."

She stopped walking, said, "I have no secrets."

"Your writer?"

She smiled, said, "Yes, perhaps, I could have told you more. Would you have come?"

I laughed, said, "Could I have said no to the Gateway to Dreams? And to bowler hats? And the smell of the forest?"

She laughed, said, "Ah, Gol works in mysterious ways. But you are not as tired as I thought, Jimmy Blue. Enough of talk tonight, perhaps? I must go to Tara. I have much to ask her. Sleep, if you shall. Your hammock is already in the hut with Baca and Pedro just over there, and your satchel delivered from its bed in the bottom of the bongo."

She raised her hand, said, "Don't worry, your notebook is there, too. But if you prefer to leave your thoughts for just one night, Marcus I'm sure will be glad of your company. I will come for you tomorrow, early."

She padded from me across the clearing, barefoot into the night.

"Good night, Maria."

I stood. A stranger. A good person from a bad land? Once more thoroughly bewildered.

I returned to the hut and drank the circle's strange brew and, bereft of breath after Marcus' welcome, emptied my head of the night, filling it instead with the colour of strange wine and the shapes of exotic languages.

After a while the colour was too much for my senses, and, despite their animation, I began to suspect my new companions had grown muted, coy with their answers, as though any second someone might enter this tight circle to censure them.

But Bernie did not show herself again and, in my confusion or through obstinacy, I could not bring myself to search for her. Instead, I slipped away to the thatched hut and, wound tightly into the bow of my hammock, I pulled the notebook from the damp satchel. The pages had begun to come loose from their spine, but they were intact, and I knew that as long as Janu fought for life, everything in this new world would remain unreal.

In the poor light of a failing torch I tried to read.

THE Cardinal woke with his chest gripped by a stifled scream. His chamber was slowly suffocating in the drone of two priests who sat at the foot of the bed reciting blessed invocations. His body shuddered once then deflated beneath the heaviness of his blankets.

The air was thick for the windows were shuttered, and the only movement in the gloom was the flicker of Marlov's eyes as they tried to grasp half-shapes in the far corners. He lay half-propped by numberless pillows and a black wooden crucifix, wet with sweat, still clasped to a breast. His dead skin was folded into the bleached linen that almost covered his vastness like some ancient desiccated shroud.

A sharp knock and his hands snatched at the bedclothes and the drone stopped. The door eased itself inwards. Dolran the physician crept into the room, his tiny triangle so flushed that his white eyes were about to pop.

Quick! Close the door! breathed Marlov.

It clicked shut. The priests raised their beads and resumed their hypnotic chant. Soon, Marlov's eyes closed.

Dolran sidled closer to the bed and his brown furs swept dust from the floor. A small, thin man, almost lost in his coats, dwarfed by this prone bulk, his master.

How, he coughed, how is Your Eminence this afternoon?

The Cardinal's eyes snapped open and he stared at the figure before him, perhaps seeing him for the first time. He licked phlegm-speckled lips. Dolran could feel his right calf muscle begin to tighten before a spasm. His eyes sought refuge in the deep folds across the bed.

How do I look, charlatan? Marlov finally wheezed. Do I look well? Do I seem quite myself?

Your Eminence, ventured the physician, fumbling inside his pockets to produce a green phial, perhaps you might take more of my sleeping draught? It should help. . .

No! No more sleep! spat the white lips and Marlov's pupils focused on some invisible horror.

The dreams, that's when the dreams come.

Nodding in sympathy, Dolran braved one step nearer. He found himself saying, Alas, these are but imaginings, brought upon Your Eminence by the fever. You really need rest. You really must . .

But his twittering sank when he realised Marlov was about to sob again. The lips formed their pout and the swollen knuckles squeezed the edge of the sheet. Suddenly, one fat mottled arm shot out and grabbed Dolran's collars.

Please! Please, can't someone take these dreams away from me?

The door banged open and a giant entered.

I believe you summoned me? it rasped with disgust. The Cardinal's face was split wide by an inane grin.

Rysto! He clapped his hands in joy, and waved his irritation at the priests.

Hush! he chided. Be done with the jumbling mumbling you two!

Bead botherers, he apologised, and beckoned his captain closer. Dolran retreated as Rysto lumbered towards the bed. He was, as ever, dressed in the full metal regalia of his position, his mighty heart imprisoned in an ornamental silver torso. He was, indeed, the size of two soldiers and his great sword hung low at his side. His entire face was an enormous down-grinning jaw.

The room had shrunk considerably.

I have a small thing you must do, said Marlov. *I must say, you're just the man for this. Yes, it will give me great delight . . . a piece of his mind for peace of mine, you might say, yes, yes. Delicious.*

He waved Rysto closer with a flurry of both hands and spoke low.

You must burn the body!

Marlov broke into obscene giggling. *Don't you see? I've worked it out. The dreams can't come if there's no body.*

Rysto turned to Dolran but the physician was staring steadfastly under the bed. He turned back to the Cardinal who was nodding his head and smiling shyly.

Whose body? he growled.

The Cardinal's face froze. And the smile had vanished. A solitary finger twitched, urged Rysto closer, to bend forward, and the hand reached up, curled itself through the captain's hair, and pulled Rysto's huge head down onto the bed.

The captain winced but said nothing. The sickly sweet stench of the Cardinal's decaying skin filled his nostrils.

Why, I know you must remember! breathed Marlov. *Tell me you don't know the crazy man you half-killed, the sweet wildness you broke by driving to suicide?*

The Guard, Your Eminence? Janu?

Marlov jerked Rysto's head onto the bed and the soldier forced himself to kneel.

Don't say the name, imbecile! Marlov cried, then in a hoarse half-whisper, *That's what he wants, you know. That's why he must be burned. You see? You see now?*

A muffle from the jaw buried in the bedclothes. The Cardinal's hand fell away and Rysto raised his red face.

But surely he is already buried?

Marlov cocked his head and peered at Rysto with one terrible goggle. He pursed his lips. Not deep enough. And now I want you to burn him! Ashes, I want you to bring me his black bones powered in a jar. You will, won't you?

Of course, Your Eminence.

If Rysto was surprised he hid it well. He heaved himself onto his feet, glaring at the priests until they dug themselves into their prayer books.

It will be done at first light tomorrow.

No! screamed Marlov and his bloated frame somehow exploded from the bed, and Rysto stumbled backwards and the priests fell against the wall, frantically making signs of the cross. The Cardinal's naked mass surged forward, clung with a single sweat-drenched sail, and he pushed Rysto from the room with the sheer force of his oncoming, screaming, Now! Now! It must be done before tonight's fall, before the dreams come.

The door slammed shut and Rysto stood breathing heavily between two soldiers. From behind him came the grunts and groaning timber as Marlov resettled himself.

You! Yes, you hiding behind the screen! Get out of here! The Cardinal's voice buffeted the door, and Rysto stepped aside as it creaked open.

Dolran looked up once with fish eyes and then he had closed the door and swam off down the corridor, eager to seek his own solace in the obscure bottles of his dungeon rooms.

Rysto swore quietly and walked off to find the stablemaster. The soldiers by the door shuffled uncomfortably. And from the room behind them the incessant muttering resumed.

I, too, could hear soft voices from outside in the darkness, a murmur almost hidden within the tinnitus of arguing insects. I lay for a long time, expecting, perhaps hoping, that Bernie would come back to me and offer some understanding.

****

Chapter Fifteen

Dreams And Leaves

BERNIE does not come and before long my words grow restless, jostle one another, and I feel myself stifled by the growing confusion on the page, wrapped suddenly inside a horribly familiar claustrophobia. I shiver but the moment is fleeting, passing through me and behind me.

I listen to the incessant crackle and whirr and whistle of insects on the other side of the veil. I know nothing of them or their world. I have found none of the answers I thought might be here. Perhaps I no longer need them.

So why do I allow myself to be dragged along like this? I'm chained to a bandwagon, a circus of strangers who believe they know me. Suddenly Bernie thinks she can see inside me.

Even the Rio Sipapo, against its natural urge to roll onwards to freedom and openness and fulfilment, conspires to pull me deeper into this closed world.

I should go home to Carmelwood. I still need you, Anna.

The notebook lies on my lap, the torch round on the page, but only the battering of moths and flies and who knows what against the net shows any interest in the words.

A vein inside my head is popping, but there is no Dolran waiting outside this chamber with a sleeping draught. Over in the corner I can make out another hammock and the misshape of Pedro's form, foetal in a spider's silver tomb, dreaming of the beaches where the girls wait impatiently, and beyond him Baca, who sleeps rolled ever tighter in a ball, unsure of himself on land, away from the rock of his bongo.

Somewhere in their wandering my eyes must have lost focus and closed, but when morning's fingers came scrabbling at the door, I found myself already awake and doubting whether I had slept at all.

Pedro was giggling in his dreams. The edge of the notebook was sharp in my belly where I had rolled on top of it. Around my itching scalp the eager light revealed the petrified forms of last night's assailants, legs and wings and snouts tangled in the netting, forever frozen in their grasping for my flesh.

I padded gingerly from the hut, scanning the damp earth before my bare feet, only to be surprised by a soft voice.

"Did you sleep?"

I nodded, shook my head, said, "Maybe Marcus's brew was too strong for my City head."

"Then this won't help," Maria smiled, handed me a beaker. I could smell the plastic softening around the scalding coffee, blocking out the dampness of the morning, already feel the gritty liquid against my tongue.

"When you're ready, we can walk to the kayaks."

Steam rose from the ground in a heavy white mist as we meandered around the trees, Maria leading, my own eyes entranced by the kaleidoscope of greens, browns, and flashes of new colour.

Gol was waiting for us by the water.

"You slept well, I hope, Mr Blue?"

"You've lost your hat," I said.

"Yes, the second one, I'm afraid."

"Why me? The signs?" I asked. "How long were you watching?"

"Only long enough to be sure you would come," said Gol, placing a hand lightly on my shoulder and handing me an oar. "Maria will tell you what you need to know."

My watch told me it was not yet six when we untied one of the kayaks and, with Maria steering behind, I paddled around Baca's bongo, negotiating passage around the trees whose tall bodies bulged with vein-like vines. My oar was tugged by the mud, struck what I hoped were tree roots.

For an hour, with the sun sieved through the forest canopy and bathing us in sprinkles and sudden showers of lemon, we made steady progress. All around us the world was waking, first with the flitter-jitter chatter of invisible birds, then the purple-flashing skim and whirr of dragonflies, now the screech of monkeys, who hid themselves like truant schoolchildren until we passed by, then shook the branches with frenzied bravado, pushing and pulling and screaming at one another.

With a rhythmic splash soft splash we progressed, until I struggled to find water with my oar and felt the plastic blade scrape on the mud and we could go no further by kayak. Maria stepped out. I followed more slowly, up to my knees in the blackness, my boots filling with warm liquid.

Maria drew a huge knife from the bottom of the kayak and strode forward.

"Come," she shouted, "the snakes are afraid of your noisy boots but the jaguar, she will always go for the one who straggles behind."

I sloshed forward.

The journey was fairly easy for the first hour. Here the trees were frail bodied and wary of one another, but when the ground began to pull itself up from the water, they grew bolder, thrust thick shoulders into our path, taunted my heavy boots with their own slow feet. When they grew too brave with their arms, Maria would swing below them, her face almost in the water, while I clambered over, yet fearful of what might be lurking in that dark liquid.

Maria did not speak, and I was grateful, for the heat was thick on my body and the breath thin inside me. The ground continued to rise away from us, steeper and steeper. Sweat mingled with water from the leaves, which slapped and clung to the skin like wet confetti.

I took off my baseball cap, a present from Baca, but the flies leapt fat from the bushes, crawled through my hair, gnawed my sunburned scalp. The cap was replaced. The sweat ran freely across my chest and shoulders.

Our ascent took three hours and for all of this time we were enveloped by the forest and I could see nothing of the mountain we were climbing. At one point, intent on a tree frog, no more than a yellow-black spot the size of my watch face, I looked up to discover I was alone. Worse, looking forward was no different from looking behind. I had no idea where the path might be.

"Maria! Maria?"

My voice fell dead at my feet, the air was too heavy and wet.

"Maria?"

"Use your feet, Jimmy Blue."

I whirled. She was just yards beyond me, several feet above.

"Do your feet not tell you we are going up? See the yellow here on the tree? No here. You see it means we are going north. You know your north? Come, it is not too far now."

She was right. Minutes later the green gauntlet reluctantly freed us, and we climbed into a steep meadow of thigh-high yellow grasses and the cool air lifted the heat away from our bodies in a continuous breeze, and I realised with wonder that we were almost atop a tepui.

Clambering, forced often on to our hands, we reached a spill of perfectly rounded boulders, each the size of a buzzcar, and there we stood, two tiny figures atop an impossible plateau, and all around, vaster than I could have imagined, lay the rainforest. It was an ocean crisscrossed by rivers, with areas miles wide dazzled by sunshine, others shrouded in impenetrable mists. Rainstorms, isolated and fierce as though rent from a cartoon sketch, drifted across the farthest plains, so that rainbows looped across the land, forming a playground of enormous multi-coloured hoops.

We sat for a long time, I breathtaken by exertion and wonder, Maria smiling as she watched my reaction.

"This," she said finally, patting the ground, "is Tepui Masota."

"It's incredible," I said, "Incredible. We're sitting on the shoulders of a giant."

"A giant, yes. Come."

Reluctantly I pulled my gaze from the vista and sidled behind Maria as she led me along Masota's collarbone.

"Now look there."

I followed the line of her arm, her finger, an enormous runway, chalk white, wide, and wholly unnatural, a wound which ripped open the forest almost from the base of Masota, bridging rivers, unswayed in its path, to the horizon.

"The Company road," said Maria. "They began last year. When soon it reaches Masota's feet it will bridge half a thousand miles from the mouth of the Sipapo, and then they can come thundering into the heart of the world."

I didn't know what to say.

"They say that once, long ago, much of the world was covered by the trees, Jimmy. Now it is only Batavia. But this needle plunges into us. It will surely suck out what life is left and push in poison instead."

Maria turned to me.

"You say nothing?"

I shook my head, said, "But who could do this, how can they? There are no laws?"

"The Company is money, money is law," said Maria, "and everyone loves to have money and more money."

"And Chavez, too?" I asked, but Maria did not reply. After a while she said instead, "Have you not felt this land ask of you? Do you not feel now the wind is urgent on your face?"

I sighed, said, "Ask of me? Maria, everything about Batavia is a question. How can I have answers? Me? All I know is Gol seems somehow to have engineered to bring me to a place that is under attack, is dying. I can see that. I mean it's written large enough down there, isn't it? Anyone can see that. That scar can be seen from space.

"But I can see hope in your eyes right now, Maria, just as I could see anger in Bernie's eyes. What is it both of you think you can see in mine? What is it that all of you think I can or cannot do?"

"You'll know what to do," said Maria. "You came here knowing that hearts can be broken, but you are already learning they may also be healed and this is good for they grow stronger. A strong heart can open itself again, yes?"

I nodded. "Perhaps. Maybe. And fragile lands, is that it?"

She smiled. "Si, just so, Jimmy Blue, and the land, too. It heals itself, in time, if allowed, helped. But would you not rather we were here to appreciate it, alive, that our children might share it now."

"That sounds like the ancient propaganda, Maria. They called it ecology. It went out of fashion a very long time ago. In my world, if we need nature there are already more than enough Morning Parks."

Maria's long hair swept my chin as she turned angrily to face me.

"Ecology, Jimmy Blue? I am not talking about ecology, a word invented by scientists to be abused by politicians. Eilidon is about life. The doctor does not talk about anthropology when he is trying to save the live of his patient. The person is one heart, the forest is one tree."

"Okay, so your little band, they want to fight for every single tree do they? Even though this Company you talk of, they are so powerful? And then there are the Abidar. While, we're here, why not get rid of all of them, Chavez even?"

She shook her head. "Chavez? The Abidar? There is only one enemy, the Company. Those who cut the trees, those who drill for oil, those who steal our animals, even those who give beds and their daughters to the incomers. They are all slaves to the Company. And with them the Abidar and the politicians. You know their name, Jimmy Blue, you just don't realise it yet."

"I do? Who are these people?"

"Siren."

"Siren?"

I laughed, picked at a clutch of dry grass stems that crumbled in my palm.

"Laugh, Jimmy Blue, but you already know it's true. The merchant class, the Company, they govern your world and would destroy mine. It is Siren who must be stopped."

"Stop Siren? The attack on the camp. This is what Eilidon is all about. Terrorism? Against a supermarket?"

"Terrorism? You like to deal in rhetoric. That word," said Maria, "once held value. Now it is used to defend persecution of the voiceless. Gol told me you saw Siren's work for yourself, that you were not afraid to write about it. Even Tara agrees that you are different."

"Bernie, her name is Bernie, and she's always spoken her mind," I said. "But I didn't think she would ever be involved in something like this."

"You do not approve?"

"There was a time when Bernie would have lain down in front of a bulldozer not torched the driver," I said.

"Perhaps you do not know her as well as you think. You should speak to her. Ideals do not live long in the forest. There is no democracy here. It is a place of life and death. Those who choose life will do what they must."

"So what more can you do, Maria? And me, why am I here?"

Maria sat in silence for a long time, and I, too.

Siren? I thought of the labs buried beneath the City, the products on every shelf, the universities, their propaganda squeezed and distilled into truth in the InfoDats…

"There was a writer who lived a very long time ago," said Maria at last. "My father used to read to me his poems. His favourite became mine also, though I think now that it can mean so many different things. There are some lines I remember, most.

> *You ask "Why doesn't your poetry,*
> *Speak to us of dreams and leaves,*
> *Of the great volcanoes of your native land?"*
> *Come, See the blood along the streets!*

"I think this writer he saw very clearly, for he knew what was coming. Senor Blue, we need someone right now who will write of the dreams and leaves and we need a keeper of our people's stories, who is also not scared to see the blood along the streets."

I stood, too quickly, and set my head spinning.

"Blood? But the killing is by you, maybe even at that camp. And the bombs on Holy Night! It's you, isn't it? Bombing entire cities! How many people have you killed? But my government is rebuilding. Every time there is a Hit, a Park is built. There are trees in the heart of my City, Maria. Why would they build Parks and destroy your world?"

"Hush," said Maria. "Calm."

She placed her hands on my cheeks and drew me down beside her and whispered into my face.

"Think, Jimmy Blue. Who bombs your people, bombs then burns and digs so that there are no survivors, no witnesses? And, yes, who builds the Parks? It's the same people, Jimmy, the same. Siren."

"That's insane."

"Yes, Jimmy, it is madness."

"Then why?"

"So we can breathe. We're running out of oxygen, Jimmy Blue, too many people, not enough trees. But no-one is going to go back to the way things were, even if we could. It's too expensive, too unpredictable. Siren has a better plan."

"How things were?"

"Our planet is messy, Jimmy. It could never be controlled, even when we were destroying most of it. Forests burning here, deserts growing somewhere else, oceans rising above everything. Siren sees a better way, not to rely on nature. No, today the Parks are our lungs. They're putting the planet on a life support system, and at the same time their bombs control the population. Who's to blame? Terrorists that do not exist."

I shook my head.

"We have to stop them, Jimmy," said Maria. "Don't you see?"

"No," I said, struggling to my feet, "No, this is mad, it's too much."

Maria rose, too, but she was looking to the horizon. Her face was suddenly white. I followed her gaze.

Where she looked there were purple clouds snorting and pawing on the distant horizon. Mists rose like boiling steam from the treetops below and in minutes the vista was veiled in impenetrable grey. But closer to us, among the treetops, rose a huge, single column of black smoke.

"We must go," Maria said.

Our descent was fast and perilous. Maria slipped often and I crashed forward, too, so that I feared one of us must snap a leg on the tanglements of roots or kill ourselves altogether by diving headfirst into a tree. But Maria would not let up our pace.

The Morning Parks

"Jimmy," she insisted, "Jimmy," every time I faltered, "Come, Jimmy!"

A barrage erupted far above our heads, louder and closer, closer, louder, until the hard rain crashed down through the canopy and the way ahead became lost in a maze whose walls were water.

Maria shouted all the more. "Jimmy!" she cried, deeper, deeper into the trees, "Jimmy!" Deeper and lower and darker until here where the rain could scarce find its way through the roof of branches and leaves and finally Maria relented and our progress steadied and slowed.

Here the birds that had chastised our ascent were silent. A heavy calm had fallen upon the slopes. Maria stopped. Listened. Turned to face me.

The gunshot ricocheted off a tree trunk to our right, showering bark into the air. I spun, bewildered, found myself peering into thick brush when Maria backed straight into me, bowling me though skin-ripping branches and we were flat on our faces in the mud where she wrapped my shoulders in her arm, her cold wet cheek against my own, her fingers barred across my lips.

Another bang, a bullet fizzed by, closer this time, I thought, and yet it was impossible to tell from which direction. Maria's arm remained around my shoulders as she moved her other hand to rest on top of my head, and yet I doubt whether I could have lifted myself from the mud had I wanted to. Panic was in my muscles. They were frozen on to chilled bone.

The third shot was a hot explosion directly above our heads and I almost bit into the earth in fright.

Maria whispered so close to my ear the air reverberated but I could not hear. She cupped her hand around my chin, turned my face to her own.

"Jimmy," she mouthed, "they are close. We must go."

I could not move. I had planted myself into the ground like one of Maria's beloved trees.

"Where?" My voice was a whimper.

"Stay close, low, feel with your feet and your hands. Always downhill. Down."

She squirmed away from me on her belly and with my eyes half closed against any way forward I followed her exact movements like a child playing out a mime.

Pierced, scraped, bruised, we did not stop. The rain fell and fell and, though the ground was awash, the sound of our movements were hidden in the torrent. I snorted and choked as mud sprayed into my face. My cheekbone cracked against a rock. All I could see were the soles of Maria's boots.

There were no more gunshots. I did not feel brave yet, but the cold had left my muscles. I told myself I was beginning to feel as though I could talk when Maria vanished from in front of me, her boots suddenly up-ending before disappearing entirely into the ground. I scurried forward, my elbows kneading frantically into the earth and felt the world fall away from me, and I was sliding headfirst down an embankment of mud, splashing into a brown pool. Maria grabbed my waist, pulled me back into the side of the deep gully.

I looked into her face but there was nothing there to show fear or even anger, merely blankness, as though she was already elsewhere and this was but a half-remembered adventure.

We did not stop. She led on down the channel of water, as the forest thinned out around us, until finally, miraculously I spied the kayak still tied to a trunk.

Maria fumbled with the rope, there was a renewed sense of urgency to her movements, and we ran, stumbled, pulled and pushed the boat through and around and through until the water was deep and we were both paddling frantically.

The rain stopped as suddenly as it had begun and I realised that in the damp air I could smell smoke. I turned. Maria was shaking her head. Faster we paddled and stronger was the cloying smell of burning wood.

"Here," Maria said suddenly and jumped, almost tipping me sideways.

We were running along a freshly cut trail, tree limbs hacked and trampled into the earth or left hanging by dripping sinews to catch and tear at our clothes. Now the smoke was visible, hanging to the higher branches like ragged cloth on bones.

Maria stopped dead in the path, her shoulders heaving and I, panting, came to her side. The smoke had lifted its filthy hems to reveal a scorched clearing, a smouldering mass of black branches and ash. Eilidon had been razed to the ground.

****

Chapter Sixteen

Truth Or Dare

GUILT, thought Rysto, must be a terrible cross for sinners to bear. He thanked the powers he should never bring himself so low to suffer such self-flagellating infirmity. Why, this Janu fool had taken his own life, and who should lose sleep for the damned? Was the Cardinal not a bigger fool who shamed his God and his Church with his weakness? And now this!

The torches held by the five riders behind him crackled and spat in agreement but could do little to fend off the quickening blackness. He slowed his horse. The path sloping up through the trees was too narrow, and invisible fingers raked his cheeks.

This night was so cold. He cursed Marlov's insanity and kicked his heels into the soft flanks.

They passed on, and up, and deeper into the midnight of the forest.

All but the last rider, who stopped when the wind whispered his name. Startled, he held out his flame into the confusion at the edge of the path. Nothing here to be met but the agitated night.

No, behind him now. Laughter?

With difficulty he continued to turn his jittery horse, which slipped once on the unseen ice, snorted, and stamped again on the hard earth. He peered stupidly into nothing.

And just then felt ice breathed on the back of his neck and before he could raise his hands the steel traced a lover's long nail across his throat, and his horse whinnied and the blade sawed into his flesh as the animal stamped against the reins.

Run, soldier, run! laughs the whisper and deeper bites the blade.

His mount strained and when his hands dropped to fight the reins the horse lurched once to the side then away. His body swung with an abrupt wet crunch before the last soldier crashed down onto the crackle of icebound leaves.

He lay there in the shocked stillness, paralysed. Until something heavy dropped from the branches, thudded by his head.

Finger nails grating his chest, slicing and slicing until they are inside him, dragging him into the solid earth, and he cannot scream for the blood in his lungs, and finally his eyes are covered.

Only blackness remained.

Only when the five riders reached the edge of the graveyard did they discover he was missing.

Maybe he's run back to his mother, scared to be followed by his own arse. It was the man called Cranor, but his voice was thin and the laughter wavered and fell dead in the thinner air and Rysto growled.

His mother won't recognise him when I'm finished. You two, dismount! I want the suicide's cross. The one marked Janu.

They hesitated.

Do it now!

They move. But this is taking too long. It really is too cold.

Rysto's eyes swallow the moonlight. They follow a white owl, sliding from the highest trees and across the gravestones beyond. He shivers, turns his collar closer to his immense clenched jaw.

Finally a cry.

Rysto led the remaining two riders. They ducked underneath branches, kicked through bushes, and entered the clearing. At the far side two soldiers held torches to reveal a lone wooden cross, the ground before it scraped bare, and the earth broken and piled in shining solid chunks.

Rysto? Rysto, why do you find it so difficult to swallow?

Foxes, he said. Light a fire, a big fire. You, get the carcass up!

The horses were tied to the stoutest branches and three soldiers began clawing with picks and spades. The rich smell of burning wood filled the clearing and soon the men were misshapes against the fire. The hole was shallow, only two feet deep, when metal hit wood

Two of the soldiers climbed out. Cranor, finding himself alone in the hole, tried quickly to scrape the brittle soil from the lid with the heel of his boot before abandoning his task and scrambling free.

Rysto nodded.

Hands reached down and dragged the coffin from its cradle.

It lay beside the fire. Waiting.

You, Rysto pointed again. Open it!

Cranor advanced on the coffin with a long iron bar. The lid was reluctant, and he strained against the wood. Suddenly it snapped up and he dropped the bar, jumped back, his mask cleaved by a nervous, embarrassed grin.

Just do it, breathed Rysto.

And yet you take a step back?

Another soldier came forward and together they pulled away the lid. And they froze. Cranor gurgled a prayer. Then all at once every one of the soldiers was running for his horse, while Rysto stood staring at the box.

He inclined forward, though his feet would not move.

Inside the coffin lay the last soldier. His head smiled up at Rysto at an impossible angle. Thick globules of blood still pulsated from between his lips. Rysto reached out as if to touch the clown-sad face, but suddenly turned.

He was alone but for Cranor, already mounted and impatiently holding the reins of his captain's horse.

Rysto forced himself to walk towards them, but his mount reared, the reins wrenched from Cranor, and the horse nodded under the frenzy of branches until the clearing filled with the sound of its crashing escape.

Without hesitation Rysto hauled Cranor from the saddle, mounted and marched the animal back towards the path with Cranor jogging by his side, crying, begging, No, captain, you can't go, don't leave me here, Captain, and all the while Rysto murmured his own litany, kicked the horse onward, faster, faster, and Cranor fell to the ground, crying no, Captain, no!

Only once did Rysto turn and behind Cranor's prone form he glimpsed a figure black against the bonfire, but the image vanished in a doubt of impure light, and Rysto was already galloping headlong down the hill, reaching out desperately for the city far below.

Cranor, claw your mind into this ice-glazed earth, cover yourself over with the black soil against the colder darkness, for the faint sounds of your dear captain's escape have vanished.

Rysto will pay? He will pay with blood? Perhaps.

But now your spine jolts at the sharp crackle of the fire in the clearing so close behind. Open eyes see nothing. But, yes, you can sense the open coffin and touch that terrible grinning face. Don't think, Cranor. Move!

Slowly, he pulled his legs underneath him until he was crouching. Barely daring to breathe, he rose to his feet. He turned once only to the glow and it winked through the gentle rocking.

Ahead he could see the smudged grey of the path and his legs began to stamp in the right direction. Each step jarred, softened only by the whimper from his throat.

From here downhill will be faster better.

But now you hear it for the first time. A deep growl, long and low growl, a growl off to your right. Walk on. Walk. Legs move. On.

He was certainly travelling faster now, and it was always downhill, down, and away, far away, better, and no more growling, and he could feel the path stretch every juddering step behind him and, though his breathing was too quick, too quick, too quick, he knew no pain could be so great against this elation of escape.

For a second time he risked looking behind. Ah but this time his mouth filled and he gagged on the terror which spewed from the pit of his stomach when he saw the figure of a man at the end of the path, black and tall, the feline pupil in the white of the moon's eye.

You would run, fly across the ground to the city, but you're blind, your legs are flaccid and not your own, your arms flail drunkenly at the thick air, your ears bubble as a shrill laughter rings around your head until you realise it is your own voice and your teeth stitch themselves shut with ragged lips.

On now! On!

Until he was crashing through branches and sudden barbs tore at his legs and the way ahead was a swirling soup of grey on grey whips. His body stopped, swaying violently, trying to bring his vision onto the ground, his hands onto his too soft knees. At last his eyes found an anchor in the darkness of a darker bole, but the path was lost. He was standing among the solid shadow crowd of trees.

The light had grown bolder, but the timid morning lagged behind, and all around was gone but for the thud thud hammer of his chest and the wheeze from his lungs. And a long, deep growl? Yes, for the second time. A growl from between the fat trunks, from among the entanglement of spidering branches, from crouched bushes one score yards from his feet. He stepped back, hard into a tree, half turned to get around it, but another snarl tore the darkness from out there, and almost immediately again from his left.

The bark feels brittle and unyielding but your nails bite deep as you sag against the trunk and will you not ask why there is no pain in the slow trickle from your fingers, Cranor? Cranor?

For the third time. A warm growl, washing to his feet, soothing, growl closer yet, and his brain cries out that he must move now, now, and he knows he cannot.

When the first head appeared from the darkness it was long and beautiful and smooth with pure white hair and ruby eyes. From the night they closed, closer around him, at least a dozen, yes twelve, each standing to the height of his chest, gazing serenely on him in still silence. Until as one their heads turned at a footfall and Cranor saw a man was behind, clothed tall in shifting grey and black, his face indistinct in the sleekit loitering of the smug night.

Do you remember me? asked the man, his voice was soft and clear and sure.

Please, breathed Cranor, please . . .

But I remember you, said the man, and walked closer, and the wolves walked too. I remember your touch.

As he spoke he brushed the hair from the side of his head and Cranor looked into what was revealed and he whispered. No. No. No, please, no.

Do not beg, smiled the stranger, it sours the taste of your fear for my friends.

And his lips touch your cheek, and the wolves, too. Howl, Cranor, oh, how they howl!

****

MARIA walked to where the doorway to the roundhouse might have been and turned a full slow circle, arms limp by her sides, palms outward, absorbing the entire scene. I stood at a distance, too numb to venture into the desolation.

The Morning Parks

Maria's face was stone, inscrutable, as it had been during our flight down the mountain. She stopped. She closed her eyes for a long time. When she opened them her step was sure. She strode through smouldering remains, raked smoking ashes, walked the perimeter of the camp, kicked at stumps of burning wood, rucked hot debris with her boot heels.

It may have taken her a minute or an hour, but all this time I stood rooted to my spot in the trail, watched her move until she was walking back to me, and when I swallowed my throat was warm with the blood bitten from the insides of my cheeks.

"I can find no bodies," she said.

I nodded, and she passed me, and I followed her in silence back along the path until it forked to the right in the direction of Baca's boat.

When Maria slowed I knew we must be near. She stopped. I stopped. There was a scuffle, a loud hissing in the bushes beyond and, without thought, I pushed past Maria and my heart leapt as huge birds exploded into a confusion of black and white wings from the bongo's foredeck, flapped away, heavy and sullen, into the trees.

But the boat seemed untouched.

Maria boarded immediately and began tearing the tarpaulin from around the outboard.

"We will have to try to get downstream, find the others," she said. "It will be difficult for two until we can use the motor."

I untied the mooring rope, fingers clumsy around the wet knot, waded into the water and clambered up over the edge and threw the coils into the prow. On top of Baca.

His eyes were open and black flies drank there like fat beasts around water holes. I backed away, gagging, and my heels tripped over something and I fell heavily. Maria came up behind me.

"No," she cried, "Madre Dio, no!"

I untangled my feet from Pedro's twisted trunk. The tight muscles of the boy's belly gleamed black and red under the divot of flesh hacked from his chest. His arms were criss-crossed by gashes where he had tried to defend himself. His face was turned from us, at an impossible angle, but even from here I could see half of it was missing.

Maria sank to her knees, sobbing in silent gulps so that her shoulders reared violently under her wet shirt. I crouched beside her, dizzy, unable to swallow the acid in my throat. She clasped my hands, mumbled, incoherent with shock I thought, until I realised she was praying.

"Get up!"

I whirled to the voice on the bank, a wild apparition in camouflage and skin and hair, all matted white with ash, streaked brown with mud. Bernie.

"They are here," she called out behind her.

Teri appeared, Marcus was already sliding heavily into the river, falling on to his knees in the water, heaving himself on to the boat, to scoop Maria from me in his huge arms.

"Get up!" Bernie said again.

I did as she ordered and she stepped back, disappeared into the shadows of the trees, Teri following, then Marcus with Maria half-led, half-carried in the crook of one arm.

I glanced at Pedro, reached out to touch his leg but could not. Even as I dragged the tarpaulin over Baca, I was turning away, clambering over the side of the boat and following the others into the jungle.

We moved in silence, jogging fast, branches whipping at us, joined at intervals by small groups of others from Eilidon, who emerged from the trees, awaiting our arrival as though by some predetermined plan. At last there were perhaps twenty, a forlorn band ghosting our way through the forest.

Finally, Bernie signalled a halt and bodies collapsed below a great overhang of rock, shielded on the other side by a fast-flowing tributary. Without word Teri took up a position at our rear, sitting in the shadow of a bole, at once invisible against its bark, and with a slight hand signal Bernie sent Guy, the young American, ahead.

When water had been swigged and all were prone, panting, expectant, Maria spoke.

"Tell me, Tara," she said. Her voice was flat, unyielding.

"We had no warning," said Marcus.

"No. Tara, you tell me," said Maria.

The Morning Parks

Bernie stood and presented herself rigidly and spoke directly into Maria's gaze.

"We have lost half of the family. Baca and Pedro were the first. Gol found them. He came running into Eilidon but they shot him in the back before he could speak."

Maria's head bowed slightly.

"Most of us were leaving camp to see to chores," continued Bernie. "Those who were there had no chance. Those of us on the north side were able to flee and escape by swimming along the shallows. Maybe they were too scared of the caimans to follow us."

Marcus spat his water into the earth.

"First they burned Eilidon," Bernie said, "then the bodies."

Marcus said, "They were destroying the evidence, Maria. I watched. They dragged them, some were still breathing, into the roundhouse before setting it to the fire. What was left of the bones and the flesh bits, they threw in the river."

Maria stood. She was nodding her head quickly, too quickly.

"Enough," she said, "enough."

Bernie nodded, said, "We can't use the boat. They've not burned it only because they want us back on the river. They are camped all along the banks, waiting."

"So what will you have us doing?" asked Marcus, "Losing ourselves in the forest? Waiting here for them to come back?"

Bernie did not answer him, said to Maria, "I know a place. West. It's safe."

Finally, Maria nodded, said, "Yes. We go on, but now all must rest."

"We start again in two hours," said Bernie.

Most were unconscious before the words were spoken. Marcus set himself the task of collecting all the backpacks and redistributing provisions.

I made to join Maria but Bernie grabbed my arm.

"Come," she said.

We walked from under the overhang, beyond Teri, who watched our passing, to the river's edge and there Bernie turned to me and said, "I am sorry."

"Sorry? Why? You were not..."

"Sorry you are here, that you're part of this now."

Her voice was firm, not cold but formal, yet she reached for me and grasped my fists in her small hands and squeezed.

"There is much you don't know yet, Jimmy. This is about more than trees and fighting loggers and oilmen in Batavia."

"I know," I said, and thought of Maria, how she had made the struggle for her people seem an ideal. Now I had seen flies feeding on the face of ideal. "Much more."

"Yes," said Bernie, "more than anyone here, more than your personal salvation."

"Listen, I didn't choose to come here."

"But you did, Jimmy. You always do. What is it that you can't stop asking questions of the world? No, no more talk. Despite everything I tried, you're part of this and you'll stay part until we can get things remedied."

She began to walk back to the others.

"Remedied?" I asked. "Are you going to remedy Baca and Pedro?"

She stopped in her tracks, turned, walked back to me with the face of a stranger.

"You don't know shit, Blue. I should have let them finish it in the Circus House. If you're very lucky, you'll live long enough to learn. But let me give you your first lesson: the men who killed Baca and Pedro no longer have arms to hold machetes."

I watched as she joined Teri. And the darkness fell suddenly without fire and without light.

I lay in the darkness and scratched at the crawling on my skin, snorted as unseen creatures clung to my nostrils, but mostly I thought about the look in Bernie's eyes when she spoke of her friends' killers and the people who had attacked me, how she stood, hands straight by her sides, eyes unflinching. And I thought about how scared and pathetic and snivelling I had been on the mountain.

Guilt is, indeed, a terrible thing. There is no strength to be found in our bearing of it. That only makes us weaker. In this breathless, lightless hiding I found I was too scared even to think too much. I tried instead to block out the forest.

But I smell the closeness of Baca's face, trace the wet wounds on Pedro's arms with my fingers. I no longer imagine terror, it is here, hard in my chest, pulling me into the earth and leaves. But more than this is the weight of guilt on my back.

Do you remember me? asked the man, his voice was soft and clear and sure.

Please, please . . .

But I remember you, said the man, and walked closer. I remember how you crawled in the dirt as they cut me apart. Do you feel guilty?

As he spoke he brushed the hair from the side of his head and I looked at Pedro's half-face, and he laughed and said, So, Mr Writer Man, do you feel guilty?

Well howl, Jimmy Blue, howl!

I woke with a start to the sound of suffocated breath, Maria crying. She had buried her head in the leaves so that the others would not hear.

I shrugged the blanket from my shoulders and went to her and wrapped her frailness in my own trembling arms until, finally, her sobbing slowed, subsided, and she fell limp into me and, at last, she slept.

****

Chapter Seventeen

The Journey

WHEN Wardlaw arrived at the remains ankle-high green shoots had pierced a carpet of red weed and were stretching their slender young necks in the sun-streamed breeze. All that might suggest a terrible violence had been committed here was a breath-held lingering in the air. Not quite the smell of smoke, nor this heaviness the embarrassed breeze tried to shoosh away, but a less tangible disquiet that made even the Abidar afraid to venture too far from the path.

"It's the silence," thought Wardlaw. "There are no birds singing."

"They must have fled. No prisoners," said the man to his right.

Wardlaw turned to the Captain of 212, who shrugged and spat, said, "My men could find nothing here."

Wardlaw nodded, even as he bent and picked something from the ashes and the shards of bones.

"Then you must continue your search, Captain," he said. "You might want to look west."

Wardlaw turned on his heel, placing the item in his shirt pocket.

****

WE are on the run. Only Bernie seems to know where we are going and no-one can be sure how close the Abidar may be, or if they are following. Every night there is an argument of accusing hisses and strangled protest, usually kicked off by Marcus, who is increasingly nervous about our proximity to the Batavian border and its string of control posts.

"Playing hiding and seeking? Running into their arms," he tells everyone in a hoarse whisper, until hushed as much by the unbearable weight of his own anger.

Bernie speaks only to Teri. Both are gone for much of the day, scouting ahead of our weary group.

Maria is looking more tired. Today she refused my offer of food, and sat wrapped in her own arms staring into the only fire Bernie would allow. Always Marcus is close by, making sure her water bottle is full, checking her blanket for scorpions, clearing the earth around her sleeping place.

Tonight, after she has ended another fight between Marcus and Johan, and shuffled off to her blanket, the huge German pulls me aside, says, "You must see to her, if I cannot. You understand?"

"Yes. Yes, of course."

"No you don't, Blue. She has belief in you, you know this?"

He claps me on the back but for the first time his touch is gentle.

On the fourth night Bernie sits an hour with Maria and Teri before she ushers everyone into a close circle. Maria takes Marcus by the arm and leads him away.

"Tomorrow," says Bernie, we cross the fording five miles north west of here. It is the Rio Vatua."

Without Maria or Marcus present, no-one speaks.

"You all know what this means, but beyond this there is somewhere we can be safe without fear. I have been there many times before. You must trust me."

Bernie takes the exhausted silence for agreement and we know that tomorrow we will try to cross the Vatua, skirting an Abidar outpost and entering a no-man's land on the very edge of Batavia. Not a word is spoken as we disperse into the darkness.

From above the rim of my blanket I can see a man's silhouette against silver-peppered blackness. Marcus stands staring into the sky for a long time. I think he is still there when I fall asleep.

MOTHER of! The lids of Cindecis' eyes closed down upon them as he sank back into the creak of his chair. Then he laughed, stroked the silver of his upper lip with a thumbnail. And the two guards shifted their weight uneasily.

So this ghost appeared from the night? Janu himself came among you and spoke? Indeed. And what did this apparition have to say? Did he ask after my health?

Calan tried some force on the heel of his other foot, glanced sideways at Henri, who now stood resolute.

This was no ghost. He was real, Captain, very real. This may be madness but you must know it is an insanity, which befell all three.

Ah, yes, Calan, but where is our third madman? I asked only that you retrieve the fool Giraud and instead you bring back tales of demons and exploding windows.

He is gone.

Henri's voice was empty. He looked ahead but did not focus and, though he addressed his Captain, his words could have been for himself.

He will to the city's convent when darkness comes. He believes he would do Janu's bidding.

Cindecis rose at once and walked around the desk. He faced Calan first.

What of this? Does Giraud intend to molest the good sisters for the sheer devilment of your phantasm?

He, that is the vision, he spoke, Captain. He said only that Giraud must free a woman. He named her not.

But of course, Calan! One of the King's Guard plans to rescue a mysterious maiden from the clutches of old Mother Symna. And what will he use do you think? A battering ram? Or will he bend the good sisters' will with a rendition from one of their hymn books?

Calan offered a weak smile.

His sword would do more against the army Marlov has hidden in that building, said Henri.

What? Cindecis turned to him. What of Marlov?

Henri looked now to his Captain. The Cardinal shares Giraud's interest in the Sisters of Hopeful Redemption.

Calan said, His soldiers are billeted in their halls. Rysto himself commands them there. We do not know their task.

Cindecis walked to the window. He seemed suddenly disgusted with his own humour.

Rysto? But this grows too strange. The joke turns sour, I fear.

Then what of Giraud, my Captain?

You must find him, of course, Calan. You must stop this madness before it sets to a gallop, and you will bring Giraud to me before he makes the King's Guard party to some insane religious circus. I must admit curiosity. What have the Cardinal and his shark in mind tonight? Whatever, we shall, of course, have no official part to play. Do we understand each other?

And if Giraud will not be found? asked Calan.

Cindecis looked into the ice, into the liquid swirl of torchlight in the courtyard below, into the confusion of grief and remorse and anger inside his own head.

Then he too is lost and we have failed another of our own.

****

THIS morning, for the first time, Maria joins Bernie to lead our hesitant file. Marcus seems uncommonly placid as he walks ahead of me, and yet I can see he is constantly scanning our flanks. He turns to me often and smiles and nods his head, but when he turns away again his broad shoulders are hunched and tense.

The crossing is reached by noon. Not a sound can be heard above its rushing. I wait my turn as one by one the others cross the hundred yards of knee deep, white froth. It is solid and cold, the water plunges instantly inside my boots, the current grabs for my feet, but most of all the noise fills my senses, thunders inside me, so that I want to break into a run, must not run for fear I will fall, as I eye the shadows in the opposite bank and then in minutes I am across and Marcus is dragging me into the shadows.

All are safe. We have penetrated miles into the no-man's land, urged ever faster by anxieties, despite being suffocated by the afternoon heat, which swaddles exhausted legs and drags down shoulders, when Marcus suddenly throws up his arms and our column halts and disappears entirely as we drop to our haunches and crouch sweating and panting and waiting in the expectant air.

There is a rummaging to our left, the heavy sashay of branches laid aside, an unsubtle crumple underfoot. Closer it comes, twenty yards from where I crouch, Marcus just ahead of me, Guy and Johan, close together behind, every one of us intent on the vegetation, now swishing visibly as a path is brokered towards us.

Fifteen yards, twelve, ten, and, as the bushes before my nose tremble, Marcus leaps to his feet and rushes forward with his backpack lofted above his head.

There is a blood-chilling scream and a huge flesh-coloured shape erupts from the undergrowth, thunders by me so that I am bowled sideways and roll in its wake. My face buried, I am blinded by leaves, breathe soil and moss. When I can scramble upright and wipe the slime from my eyes I see first Guy, his face horribly convulsed, slapping Johan's back and I fear the boy is dead until he lifts his chin from the ground and I see he is laughing. I trundle around on my hands and knees and see Marcus, too, bent double, his huge Bavarian lungs choking silently.

He points as best he can and I half stand to glimpse the hairy buttocks of a barrel-shaped creature as it charges away from us into the bushes, disappears in a fury of green confetti and terrified screeching.

Bernie and Teri have joined us. Bernie slaps Marcus on the chest.

"You should stick to fishing, my friend." she says, "the tapir are too fast for you."

Teri, I notice, does not smile. As she walks away she is replacing something in the right leg of her combats, strapping down the pocket.

"One more mile, one only, and we camp," says Bernie, and one by one her entourage stands, for the first time in days listening to a voice that is loud and unbowed, and the tension lifts from all of us.

Marcus, fetching his backpack from the bushes, is smiling even as he shakes his head.

One mile more. I rest by the side of a fallen tree to catch my breath and rub my bruised ribs. Bernie joins me.

"Why so glum, Blue? After tonight's camp we're almost there."

I salute her with my empty water canister.

"Yup, almost there. Wherever there might be."

"You're not enjoying the ride yet are you?" she asks.

"Okay, Bernie, or Tara, I'll let you know when I begin to have fun. Until then I'll just go on playing follow my leader."

"You follow well."

"Well, I'm sure I'll be first to be told if I let anybody down."

Bernie takes a swig from her water bottle and passes it to me.

"Listen, Blue, half of them still don't remember your name never mind know why you're here."

She elbows me hard in the ribs, says, "Hey, whatever Maria may have told you, she and Gol didn't choose you by chance, so you're not a complete loser. But you should know that Maria finds it difficult to get too close to her own. They have a habit of letting her down."

"She doesn't trust her own people, the people she's trying to save?"

"She has no reason to trust. She has already lost all of those she ever loved. Her father especially."

"He was killed?" I ask, "By the Company?"

Bernie takes the water bottle from my hands, screws on the lid and stands up.

"You could say that. Her father is Chavez."

BEYOND the abandoned gardens, its brittle shrubs, through the mad maze of frosted slabs and crosses, underneath rolling crests of mist, to the doorway of the crypt. Half hidden here in the shadow of the portal, Giraud. For a long time he has watched the clouds roil and crush themselves into a grey and black-whorled pulp above the convent.

His unshaven face is thinned and scarred and the knuckles above the hilt of his sword are raw. But he has waited without movement or even the menace of sound. As the day sank slow under the fat knuckles of heaven.

At last a light blinks in the faceless stone and his gaze snaps to the building. The yellow point grows fast in his eyes and the steel slides with a long contented sigh from his side.

****

Chapter Eighteen

The Sapphire Pools

MARCUS tells me we're now trespassing in a land where we're just as likely to be shot by smugglers as the Abidar, yet his mood, the mood of our entire band, has altered considerably since the encounter with the tapir. This morning Bernie announced we would begin our final trek. We would be safe before nightfall. The promise itself is a tonic for our spirits and a balm for weary limbs.

I have not been able to speak to Maria since Bernie's revelation, but I am unsure how I will ever be able to broach the subject. It is not something Maria can carry lightly and I fear breaking the newfound strength in her stride ever since we crossed the Vatua.

She even allows Marcus to join her and I can see them deep in conversation, as much as our exertions allow, for the first time disregarding their surroundings to make time for one another.

I walk with Bernie. She, too, is relaxed and seems increasingly keen to engage me.

"Here," she says, loading an astonishingly heavy backpack into my arms and unrolling her sweat soaked top over her head. As her firm white breasts are revealed I turn, embarrassed, and she laughs.

"Jeanie Mac, the Saturday nights you tried to get your paws on these and now you can't even look?"

She tugs at the pack to remove a dry vest, but before she puts it on I place a hand on her shoulder, turn her slightly. It is faded, like my own, but the tattoo of the eagle and the lion is unmistakable.

"We're coming to the point again soon, aren't we," says Bernie.

"What do you mean?"

"Why you're here?"

"I ask too many questions, remember?"

Bernie stops in her tracks.

"So, I'll begin then, Jimmy. Why did you come?"

"The scenery. Adventure. Meet old friends."

She laughs, shoulders her pack, strides on.

"I saw you, Bernie."

"I know you did, Jimmy," she says over her shoulder, "but you've missed me so often before. You were very unkind to the poor orphans of Batavia."

"Orphans? Orphans. That was you, in the City, the girl in the vest?"

"Questions, Jimmy, questions. Tell me about your story, the one you hope Anna will like so much. It's a love story, right? Is this catharsis, then," she asks and slaps away a branch. "That's what this is all about?"

I say nothing. I'm shocked, not by the fact it wasn't only Gol who was watching me, but that I haven't thought about you, Anna, for so long now.

"So many bad bastards at work in this world and you're inventing more, Jimmy Blue? So come on, then, let's see this work that helped Gol convince Maria you're the man to change lives."

She whistles loudly, just once, and the company halts, dropping where they stand for their five-minute respite.

She takes my notebook, finds my marker, reads.

IN the main hall, at the head of the ancient oak table, where once long ago the good sisters dined in the perfect regiment of their calling, long ago when such God-fearing women were many and virtuous and willing to serve and this world seemed a place fit for this man, sits Rysto.

"You're kidding me, right? "

"They're not my thoughts, they belong to a character," I say. I feel like a student again, my work berated by a master. "You're taking me out of context."

"You were out of context the moment you arrived here, Jimmy."

She settles sideways against the bole of a tree, looks at me and smiles, says, "Don't worry, I'll do it quietly."

There is a silver goblet stuck in his fist and dark stains burgeon from his lips. He watches the flames fight for air in the huge hearth, entranced by their movement, whipping one another, beaten down by the shadows above, always beaten down.

A knock startles him on the door behind.

Someone stepped into the room.

We are secured, Sir, said his lieutenant. The guard doubled in the lower rooms, torches lit in the uppermost corridors.

Silence.

Then: Are my instruments ready?

All is prepared. Sir ... and Cranor has been found, Sir.

A thin smile quivering, Rysto's eyes swivel sidelong to the soldier. And how is the horseless renegade?

Sir, they say his body is untouched, unmarked bar punctures in his throat and cheeks. And yet he was near death. His body, it was purged of blood. He rants now. He speaks continuously of ... the soldier hesitated.

Rysto's head snapped towards him. He says, Sir, that one comes whose kiss will not be stopped by mercy. He gives no name but says Rysto, you, Sir, you will feel his touch.

Get me the witch, screamed Rysto. Get me Symna! Now! Leave me now!

The soldier retreated hastily and the door closed.

Rysto pushed the silver rim to his face and looked inside. He studied the vague glint in the purple liquid but perhaps his own image disgusted him for he stood and the chair flew out from behind him and he slammed the goblet into the fire.

He grins as the wine swirls and steams over the embers and he turns to the triangle of glass set high in the wall and he sees the night will soon claim the sky and he cries, Let him come then! The forces are not his alone! Let him come!

"You're not half full o' shite are ye, Jimmy?"
I smile now.
"What happened to the hippie girl, Bernie? Before all of this."
"You left her in Malones, remember? But there's a lot of folk would still love to find that girl," she says. "I've been running away from her myself for half my life now. Tell me, Jimmy, have you been home at all?"
"Cashelan? Not for a long time. It's not so easy to travel these days. Taxes. But last time Colm was asking for you, though I couldn't tell him a thing of course. He's fat as his own head but with the meatbeer in him he's still the finest singer in the Kitchen."
Bernie laughs again and it is a sound I remember.
"He always was that. One day," she says, "I'm going back and the only place I'll be running to is down to the Kitchen and Colm better look to his laurels."
We look at each other for a long time.
"You're never going to go back, are you, Bernie?"
"Maybe you'll just never know I've been, Jimmy Blue."
She whistles and Teri appears beside us and we set off.

LOVE and Rosalia in the same breath but Janu feels their last together a thousand times over, as he lies foetal and forsaken in this clay. Why must he see her face without the fingers of love to feel her skin? Why should her voice tear him from the ground only to leave him here blind and scrabbling?

His dreams of her were once as delicate as dew, gone with the growing of day, but now so cruel they linger here when the frosts have made brittle all the world.

And the slow spiralling of worms brings its own vivid phantasmagoria. Tunnels, flames and flight, rooftops, bones and fright, the agony of terror in eyes that once were mirrors of happiness. Such strangeness to move among the world without leaving this pit, where his rotten limbs are shivered by the cold venom of betrayal, his heart pummelled hard to the core by the necessity to beat to a rhythm of hatred.

But if this fresh odium of life is to be his strength let none be brave, for tonight he will wear these leprous hands without conscience, as gloves stolen from his enemies, and the lives who feel their touch will know the imprint of their own wrongs.

Travelling without moving, flying faster than hatred, a being created from the impatient energy of vengeance.

But we do not flee, we follow, desperate through this maze of cityscape, once safe and solid in charitable veils of the midday sun, now dark and viscous and watchful in this nightmare, so that towers swoon and sway and the narrow streets below writhe and stretch and devour their own tails, as the watch fires pulsate and the boom and the beat grow fast and fervent and the lines of strung-out lights grow long and circles widen and the air crackles with the energy of a thousand million voices of hate that will never die but will soon live forever, suffering in the ether.

How fast we fly.

Ah, these gargoyles of humankind are so brave when Janu has passed. One wet tongue has almost betrayed its ugly owner on my cheek. Beware most their gaze. Only their eyes are real, only their eyes know our trespassing.

But where? Where are we going at such frenzied pace?

The islands of the dead are numberless, true. But on this night hard promises will be hard kept, and the softest web is already spun and the spider races to its centre. See yonder, see the blackest basest heart of this city?

So stop.

Here.

Now.

The Convent of the Sisters of Hopeful Redemption.

****

STOP! The cry goes up. There are whoops from ahead but we can see nothing yet, for the scant tracks and tunnels made by animals gave out long ago and the path cut into this dense bush is necessarily ragged, our path circuitous, and continually we trade places to the end of the line for behind us all branches must be carefully remarried. No-one must follow.

Marcus shrugs the pack higher onto his huge shoulders and stomps hastily onward and it is together we step into the camp.

The trees have stopped shy of an opal-coloured rock face and here the water streams and tumbles and rolls around the jumbles of round boulders into three huge pools of sapphire liquid.

On this near side of the water's falling, hugging the cliff face but warmed now by shafts of the afternoon sun, are a row of a dozen or so tiny thatched homes, their lean-to walls made from palms and branches intertwined into the thick limbs of thorn trees so that they form a natural, green wall.

Maria embraces first Bernie then Marcus.

"Right, you filthy heathens," cries Bernie, "bath time."

Marcus is already ripping off his shirt and trousers, clambering atop the highest rock, and with a holler that bounces off the cliff face, dive-bombs naked into the last of the sapphire pools.

Amid a confetti of discarded clothes and cries, Maria walks towards me and takes my hands in hers and says, "Our new home."

****

Chapter Nineteen

The Homecoming

COMING home does not always mean returning. I remember how we felt when you and I arrived in the South Plains, a holiday, our first time far from the City. Everything was skin-burning and surreal and beautiful. During the day the sky was so faraway blue it made me dizzy just to look up, and the night was a puzzle, until you said the stars were simply hot lamps hung all in the wrong places. And yet in those first few hours and days that turned into longest ever nights, the arid air, swollen smells, rattletattle tongues, everything about that magical place made it feel strangely familiar and we both confessed, we would stay, if we could, forever.

Of course, nothing is forever.

The refugees of Eilidon had been at the Sapphire Pools for countless days and nights that were now weeks, if not months, but even on that first afternoon Bernie's forest sanctuary made me feel I had come home after a long time of longing.

One day many years ago I'd been sitting in an airport lounge, leaving my City to look for some piece of me I could recognise and reclaim and give to you. I had not realised that I had packed up and brought the entire City on my back. Now, finally, it was being shaken from me. By violence and death, now by serenity and a beginning.

Living beside the Sapphire Pools I felt I was no longer myself.

Maria looked puzzled.

"No, you are the same person," she insisted, "Maybe you know yourself better?"

"So why do I feel it, I don't know, like I'm alive, you know, inside myself? That sounds so lame, doesn't it?"

"No, no don't you see?" she asked. "It is this place entirely, the land all around of us bearing its fruits in you. Gol taught us that when the trees grow everything else is part of them. It is not possible to feel alone or apart."

"And the people? Eilidon. You?"

She smiled, "Ah, you know this already. We are always growing into one another, Jimmy Blue."

She gently grabbed my unkempt hair and pulled my forehead to hers.

"You see how I grow like a poison ivy all around you?"

She was smiling, with her head tilted just so, slow-swirled black locks curling into the v-shadow of her white shirt.

I reached out for her hand, I wanted to touch the small slimness of those fingers. I do not know why I stopped. I could already feel the smooth warmth of brown skin. It was not fear that she might pull away, which stayed my own hand. It was a dread that if I dared touch, everything would dissolve and be gone.

Sometimes it is best to be outside the moment and inside of its happening.

Even as Maria walked away, I told myself for the first time that I'd chosen well to be here. I was wide awake to moments, knowing them for what they were, not wandering what they might be or remembering what they had been.

In those long days by the Pools there were many such moments, moments that every day grew not as memories but as crystals, small, translucent, powerful to touch. Maria washing her hair in the shallowest pool until the tumbling water blends sapphire, black and blue. Bernie trying to teach us the words to an awful song until Marcus tackles her, but she is on top of him and he bellows with laughter even as she bloodies his nose. The long evenings when the sun refuses to lie down to sleep in case it misses on second and I'm walking to the west lookout and steal by Bernie and Teri who are flat on their stomachs, staring into the pool, and Teri turns to ruffle Bernie's blonde spikes with sudden, unexpected laughter.

Marcus is more direct in my education. He shows me how he can tickle fish into his control, quicksilver in white hands, the beating alive and wet in the air. "This is their dance," he cries, spraying cool water into my face, "this is their little victory, see how they are being, this is why they swim, they are so happy, you see?"

Even as he batters their fragile, happy dance against the rocks I cannot disagree, for I could never wish to confound the giant's immense joy.

I sit often with Johan and his girlfriend Detra, the quiet spoken Danish girl, as she tends her terraces of herbs in the north east corner of the camp. Detra never exchanges more than a greeting, for, excruciatingly shy, she finds it difficult to talk and will turn her head away, yet I can watch her work for hours, listening to her hands and fingers prod the earth and nurture shoots, learning how she plans to coax delicate leaves from the heart of the savage garden.

We are quiet in this place of the Pools. There is no revelry as on that first night at Eilidon, nothing that might attract attention. But happiness is in our flesh. It is in the simple meal every evening, the fireside laughter and, entwined as we are with this place and each other, in the space we give one another to enjoy our private universe.

Every day I record in the margins of my notebook what I see. The birds, the flash and stramash of their sounds and colours, the smallest plants at my feet, how they open and close their delicate treasures as the day waxes and wanes, the tallest trees which have surely been looking down upon all since before our kind ever came here.

The leaves of the book soon grow alive as they ingest my surroundings. And, meantime, the insides of the old tome happily whore themselves around camp. Once and awhile the words come back to me, more ruffled and dog-eared, and every time I am happier with their passing from me. I know when they return that new and eager fingerprints will have made their tracks across them.

In the hours after evening meal Marcus delights in baiting me like one of his silver prizes, asking what manner of men and madness have I created. Even though I cannot answer, I am happy to read more, for I know Maria enjoys the ludicrous ramblings, contrasting my imagination against the reality of her world, perhaps holding up my words like a negative to what she hopes I will one day offer.

But the greatest happiness of all is when I am on vigil, for in those hours of sky lights and songs of the invisibles, Maria often joins me as I sit cocooned in the flared roots of the dead Garia tree.

"I do not want to sleep so much here," she says.

If she can, she identifies the mysterious night calls, weaves stars into tapestries, weaving among all Baca's tales from their long journeys together on the river.

"You miss him."

"Yes," she says, softer adds, "Sometimes I dream he and Pedro are still searching for us on the river. I hear them calling out our names into the trees."

I want to tell her it is alright, but this is the girl whose own blood is the nemesis of her land and people. I have no right to tell her such things. But sometimes I put my arm around her small shoulders and we say nothing until soft scrunching footfalls and Johan's whistle mean we each must retreat to our own cocoons of netting and coarse, skin-chaffing sheets in the darkness of a thatched hut.

Often afterwards I lie awake for a long time. And I am afraid I am losing myself, not in Maria, because she would never ask that of me. I am losing myself in this world she is giving me.

Then one morning, before the others have risen, as we sip coffee, Bernie says something strange as she stokes the coals of the fire with her boot.

"You've forgotten your love story, Jimmy."

"I don't understand."

Neither Janu nor Rosalia were slipping from me. In fact, they had grown to be characters in the camp's nightly reveries.

"Are you happy to stay here simply because you don't miss Anna any more?"

Anna! I had not thought of you for such a long time. Bernie let me be, but for the rest of that day the shame hung inside my guts like a forgotten bandage.

At the meal Marcus surely noticed for he tried to cheer me by pestering for the next chapter of the Big Book, as he called it, succeeded instead in sparking my mood.

"Will they come tonight, Jimmy? The…"

"Musketeers," whispered Detra.

"Yes, do these men with the big swords who fear nuns. Are the nuns warrior women under their halibuts?"

"Habits!" came the chorus.

"Yes, I think they will come," said Detra and there was a chorus of support.

"We can be in no doubt then, that your hero will meet his true enemy?" asked Teri.

Her words surprised me. They were perhaps the first she had spoken directly to me. Her accent was refined, a perfect, clipped English.

"Janu knows his enemy," I said. "Neither of them can avoid that truth."

Teri said, "And you, too, Blue, do you know your real enemy? Can you avoid the truth?"

I could feel Maria watch Teri over the glow of the fire, as I said, "You can't catch the truth. It's too heavy, even for you Teri."

Marcus guffawed.

"It would break your arms," I said. "It falls to the ground like gravity and buries itself."

"Indeed. And how do you know this?"

Maria shifted uncomfortably, but my own mood was heavy inside me and I would not be diverted.

"Because, Teri, the truth always comes back to the surface, even through ashes and rocks. It needs the light. Perverse that way. It's in its nature. The darker the truth, the deeper it hides, yet the more it desires to be known."

"Ah, and isn't the truth just dying to be out tonight," said Bernie as she crashed down beside Teri and put an arm around her. "Hadn't you best read to us then, Senor Writer? Do you want to dig up Janu tonight?"

"Ya, ya, silence for the Big Book," cried Marcus. "Begin!"

"Please, Jimmy," said Maria.

She placed a hand on mine and I thought perhaps that she, too, wanted this distraction from her own truths more than anyone.

MARLOV claws at the naked folds of his deflated trunk, frantic to wear his insides out so we can see his suffering, witness how guilt has slept and gnawed fruit from his belly, how the skin hangs in disgust from him, mottled and peeling. His hands tremble. His bleached lips stick to his teeth so that vials pressed there by Dolran, long since fled to the country of his sorcerer fathers, have done little but stain the bedclothes.

But look where his priests will not. Into those orbs and the true colour of Marlov's mind. Blind and black as stagnant water. And though they seep slow there is no measure to their fill. Without sleep without end they spill for his answer to every night is to weep for all of now, emptying himself of all warmth.

But reality is left cold and alone and here beside him in the pit. You can't hide from your insides.

Barricade the last window with the thickest wood, cloak the air in this reek of incense and sweat and urine, but you can still feel it roll from the hills, stampede of howl and horror, alarum, laughter of the pack.

Madness comes searching nightly, roaming free, even into the city, even among these portals, now that days are weeks and still no word from Rysto, and his men gone, all gone, every one a traitor, leaving families to evils which beset all when food spoils, the winds scream, and the catacombs cough so that the streets fill with abominations and the river runs red, and the dogs run and splash and feed.

'Struth Rysto will come back, the Shark is hunting, stealth, say some, while others whisper malice and mystery, no, no, Cindecis roars through the night and Rysto must face the Captain, God and justice.

But, Marlov, you know, don't you? Rysto is gone. And that is because of the other, because of the one who comes. The one whose name torments. The one whose mantram stamps footprints on your brain as it crosses and recrosses every thought. Janu. Janu. Janu, dancing on your sanity. Yes, Janu, Janu. How can you laugh, Marlov, in the delight of it all?

Laugh! cried Marlov and the priests woke with a start and looked up bewildered at this first word in so many days and nights.

Excellency?

But Marlov said nothing more. He sat, and stared, and wept.

And when they woke hours later the bed was empty. The priests scuttled to the door and discovered the guards, too, were gone.

"Now we get to the place!" cried Marcus and was hushed by, of all people, Detra. When the laughter waned, I said, "Now I will make this man of the cloth prey for you."

Only Bernie groaned in the silence. I knew what she was thinking, that I was no funnier now than when I was her travelling companion many years ago. She was right. Puns? You hated my puns more than anything else, didn't you, Anna? The joke was that I was no longer trying to be funny.

My mood had grown filthier and now this new remembrance of you made me inexplicably angry. The more I read, the tighter I strangled my voice.

NOWHERE to go but the fist had gripped his heart so viciously only movement itself was release. His bodyguards, half-demented nightly by sordid rantings and little deaths, without word decided best allow this half-robed figure to flutter past. For a while they followed as Marlov moved through the palace, flapping feet on flat cold floors, while they shuffled behind, until he halted, turned back on himself, bowled through them. Again. And again. And again.

When it seemed obvious these great loops were to continue into the night they grew weary of his blind wanderings, grew angry of his sudden blundering charges, grew to think of their bunk house. Then let the madman pace. He will not get past the gates.

And so they were not there to see him shocked still at the far end of the topmost corridor, arms and legs too wide, ears unfolding to the patter of sounds upon his consciousness, sounds so subtle and yet so terrifying they threatened to overwhelm the name. Sounds of soft, padding paws and the wet hiss of breath.

His own screwed into his chest. Sounds grew.

Behind him.

He turned and there at the end of the corridor sat a black wolf, the height of a man, red eyes, easy breathing, with only the hint of tongue below the ridges of its long lips. Shadows became wings became two more wolves.

The first stood. And all three moved. Towards him.

Through the marble halls Marlov scurried, unable to catch the whimper in his throat. His bedridden limbs were stiff and might have ached but he knew nothing of it. Only this. No, not this. He had not expected this. Your creed, recite the litany! Janu, Janu, Janu, Janu!

His cries echoed, rushing up, rushing down, crashing back upon him so that his own fear terrified him most with its noise, raging through rooms which should be familiar but were blurred in a torrent of knife-edged furniture and sudden doors with handles that slipped so that he half hung on their brass and swung himself on and in and through to the next whirl of walls and cloth and paint and bewilderment of faces, laughing down upon him, reaching out, and always always always pads of feet, hisses of breath.

On to the last, the bare-bricked passage, an artery into the heart of the chapel itself, lit by gold dishes of holy oil, and in horrible genuflection each flared and flickered and died in his passing so that when he reached the doors to the sacrastery and put his hand on the latch he stood in utter darkness.

Locked.

No, it was locked.

Utter darkness.

Sounds, soft footfalls.

He whirled. Nothing nowhere but the intense throb of green light that chased his eyeballs, confused him, but then there the flash not fifty yards away of six gleaming rubies. The breathing was no longer easy. It was hoarse and wet and he knew their tongues were free and pink flesh was already curling gently through the sharp white pillars.

Utter darkness. And now they come. What are you going to do?

But it is locked. Locked. Fingers slip and squirm on the iron ring, but don't whimper for hear how it excites them, their snarling, faster forward, until you can feel the muscle and bone roll beneath their hair, smell the hot lust in their breath, sense huge bodies scream towards you, how they leap, and the door falls away into sanctuary, banging knees, kicking heels, the door slams fast and the wood is battered three times.

Marlov lay balled on the floor, his frame swelling with great bellows of sobbing. And through the veil of fat tears he saw lights forming. Slowly they coalesced into a pathway of candles laid neatly from his fingertips to the next doorway and into the gloom beyond.

Sniffing and scraping tormented the door but he could only crawl along this yellow aisle, his wet robe dragging candles so that their flames spilled and hissed but refused to die, transforming him into a peacock with blind meteors in his sad tail.

At the inner doorway he clambered to his feet and his vestment burned and fell from his body leaving him naked. The chapel's gallery of a thousand thousand stars spun slow arcs, and though distant in the greystone gloom which hung from columns and niches, those heavens looked full now upon his nakedness and their light grew strong and knowing.

He stepped, past row upon row of benches filled with wraiths, growing before him, heads on the slow roll of dark *waves, and his being pounded with the blood which laid siege to his heart.*

Stop.

What stands by the font?

Not shadow.

And yet His Excellency Cardinal Marlov walks on. And so begins the slow drip of water in well, low moan of Gregorian whispers in dread.

I know you. You, who cannot be. Janu, Janu, Janu, Janu.

Falling.

Onto his knees so hard noise resounds through him and yet he feels no pain for the sensation brings images from his youth, the pleasant torture of penances when it was rewarding to be scared.

Begging forgiveness not with thoughts or words but this mantram, this terror which has become his litany. Janu, Janu, Janu, Janu, Janu, Janu, Janu.

On your knees, too terrified to look up. Ah, but you can imagine the hand reach out, hear the swish of the cloth, feel its breeze about the skin of your head. About to touch me, about to touch me, let it be now, please, now, and suddenly your heart swells and swells and simply explodes in release.

And, finally, Marlov looks up and sees the statue above him and looks into the smile of a saint who has not moved and he blesses Janu, Janu, Janu, and smiles, too, even as he slumps dead upon the floor.

"Ah the big, fat bastard man!" cried Marcus.

"If only it were that easy," sighed Johan. "Unfortunately, all of the Company badness does not come in targets so big as Marlov."

"And you, Teri?" I asked. "Do you believe the evil done by the Marlovs of this world will be avenged?"

Bernie replied in her stead, "Still seeking a spade for those truths, Jimmy Blue?"

"Isn't that why I'm here, Bernie? Sorry, Tara. Yes, let's see if we can dig up this little nugget first. What should we call you?"

"Friend," said Maria. "Call her friend."

She stood, put her hand on my forearm, said, "The fireside is for friends. But the wind is blowing the smoke south and tonight maybe we should not sit so long."

"It's okay, Maria," said Bernie. "Tonight it's okay. Relax, Mr Writer. Let us hear this whole tale once and for all, before this warrior queen has to go and stand guard over your City skin."

I shook my head and smiled. If she knew anything, Bernie knew me well enough to be sure I could not hold anger long in the face of her boldness.

"Then tonight, Miss Bernie Tara MacSharry, I present my most gruesome tale, Beyond The Sun, a tale of love lost and love won. Stouter hearts shall sit long tonight, though I will forgive you if your weak disposition means you must leave us early."

I bowed to applause. And began.

THE convent's stomach was seething hot and its walls, splashed yellow and red around the huge gurgling hearth, seemed to convulse. The soldier, no more than a boy, shifted uncomfortably by the far wall, caught between these blasts of raw heat and the icy air searching for his bones from beneath the outer door.

His older companion sat slumped enormously at the table with his head buried in the crook of his dead arm. The only sounds were the death throes of the sticks squirming in the flames and the simmering of a giant steam-shrouded pot.

And a slow scraping at the lock. Again.

It might go away? The soldier hoped, and held his breath and hoped, but, no, this sound grew louder, grew so deliberate.

One short sharp knock.

The soldier jumped from the door. The man at the table started from his slumber. Whassat?

The youngster put a finger to his lips, pointed.

Well? said his companion. Go to it, Grub!

He shook his head, hissed, We're not supposed, got to warn them first, eh, Barth?

Right you are, boy, run get the big grown-ups! And then we open up and it's only one of them sweet-for-nothing husks been out for a sly bottle. Go on, wet boy, you don't even unlock it, you just shout through to the little old lady, see?

So Grub did turn and he called out, *Who's there?*

Silence.

Barth yelled, *If there's no-one there then you can't come in!*

Silence. He guffawed.

Well, just bugger off back into the darkness, see!

He laughed again, shrugged his shoulders, leaned back on his stool.

There was a knock at the door.

Look, cried Barth, and his fat cheeks were flamed by the fire, *there's no-one'll enter here this night, so if you don't want stuck and squealin' and put in this here pot, you'll get the hell away!*

But Hell has come knocking.

Barth lurched to his feet at the sound of the man's voice, knocking over his stool. He tugged a sword from beneath the cloak on the table, stomped to the wall. There he stood with his back against the shadows, offside of the door, signalled Grub forward with a thumb. But the boy stared at him with his hand hovering over his own hilt.

Do it! sneered his companion.

Grub leaned down. He slipped back the bolt. He turned the iron key. He pulled open the door. And he stepped back.

The figure filled the doorway, wrapped in a thick grey woollen cloak against the winter's reckoning, but his face was uncovered and the man's eyes glowed instantly with the light of the kitchen. He smiled.

May I come in?

Grub's gaze flicked unconsciously to Barth who nodded slowly, heaved his blade above his head. The boy stepped back, stepped until his backside bumped against the hard edge of the table, knocking over a wine cup. It spun noisily on the oak, staining the wood with a shower of scarlet wine.

The stranger entered.

Two steps inside he said, If you strike me from behind fat man, you will not deserve to live.

Barth's sword wavered, hesitant, hanging miraculously in the air.

The stranger leaned towards the youngster before him, said, Know that I am Giraud Savane of the King's Guard and I will not be stopped in my task.

So slowly time moved, so surely Barth sliced down, so swiftly the stranger swept his sword behind him and cut the man in two, so that Barth's torso fell to one side and his legs the other and the flagstones splashed with the blackness of his heart and its spidered lines. Spirits sizzled and spat on the hearth.

Now, boy, turn from me. Do as I say.

Tears ran from Grub's cheeks as his sword clattered onto the floor and he turned and his palms flattened on the rough table top.

Giraud said, You will sleep, for I see your heart is yet in its right place. And at once he would bring the hilt of his blade knocking on the back of the boy's skull, but Grub's fear had dropped him to the floor before his senses could feel the bruise.

As Giraud left the room he unfastened his cloak and it fell to the ground, and with his insignia unveiled he ascended a flight of steps and opened another door into a long high-ceilinged corridor, bright with torches.

Cardinal's men. At the far end of the corridor were squat double doors but before these a knot of Marlov's guards, but he walked on, straight to them. For a long while they did not move, and perhaps they could not believe in such a bold act for they seemed figures caught in a frieze, as Giraud strode forward, his gaze nailed to the doors, and only when he was among them did they break from their trance and their blades sprang like startled peacock feathers, but their cries of outrage were entwined with sudden cries of pain as

Giraud waded in, hacking, stabbing, and weaving a silver trace through their stunned defence.

Two soldiers swayed in front, too close together, jabbing across him, and he simply stepped into them, bringing his blade on top and with his left he sliced roughly across their throats with a serrated knife. With this same swinging hand he pulled down to his left side, ripping wetness from a third chest.

He stepped back once, twice as the two soldiers fell, clutching through the blood as their voices sprang from their throats, and he grabbed the third and swung him into two more too slow to react, too engrossed in the horror befalling their companions.

Stones were awash with the hot fetor of combat and Giraud's boots sloshed around the flailing to the one man before the doors, to the soldier who stood transfixed, his sword arm trembling.

It was then a flicker of yellow was shooed from the darkness of an archway, chased by a furious agitation, a force of anger that cascaded into the passageway.

Here Giraud halted. Here were at least a dozen soldiers before him. Here he glanced behind where two injured men had clambered to their feet, tunics black shined with their companions' blood. Here was getting very crowded.

THEY did not advance slowly but surged forward en masse, clotting the corridor with their bodies, blades, and exultations, and just as suddenly stopped. Their mouths were clamped and their eyes pulled beyond their prey. Giraud glanced behind to see Henri and Calan framed in the doorway.

You started without us, I see! smiled Calan, freeing his sword as they strode down the passageway, side-stepping the barbaric contortions.

Thankfully, you left the kitchen door ajar.

They joined him, a brother on each side, and the three Guards stood together against his assailants.

My work here is not yet done, said Giraud.

Calan turned to him. But what were you cooking? You left too much fat on the roast.

Guard yourselves, grimaced Henri, we shall see this madness to its end before taking quick leave.

Without pause three lunged forward and as one they hacked a path towards the door. The sharp clash of steel pierced the stramash of torn breath and desperate, shocked cries, and foretold the thud of more short, wet life onto the stones.

Soon their shirts were ragged, dripping heavily with foes, but the doors swung before them now, into the murk of a wide, circular room. And here, on a wide white cloth in the middle of the chamber, what horror they see. A crouched Mother Symna. Her brown claws wrapped viciously around the hands of a young girl, who kneels, naked, with a long silver crucifix slivered between her wrists.

Blood rolls gently down the girl's slender arms to her elbows and drips into a chalice held by the Captain of the Cardinal's Guard.

In the name of God, what evil is this? cried Henri, and twelve sisters raised their heads from their circle of prayer and the room was lit with the hard-edged fire of red eyes peering at them from within black hoods.

The girl, too, turned her head, but her eyes were round and disbelieving and filled with horror, and her small round mouth was empty.

Rysto raised his head more slowly, and when he faced them they could see his orbs were vein-cracked white, as though he were taken down into the abyss of a trance. His lips curled from his teeth and his cheeks cringed and his lungs hissed.

Suddenly more footfalls charged towards them from the corridor and yet more from an arch on the other side of the room.

Giraud spoke. She is not the one. Come!

He strode towards an archway on their right and Calan hurried after, clutching at Henri's sleeve for he knew he would not wish to leave the girl.

They are too many. She is gone, theirs.

And he dragged his friend by the arm.

Yet Henri could not escape the girl's eyes; he could feel them bury deeper into his brain, driven by the force of her disbelief and despair. He was followed even as they climbed the spiral of a staircase, higher, still higher, as hideous forms leapt up after them.

Their flight, for so it seemed, mazed through numberless, twisted arteries, up spinning stairways, far beyond the room of the sacrifice, and still those eyes beseeched and wrung his mind.

But now they could fly no higher for they had reached a stone burrow which was halted by a dripping black wall - the mound of rock to which the ancient bones of the convent had been fastened. There were several doors set like rotten teeth on either side of the passageway, but Giraud did not hesitate. He led on, right to the last, attracted by a force felt by him alone.

Henri reached forward and grabbed Calan by the shoulder.

I'll wait. Someone must guard our escape.

Calan nodded and Henri turned his sword arm back down into the stairwell.

When Calan reached Giraud, he was standing motionless by the door, staring into the wood, hesitant for the first time. Calan twisted the iron ring with a violent wrench but the door held. He looked to Giraud, who said simply, She is here.

Calan shook his head, leaned his blade into the wood. Again and again the blade gouged deep and true, until finally, the lock fell at their feet.

RED stop go now go now green red stop and when you glance sideways through the white misted rectangle grey on grey on black. Outside. What really lies out there? Nothing real.

The Morning Parks

The old city, discarded bricks and broken panes, mottled skin through which this snake shunts and squirms and beeps and squeaks, casting off its ghosts with noise and fumes. Fleeing yesterday's slow wraiths. Honkhonkhonking like geese fleeing for the mythical sun of the south.

"Wait!" cried several voices in unison.
Marcus said, "But I thought this tale was in the past."
"It's in the past and in the present," I said.
"It's all in your head," said Bernie, to laughter.
I smiled, embarrassed, "That's why it's probably not quite right."
"It's fine," whispered Detra, "it's a fine tale, Jimmy. It makes the night seem cold and hot all at the same time."
"Get on with it, Blue!" cried Bernie.

Pedestrians, too, waddle into winter, but silent, laden, baggy, bundled. Cold noses and warm breath. No hands. Processions of hurried legs and wary slipping feet.

A newsreader berates us with his angry mime, nestled in his tinsled manger of gift ideas, but here we're safe from temptation, frozen on the other side of this double glass cocoon.

Happy that yesterday's news is stuffed into our boots.

But come, abandon the doorways where the wind will only find us in the deepest darkest hours. Come back here, yes, come down the old alleyways where the wild flowers grew long all summer, and see now how snow swirls above their dead heads, anxiously in search of sleep.

Sleep. Yes, lean awhile.

This fence? Oh, 'twas once a very high wall, since you ask, but the crumbling caused offence for their very holiness, windows almost they were onto the ancient abandonment of the convent, scene of horrors past.

No, bar the way with iron! They said. Well, some say they said.

Now long overgrown, you see, so that the barricades are latticed as much by sinews twisted from the ground. But if we pushed harder the gate might give, might be happy at last to surrender. And what harm now if we climb in?

Here in these very grounds once her gardens grew, that old nun of the nursery rhymes. Of course, it's all concrete, crazy cracked, bitter black under the ice.

Mother, mother, not in bed, mother Symna lost her head.

That's what they sang. Cruel children. Could they really know?

Yes, put your face to the stones. What could they know? What do you feel? What do you hear through these walls? Moans. Whispers and moans.

Footsteps deep within. Someone is coming.

STUPID, thought Henri. *A virgin branch smeared with flame from a cone of oil set deep in the stones. Thrown back down into the stairwell. Stupid.*

Blind to any true sense of direction and the uneven and broken steps hammered his knees as he stumbled heavily into the unknown. Why always in darkness? Was he never to see the courage of swords played in the honesty of an open battlefield? Down, down, and these steps are too many, too far, too much darkness.

Stupid.

He paused, hovered on the edge of just one more step, would have turned then to retreat but an uneasiness stayed him. Until gradually that feeling became sound. A murmur murmuring from the bowels of the convent.

And the girl's eyes bleed for pity.

Endless walls snake by headlong into the fathomless mantram but from among those whispers and moans in the dark recesses he races none creeps forth to challenge his wild course.

He had entered the room of the sacrifice before knowing it and there before him lies her body, discarded, fading, helpless in the last trickle and beyond this pool, eyes like stars in its perfection, kneel the sisters, and from their hidden mouths comes the gangrenous drone which radiates into the heart of the stones. And beyond them, beyond the abominable Symna who squats like a mature boil with her head bruised and swollen to the flagstones, stands Rysto, in a circle of light for which there is no flame.

Revolving slowly, round, and slowly round, his eyes hooked into the emptiness above him, hands fused to the chalice, whispering such strangeness the very floor pulsates in its tone until circles bubble the pool of discarded blood. Mouths are biting at its surface from below.

Snared in their trance the sisters are oblivious to Henri as he crouches by the girl and slips his fingers into the thick warmth under her skin. But as he bundles her up into his arms and against his chest, the room explodes from him with the heat of a million stars and he stands blind and bewildered.

Seconds pass forever as he backs away, feet slipping and the wet body unsure in his grasp. Blood from his fingers weeps with the sting of tears but his vision will not clear and reality is far from here.

Defiantly, the room begins to reshape itself, the walls sucked into focus, and the fierce heat beaten back until it is a curtain of glowering white. Before that glimmering, six feet from him, stand the twelve sisters, red beads upon him.

Dead is their chant.

Towering behind them is the black soul of Rysto's eyes, his face twisted in an agony of pleasure, his lips chalice purpled.

And in this horror, transfixed, the girl dying in his arms, Henri saw shapes form and move behind that white veil, bloated forms with crooked limbs, beings which could not be human, waxing, dancing closer, faster filing into the room.

Yes, said Rysto, his voice sated. Bid you welcome to my new friends. And farewell to those that were.

And he lifts his right hand and here is Mother Symna's smile, whose will is done.

HIS body would twist away and fling itself into flight but his mind would not turn its back to invite immediate death, and his heart would not let go of the poor creature. Step by careful step retreat and step by step the dark sisters shuffled. Nearer, nearer. Rysto, too, swayed drunkenly forward until Symna's head was discarded, rolled towards him, forcing his back against the doorframe.

Grabbed by the shoulder, a voice in his ear, Move!

Hauled backwards, he almost lost hold of the girl, and a figure leapt by him, slamming the door fast, throwing a bar in place, turning.

Captain! and both stumbled away from the door, aware of the horrendous force growing inexorably against the wood.

Cindecis' pale face unnerved his silver locks. His tunic was ragged and raw furrows sliced down from his cheeks and mixed blood and spittle in rivulets braided through his beard.

The others? he cried, Where? And he tore the flimsy body from Henri's arms and draped it over one shoulder.

Behind them the door shuddered and a long, terrible scream pierced the wood, shot from a deep abyss in that dark, closed room.

Lead me! roared the Captain of the King's Guard.

Running scared back through the long winding ways, Cindecis pushing Henri whenever he falters, which branch, this branch, that, in the maze of torches and terror and dizzy, sweating shadows, and Cindecis oblivious to the weight he carries, but the back of his neck clamped and prickled by that awful presence so close, too close behind, as they launched themselves up another flight and there was the distant crunch of wood.

Pause. Scream, a cold scream, a screaming wind, a cold screaming wind overtook them, filling the stairwell entirely with a sickening smell of offal, the stinking stench of Hell.

On! For God's sake, boy, run!

With every desperate stride the air is thicker with the drum of a hundred footfalls and the tumult of manic exultations that come from no human throat. And all this squeezes inside Henri's brain as he halts and stands panting, with his back to the stairs.

Just these, he cried, the last room, but his voice silent.

Take her, said Cindecis and dropped the girl back into Henri's grasp. I watch our retreat.

Henri nodded, turned, stomped. His Captain followed, but slowly, half his face bent to the gloom below, and now he fought to keep his sword aloft and fast into that impending maelstrom of howls and fetid air.

It happened when he reached the last step and Henri had already advanced far down the corridor. A long, hairless dog skull with burned black holes emerged from around the curve of the wall a dozen steps below. White needles. A long-jawed smile. Now with two companions, sniffing, staring, smiling.

Cindecis struggled for his next breath as these heads strained forward on long twisting necks, pulling against leashes made of coiled pink gut. They rose towards him on the bodies of huge skinned hounds, muscle-knotted front legs knuckled with spikes, talons scratch the floor.

He backs away down the corridor and the beasts rise from the stairwell, slavering and straining, scuffing and slipping.

And from shadow climbs their master.

WATCH *out!*

Calan's blade was above his head and would have divorced his friend from the girl had Henri not cried out. Calan stepped back in disbelief.

You just couldn't resist it, Henri! Another one!

Inside the room Henri lowered the girl onto the mess of straw dragged from the pallet. A confusion of rags untangled itself from Giraud's arms to reveal first a pair of thin, trembling hands, then a tiny streaked face.

Rosalia! cried Henri.

She struggled from Giraud's embrace and crawled across the floor, but her focus intent only on the unconscious girl. She gasped when her fingers touched the wet wounds and immediately she began tearing strips from her own raggedness to bind the wrists.

Henri looked up at Calan, who stood by the door, said, They're not far behind. Can you see him?

Who?

Cindecis.

Cindecis is here?

Calan stepped out into the gloom, at once was thrown back into the room.

Sweet Mother! He slammed shut the door.

Cindecis? cried Henri, starting up.

He was stayed with a hand hard against his chest.

Gone, and for his sake I hope escaped. Whatever abominations fill that corridor were not shaped by God's hands, and there is no-one between them and this room. Help me here!

Reluctantly Henri grabbed the other end of the pallet and they hacked at the frame until they had enough cross-sections to wedge against the door.

As he smashed his knee through another plank, Henri nodded to Giraud. Now where will you lead us? Is it suicide you have in mind for us all, my friend? The fires of Hell seem warmest wherever you are.

Giraud's eyes flicked open, glanced only to Rosalia, who lay against the wall with the girl's head in her lap.

Night falls fast. We will be protected, he said.

Suddenly inspired, he leapt to his feet and grabbed Calan's throat and jerked down.

Hang this over the doorway.

He opened his fist and a silver cross danced from his fingers on a length of cord.

Just then a soft tapping at the door. No-one moves. Tap tap again. Tap tap. Tap.

Calan edged forward, hunkered down and peered through the chink left by the missing lock.

It's Cindecis! he laughed and began pulling away the wood.

Care! warned Henri, as Calan creaked the door inwards.

Before them was a figure. Calan thrust forward a torch.

My Captain!

But his Captain's arms hung by his sides, and now they saw that his torso had been ripped open to its cage, and his gaze went through them. And in that same instant his eyes fell from his skull, replaced by two pink talons, and his body simply fell away from his head.

In the doorway stood instead a tall crimson-boned man with no skin and one claw still stuck inside Cindecis' skull. The muscles stretched across the head lifted to reveal short triangular teeth and a sibilant giggle as its shoulders shrugged apologetically and the other claw lifted Cindecis' arm as if once more to knock upon the door.

There was an almighty shriek as two more of these beings appeared in the doorway and all lunged forward, but just as quickly Giraud's hand thrust between Calan and Henri and the cross flashed in the torchlight. The devils shrank in terror and disappeared into the darkness. The clatter of their hooves sounded far off down the corridor.

With his knife Giraud pinned the chain to the lintel. The door was barricaded once more. The cell throbbed with harsh, terrified breath.

Until finally Henri rose and pushed Giraud to the wall. His voice trembled with the tremors of his body.

What madness have you trapped us in? he sobbed. *Did you see? Our Captain! Did you see?*

Calan slumped, his hands on his face, rocking back and forth on his heels.

Now where is your phantom? railed Henri. He released Giraud's tunic. *Where is Janu now?*

There was a gasp from across the room. Henri turned and Rosalia looked straight into him, her hand to her mouth.

No, moaned Giraud. *No, we must not speak of . . .*

Hush! Calan scrambled clumsily onto all fours like an uncertain toddler. *Hush!*

Louder, louder, the sharp click click click of hooves in the corridor, many hooves, nearer, louder, click click, click, nearer, so many.

Calan, in a whisper, *They come once more.*

THE ground leaps to swallow the sky in its black maw. And the solitary sun of a distant galaxy, a gem in the depths of a black pool, is extinguished in the blink of a slow, languid eyelid. The owl's head turns swift, a single feather flutters, ruffled brusquely by the rude breeze. Almost invisible against the moonlit alabaster of the mausoleum, safe in the crook of the shield above the knight.

The sleeping knight, tall, whose broad hands are crossed hard on the hilt of a mighty sword, whose cape of virgin white fills the portals, cascades down seven broad steps and sweeps the frozen floor of the graveyard.

The knight who wears no helm and from the rock his locks flow in carved curls of time-blackened marble. And the skin of his noble face is without flaw. The single drop of rain on his cheek could almost be the softer quicksilver of a tear, and the breath of air silence sighing from the heart of voiceless stone.

And so the owl makes no sound when the knight's eyes open blue black upon the night, and no bell beat of wings alarms the world when the great broadsword is scraped from the stones and rises slowly against the silhouetted grossness of the convent, abode of the Sisters of Hopeful Redemption.

But far away in a closed chamber, where long ago the priests have fallen aslumber, necks noosed in their beads, where candle wax hardens below flames snuffed cold by the suffocated hopes of an elusive dawn, his Eminence Cardinal Marlov starts from his numbness and in the sudden single swollen beat of his chest he feels the clasp of terror and he knows that dead of night is now.

I'm tiring, and I know Marcus is fidgeting. He would take his turn with the Big Book. He doesn't understand half of what he reads, he had confided one morning, "but it is good for my English". And so, as soon as I pause, I signal and he's already beside me, a finger searching for the last line.

Maria puts her arm around my waist as I sit down.

"Are you ready?" she whispers.

"I'm never ready for Marcus," I reply, "I don't think half the forest knows what hits it."

The giant breathes in through his nose, plants his feet apart and launches into his storytelling, his huge arms swinging against the stars, his voice booming into the jungle.

FROZEN fast with fear, the room is one immovable instant. But minds fill not with invisible dread, they crawl with the imprints of fangs and claws and the defiled body of Cindecis. Only Henri moved, slowly, seductively unbuckling his scabbard and allowing it to fall from his hip. With his right hand he raised his blade and admired its keen, cruel length.

First Janu. Now Cindecis. No more. Calan?

His friend nodded and let slip his own sheath and unclasped his scarlet-steeped shirt until the intricate tattoo of the King's Eagle displayed more darkly on the glistening of his breast.

And you, Giraud?

Henri looked down on the pallid opal of Giraud's face not now with anger but determination. And Giraud too nodded once, opaque orbs free from their former glints, reflecting only this cold resolve.

Then we are one.

Henri ripped the wooden barricades from the doorway, clawed at the wood with glad abandon until only the black rectangle remained. And therein sat expectantly the stones of the opposite wall, ordered yet unsure, hesitant shapes in their torn frame. The cross and chain were gone, the knife ripped from the wood.

But sudden clear and solid certain were the sound of footfalls and the world swirled around their heads with half whispers, now slid from their grasp on sibilant giggles.

For Cindecis, said Henri quickly, and he stepped at once from the stone womb.

The awful remains of Cindecis had been dragged from them in a royal red swathe and Henri stepped onto mirrors. But as his eyes slid before his boots they were halted abruptly by a twin barrier of stunted hooves, clip clip clip clip clip clipping charily each on its merry echo. Hovering above the dance were burning satellites, bulged from cracked sockets, spinning crazily towards him, and fang-filled gashes split skulls with sniggers and hisses and curses and gnashing.

His left flank was Calan.

We must leave now or die here, said Henri. *The other girl, does she live?*

It was Rosalia who whispered she breathes but soft.

Without word Giraud scooped the limp body into a blanket, draped it over one shoulder. He moved into the passageway and became Calan's back.

Guard yourself! See how close they come.

Take this, Henri urged, cupping Rosalia's numb hands until icicles became gloves around the hilt of a curved dagger. *You are my right side. I run, you run.*

We shall charge? whispered Calan.

On my command.

Slowly, surely, six, eight, ten, the devils' number lost in a sudden flurry, and among them three, four, five of the weird sisters, clothed only in the life startled from open mouths and across their breasts, from temples torn to the bone into eyes white and wide and weighed upon the guards, as though the kernels of their souls had been sucked straight from their chests, leaving these ravaged husks, infernal machines.

Now!

Thirty heavy-legged yards and already blades sing, absolved in the waters of open hearts, the air stirred thick with noxious hideous scream, the death wail of the sisters, the clash of bone and steel, while the mirrors of the underworld splash with the meteors of vile debris.

So many! And still they come. See these geysers of red skin erupt from the stairwell, vomit into the corridor on all fours, talons flaying forward for flesh, bodies lunging with no regard for the fate awaiting on bloodslick spikes.

The pulsating heart gouged deep from home and the devil watches in laughter as its beating organ implodes on the end of Calan's sword.

He cries out Why do they not fear death?

That is why.

Giraud 's free hand hammered another devil into the wall, caressed purple pulp from its throat until it slumped empty to the ground.

He pointed over Henri's shoulder. They fear the wrath of their master more.

Henri whirled and a devil's severed head, viced to his ankle by its teeth, whirled too, until they both stared aghast, for there, at the top of the stairwell, twenty yards hence, are the two hairless hounds of hell, unleashed, slavering, obedient as stone on either side of an enormous figure, a devil far greater than all before, a devil whose gargantuan maned head boasts a tangle of knotted ivory horns which scrape showers of black flakes from the roof, whose paws boast talons each the length of a sabre and click like hungry scissors.

But worse yet is the sight of the being's chest for here, writhing in three bleeding wounds, are the faces of three Sisters, mewing silently for merciful death, and their eyes roll and their tongues dance with unheard screams.

Hissed this devils' master and foam flew from his fangs, hissed and cried. And he opened wide his maw and he took one long step and one huge hoof clumped onto the stone and the passage trembled and at this rumble of fear his hounds leapt.

Wild was the first wide arc which Henri swung and the hounds flew free on either side, while the giant took one more step and ten long knives rained down, scything furious sound inches from the crinkled skin of the guard's astonished brow.

Straight to Calan one hound lunged and there's no time to bring his blade to bear upon the creature for already it's upon him, slapping him to the ground and only the sinew and crunching bones of his forearm bar those teeth from sinking yellow to the gums in the soft apple core of his throat.

The second hound aimed for Rosalia but terrified she sank onto her knees, trembling arms above bowed head, and though the crescent's hilt of twined steel and jewels almost breaks through the brittle bones of her supplicant fingers its blade bites deep into the beast's rattle of ribs, the cage cracks open, the body crashes down around, asunder in howls, in rage and pain, and red flowing dead.

Giraud was on one knee, scraping, scrabbling, but not desperate, he steadies his fragile burden, while thrusting back into the darkness, snapping at two persistent monsters who slither hither on the ground, intent on clawing the girl from his stooped shoulder.

Calan, feet away, groaned, Giraud, playing with the children? But his breath was snatched and shaken between fangs and fetid breath, until he hoisted one knee feebly up into the hound's hanging belly bulge only to feel these needles pierce deeper into his arm, stop, get this bitch off me!

Henri cried out suddenly, Go round! ducked below another rake of nails and rolled backwards from the whoosh stomp of a serrated hoof. He clattered into the wall beside Rosalia, untwisted his limbs, kicked at the bloody lumpen mass before him and the awkward dog-beast rolled slovenly away to reveal the girl's frozen form.

The stairwell, he hissed, go round me! and he rocked forward onto the balls of his feet, his sword singing happily, forth, back, forth, back and forth, a hunched peasant sowing seeds, advancing on the master who stands on sudden dissenting legs, confused at the swift audacity of this outrageous human.

Unburdened of her kill, Rosalia crawled to Calan, grabbed hold of the hound's hind leg. The beast shook itself from Calan's arm and turned its head, its nose, its bare red grin and crimson eyes and fixed all upon the girl.

Without hesitation she swung her knife hand up. The hound screamed once, convulsed, its back a bridge of bony knots, and scuttled off down the corridor, bowling over the two startled devils so that their bones skittled onto the flagstones.

He's a bitch now, panted Rosalia.

Surely she cradled Calan's unbloodied limb, helped him up. His sword arm hung forlorn and passive.

So take the girl, urged Giraud, placing the body over Calan's good shoulder.

By now Henri's momentum had backed the demon to the wall but his arms were solid sore, tempered by the relentless hammer, when Giraud appeared at his side, said, they're safe.

And these? wheezed Henri. Sisters?

Lost, said Giraud, as his sword chopped three talons from the master's paw, tossed them twitching to the floor.

We can send them back.

So be it, breathed Henri, and in this gasp they heave heavenward and plunge down deep into the devil master's chest and an explosion of searing seething orange engulfs their brains as the beast disgorges its stolen spirits in a blast of skull-sized meteors which hang defiantly in the air before imploding back into the charred, smoking abyss of the carcasse.

Though stunned, the King's Guards did not pause, but stumbled blindly to the stairwell and themselves were sucked back into the bowels of the convent.

RYSTO?

Rysto. Yes, this is I.

Who asks? Will no-one come forward? No-one of belief, then, for your fear of the unfamiliar hides you well. Then ask, was this cup mine to drink? Will you not come hither also to feel the warm taste of our lost daughter? Plug your outraged squirmings into this dammed river, but flow she will through your fingers, and mine is the burning tongue, mine the hot kiss of freedom.

Burn me, do, salves me, not. Only her. I am her vessel, you see, an instrument, empty but of sacrifice.

Rysto stands in the centre of a whirlpool of purple life, a grinning face deep inside itself, blue circles white in the silver rim, chasing frothy bubbles. While everywhere the world spins troubled, herein worlds collide and spark, ignite.

Burns me!

Not now, the shark must swim, thrash to breathe, to move, must move, oh yes, move on, and on, always moving. Trapped, no, but a trap, yes, now that they come to me.

Rysto?

You will see. Come deep, deeper, round and down, deep down where the currents can trap and turn and drag and drown.

Here let hammer blows resound, bell beats begin, the stamp and chime and clang of the crystal ship wrung by wraiths. Come closer, gather to your master's rhythm.

Rysto?

No, now Rysto calls you. Hasten! Yes, you! Oh, yes, I see you now.

HENRI'S *veins surged not sweet and victorious with adrenaline and his heart pounded not proud in his heaving chest. No, his blood crawled slow and sour, thick with atrophy, emptying his head until his senses were all but overcome by loneliness, congealing in his limbs until they were swollen and numb to every step he ploughed.*

Calan, he could see, walked in the body of a drunk man, one foot racing the other, an arm lagging low in its scarlet glove.

Swallowing against every great new gob of nausea, Henri leaned on the ripped knuckles of a palm against the cool moss and shouldered with a grunt the body of the near dead girl.

Calan, too, grunted, where? Where is the ghost of our friend now? Where is his powers of darkness when we are surrounded by evil?

No, said Giraud, do not speak! It is the night, he whispered. He will come now.

Who? whispered Rosalia urgently. Who will come? Her words were harsh and urgent but her head was bowed as though truly she did not seek an answer. Her body quivered with the shock of each breath.

No, Henri said quietly, enough. This is not the way. We must on and pray we soon find our own escape from this nightmare.

Escape? 'Twas enough to move, to sense the little victory in every footfall.

And so once more they filed into the darkening descent, bleeding back down through the twisted wormholes, sucked ever deeper into the throbbing blackest of hearts.

Rosalia led with a replenished brand in one fist, free fingers nipping lightly at the crook of Calan's healthy arm, slowing when oft he stumbled and soft groaned.

Henri's eyes alone were alive, darting defiance into the darkest corners, but they stared back, making him blink angrily until they withdrew finally, insolently behind their veils.

And then came Giraud, stepping solidly into his feet, sword held like the stick of a blind man who cares not what lies ahead, yet whose head cocks now this way here now that, attentive for sounds unknown.

It was Rosalia who stopped, stifling their gated shuffle to an awkward halt, killing all sound.

Calan who gagged and gasped from beneath his brow, 'tis the smell of death.

Henri who stepped forward, took the torch, ventured onward, not too far, no, out along the passageway, stumbled and spewed his curse.

The others who watched as the light lowered, vomited its own thick gaze like yellow oil across the floor And there, where Henri crouched upon his haunches, sprawled a slow carpet across the distorted lumps. Mounds? No, men, soldiers, so many men, piled on one the other, arms and hands planted at absurd angles in the flesh for a stunted crop of stiff, incomprehensible gestures, whose faces were frozen in a lurid tableau, shocked beyond life even as it had pulsed from their broken hearts.

Henri stood straight, his back a thick broad shield against the horror of this new and vile assault. While he prevails there must be hope. And see he stands. And then he turns to his companions and he smiles and they know his steel has been breached.

This will never end, he grinned. Never. You see, and his arm twitched towards the dead, now they are killing their own.

The sudden splutter of his torch was a baton tap, a cue for the slow waltz of madness to hijack this poor party and spin it from the repressed adagio of fear into a cacophony of horror. At last, nothing could be done but to let themselves be taken by the swirls. Sweep of violins slide inexorably into howls of despair, cymbals roll thunderously into the crash of terror, horns, everywhere horns, the cry of the hunt, the dread sound of dervishes, cries of the alarm.

So onward they danced, Rosalia leading their macabre slow step, tip-toeing apologetically through this narrow field of death. Rosalia, with her sleeve held across her ashen face while sweet poison burned her throat and lungs, Rosalia, in whose pale opal frame opal eyes betrayed a familiar blue softness, Rosalia, so that from the impenetrable surrounds a whisper sighed her name, Rosalia, Rosalia.

And she knew, suddenly she knew, Rosalia, he sighs, and her dance grows stronger.

Rosalia.

Ahead and on, and on, on, on, and if not light itself then its promise surely is opening their way, for it draws their circle of steps into conclusion.

When suddenly Giraud cried out.

Even before his voice reached their ears, an explosion of orange raced ahead to snap shut their eyes, and spun them in dizzy circles, so that when finally their eyes found their companion, Giraud was a strange haloed image anchored to the floor.

He has tripped? But, no, see now what holds him to the floor, see how his ankles are caught in the grasp of a soldier's hand, the hand of a soldier who clearly has no head.

And, as full vision returns, the world dilates and time lengthens and Giraud's friends, who were almost free, see that the corridor is lit by many torches set absurdly high in the walls. And now they see that where once lay the carnage of mangled bodies stands an army of silent, staring corpses.

THIS instant did not stretch into infinity. There was no breathless pause wherein each heart was betrayed by its serpentine life of memories. No eternal second wherein each soul could shrive itself for mercy. No endless moment wherein bravery welled forth from hitherto unknown depths and screwed itself to sudden instinctive conviction.

In that instant the hideous army rushed towards them, cascading over Giraud's crouched and helpless form.

But for his obstruction the others would certainly have been overwhelmed too, such was the force of that swollen wave of distorted, blended torsos. Instead they found themselves propelled headlong on its crest of naked limbs and bare blades, inches from the silver-tipped embrace yet always just beyond the grasp of its fingers.

Swept until seconds later a toothless maw gaped wide before them, a red portal swallowed them whole, and Calan swung around as he was sucked through its ragged lips, and he slammed his good shoulder against the door, and so slowly it swung into the frame, so slowly slammed shut, and

Henri helped drop the heavy timber beam into place before it thundered under the rain of blows from the horde.

Calan stood shaking his head, his entire frame convulsing in perfect unison, as he gasped, Giraud? Giraud?

He stopped. His body, too. Petrified by disbelief.

He stopped and he stood and he stared.

As did Henri. And Rosa, kneeling by the discarded body of the girl.

Spin. Spin three hundred and sixty degrees.

A chapel? A vast octagonal room with the altar offered up on a high dais in its centre. Torches wink in the alcoves, so many they shine like a honeycomb of pure gold from floor to the ceiling, itself crowned by an enormous crystal dome made of many shapes and colours and bejewelled by the moonlight sparkle glinting all around the dark glass jigsaw of a huge, cowled saint.

Spin again, more slowly.

And see on every wall a portal identical to the one through which they have entered. And in every portal the door ajar. And in every doorway a mass of demons and the undead, silent, sentinel. Ranks of stone staring in vigilant expectation at this huddled knot of ragged-breath penitents.

At their backs the newcomers feel the corridor grow turgid with the torrent of bodies and the quick smothered screams of the zombified soldiers. But here, in this dead calm, no breath dares the still air.

Until, finally, a slow click, over there. Click, over there. Click, there, from behind the altar. Click.

Steps Rysto.

Draped in immaculate white cloth, bathed in crimson and cream light, his face halved perfectly by a beatific purple-lipped smile.

At last, he sighs, we are all one.

We were all one. Bernie stayed for almost the entire storytelling, joining in as the crowd heckled, corrected, urged Marcus to his greatest ever night with the Big Book.

This was the first night Bernie did not herself keep vigil for the camp. It would be the last night of fireside tales at the Sapphire Pools. Holidays are not forever.

****

Chapter Twenty

The Difference Between Life And Breath

THAT day began like any other, only more so. What I mean is that when the sun stole through the open doorway and across the damp earth it touched me lightly, so that I lay yet a little longer, knowing my guest would not mind waiting. And I slipped back into unremembered dreams.

Later I sat slightly longer than usual, perhaps, though it was Marcus who had lit the fire and his coffee was renowned only as liquid charcoal. But I had fine company, for Ron and Rod, the resident monkeys had joined me. Up popped two tiny twitch-whiskered heads, followed by four orange-banded arms begging for chunks of casabe cake.

Detra's herb patch was beginning to fulfil her promises.

"Just there, yes," I said. I could see the feathery leaves of coriander. She rubbed a thumbful against her palm and offered it to my face. I can smell their fragrance, though they must all be gone now, of course, every one bullied and smothered by a thousand others' sun-gulping tentacles.

Later Maria and I walked downriver, to spot for any signs we might not be alone at the Pools, though both of us knew we wanted only to be together, to walk and to talk.

"No, it is not wrong always to cut them down, but it's not as simple as saving them," she said, exasperated with me again. "Gol told us that in the beginning, long ago, those who wanted the rubber sap were not wrong to ask the tree for some of its blood. But then they asked for too much, too often.

"But now Siren's mining companies, the oil prospectors, when they see trees all they see are obstacles to be moved out of their way. The loggers, all they see is timber, stacks which must be cut and moved then floated downriver to make credits."

"Did they never listen to you?"

"When they bothered to show at our meetings in the city, a long time ago, they would talk only to Gol because he came from their world and wore expensive suits. He was a law broker. They told him about tree extractions as though they were cutting out a patient's cancer."

"And what do you see when you look at the trees? Do you see the tree of life?"

"Baca's tree? Gol learned everything from Baca, and his people. They were good teachers for all of us," said Maria. "Me, when I see trees, I see the scaffold around which a whole world is built. Tell me, this is not so difficult to understand when you live in the forest is it?"

"No, no it isn't difficult at all. But how did it first happen, that you became involved?"

"The same as for everyone else," she smiled. "For love. Like you, for a love I had lost."

"I'm sorry."

I wanted to help her. I knew she wanted to tell me.

"Your father," I said.

"So you have been digging for truths, Senor Jimmy Blue."

"I'm sorry . . ."

"No, no, that is good. I asked Tara that you should be allowed to know everything. You must know if you are to write everything. I have wanted you to ask."

She leaned against a Capiron tree, spread her hands behind her against the smooth bole for support. I hunched down opposite on the crook of a dying neighbour's arm.

"He was only a minister, responsible for city utilities, but even then the fights grew around our table. We enjoyed them at first. Sometimes even my mother would sit longer just to listen to us argue. She said it was better than watching holoflicks.

"You know, I think he was proud I showed such interest. I have no brothers. But when he realised he could win more power, our fights stopped. He would not be questioned."

Maria put a hand to her cheek, stroked the skin as if remembering a touch.

"I knew then I could not stay at that table."

She stood straight, rocked forward on the balls of her feet and swung down beside me on to the fallen branch. She tugged at the shirt clinging to my shoulders.

"It is quite simple. I am my father's daughter. I have his blood and so he will have my heart. How could it be otherwise? But my eyes, they are my own and they have been open a long time now and . . . I have followed my own path, no other's. Come, let us walk more."

When we reached the Twin Garias, the farthest point Bernie would allow anyone to venture from the Pools, I asked what had been troubling me.

"I understand. Trees and mining, okay, but the killing . . . is there no way to stop him, no, what I mean is stopping these things. As his daughter, I mean."

"You do not understand, Jimmy Blue. My father is no killer. If the world spins around him it is not because he says it must be so, it is because that is how it has become. He is no hub, he is only trapped in the centre of a mad carousel."

She placed her hand on my chest.

"But you must understand, I hold no anger for this man. None. If it were not mine, it would be somebody else's father. This is not the country he wanted, and now it is no longer his. No matter that he is seen in the seat of power, it is Siren who stand behind him. Remember it is he who every day, every new day of his life is missing so much and gaining nothing. Nothing, for what can he gain?"

"His daughter?" I asked.

She looked away, shrugged too quickly.

"Many years," she said, "and he has not called me this. When last we spoke I could feel the emptiness inside him and it threatened to swallow me too."

"But surely anyone can change? Can he make new policies, turn out Siren, go alone?"

"Laws? Jimmy, do not talk of this."

I shook my head, said, "I knew a girl once who said the world was destitute, that it needed new laws."

Maria said, "No, Jimmy, she is wrong. We cannot make more regulations for our world. How can we make rules for the way trees grow or rivers run? What we must change are hearts. This is why you are here.

"All that matters in the end is that you let people know, allow them a chance to know beauty in this world, not in the Parks, in the real world, Jimmy, in each other, even with all of the mess and the failings. When we are allowed that, we can turn it into anything. Love even. Yes, let's call it love, Jimmy Blue, because without love everything else is just getting by, isn't it? Whatever happens, you must tell people this truth."

THE girl was not dead. Her body was lifeless, a supple yet empty shell slumped across the brutality of flagstones, and her screams were stranded in the pit, waving yet anchored to depths of terror in which she could not see or feel her legs, in which she flounderd without the wings to follow her heart into oblivion.

Therefore she saw everything. She watched through barred windows as the horror began to unfold.

Rysto creeping upon them, the lead who has entered the stage to discover an inexplicable pause in the dance. Her eyes followed the inexorable fall of his feet as he circled breath-wracked bodies, each frozen in semblance of balletic paralysis.

The bedlam behind their own entrance had ceased in one long shiver. But here the music just begins. In the shift and shuffle of many feet death comes calling, fresh and fecund, creeping, oozing from the portals. Surer wash whispers on the hungry tide, louder rasp tongues, braver this insistence of sibilant hideousness, this slither on stone, this rope of flesh, this slow circling noose.

Calan was stabbed first. The tiny star flew from Rysto's fist and disappeared in the guard's gut, below his heart, for Rysto was yet playing with them. Calan slumped to his knees, clutching through blood. His sword clattered before him but could not hide his gasp. Rosalia fell, too, clasping herself around his shoulders.

Rysto laughed.

Will you not dance? Finest of the King's court, will you not dance? Show me no manners. You, de Gracia! Has Marlov left any royal blood in your soiled finery?

He launched himself at her, a blade snatched from behind his back, but Henri backhanded and the steel sparked down the length of his sword. The guard reeled, unable to free himself from the spin, but he cried out, come, come again, I fear not your abomination.

Rysto roared and the throng resonated and shimmered.

Abomination?

His eyes, dead in their whiteness, could see too clearly for he crashed down upon Henri and the throng grew braver, tighter.

You, you are the unbelievers! screamed Rysto and his blade whirled. All of you!

Henri staggered, jerked backwards as a second swing filled his space, stumbled, rolled away as the third thundered into the stone by his head. Over and over and over he rolled, his world hubbed by Rysto's face, punctured by the swoosh, clang, swoosh, clang of the terrifying toll by his head.

And as he fell onto his back one last time he looked up and knew he was to die for the strength in his arms had abandoned him and the madness in Rysto's eyes showed only stronger exultation, a glee that his specimen lay poisoned and pinned.

The point rose out of focus until it was lost above Rysto's head.

Calan groaned as he tried to crawl towards his friend.
Henri looked to heaven and breathed a prayer.
And heaven fell to earth.

It exploded from the silhouette of the cowled saint and the entire crystal cupola shivered in the wave, came crashing down in a shower of meteors around their heads and the air was filled with screams as the devils were speared by the shards of many-coloured fire, were burned and broken by incandescent shafts.

While here in the centre of the chapel all are untouched. Though the girl cannot move her hands to protect herself not one flame touches her skin. This heart of the inferno is a cold and cradled sanctuary.

When finally the kaleidoscope stopped its lethal whirl the girl blinked into the delicate sounds of settling glass. And she saw that a saviour had come down among them. In the dead centre of the chapel stands the cowled saint.

****

A SAVIOUR, or even the daily hero, is not normally discovered in such a magnificent pose. On my wanders around the Sapphire Pools and beyond, out on to the secret forest trails, I was witness to men and women who were heroes but in their demeanour seemed anything but. Marcus snore-bellied and butt-naked on his rare wash day, with his voluminous grey underwear slung across a bush. Detra fidgeting and talking into her own shoulder when the herbs wouldn't listen to her. Teri slim-mouthed and impossibly serious yet ever vigilant at her post high above the first pool, her smiles kept for Bernie alone. And Bernie, a girl who took the air around her and shook it upside down before breathing it in and exhaling in your face.

Perhaps Maria. Perhaps she alone. Impossible to ask why or how she could find goodness in everything. Travelling outside of herself, finding beauty and sharing it, she may have been carrying the weight of her world and her surrogate family but she walked always with grace.

Looking at these people I knew I had boarded a strange boat, joined a crew collected from every possible quarter, old, young, or perhaps neither. Here they remained together in the calm, waiting patiently for the first chance to return to a storm that had claimed the lives of friends, intent upon a course unknown to the rest of the world, confounded by those they sought to help.

I did not imagine anyone could win, never mind find such unconscious nobility in the trying. But here? Here it seemed illogical not to try for the impossible, for the impossible could be no more a stranger to the senses than reaching out my hand here to this single leaf, which is green and gold but when the night shines through it is a black flag. And when the morning dares breathe again it will shed its armour and delight in its own diaphanous skin and web-veined heart. Today it is acrid in the dry sunlight, but when the rain comes it will grow tumescent with citrus. It is a leaf I recall Baca chewing for hours, to get the zings in his wings, he laughed, though it made me gag and my gums turn brown. A leaf that is softer than the second before a kiss and stronger than the force of its meeting.

Sights, sounds, smells, tastes, textures. All of these were neither hopes nor laws but simply the daily event of being. They were elements entering my body and, as such, became needs. It is not about wanting to save such things, it is about realising we cannot choose to live without them.

I think I understood then why Maria needed me to come on this journey to Eilidon. This was a lesson in a self-defence of the senses, the difference between life and breath, living and breathing.

SHOCK has left the chapel in serenity. But for the occasional frisson of glass betwixt stone and twitching limb the world is silence. Only the hooded figure stands amidst the ruins, shock still in a funnel of moonlight, robed impenetrable as the grotesque frieze burned indelibly onto the walls.

Slow was the reawakening of fear. First the sporadic cough spit of a demon spared the worst under the shield of its neighbour. Then one by one others struggled from beneath shatters of glass and flesh, shaking steaming fragments from their unhinged lengths like huge hairless hounds come in from the rain. One grinned at the sight of a translucent pole sticking from its belly, laughed when fingers were severed wresting the glass, and the sound woke more, and soon they too were standing.

Rosalia tugged herself from under Calan for the guard had thrown himself on her. Now he grunted, an old man wrestled from afternoon slumber, groaning until his eyes found the figure, screwed upon the demons prowling on the hazy rim, and fear stole bitterness from his mouth and stuffed his mind with the undeniable image of Rysto about to strike.

Of Rysto there was no sign, but Henri's body lay discarded nearby.

No, said Calan.

When suddenly his friend sat up, picked a sliver of hot glass from his tunic arm.

Bloody hell, said Henri. Calan! I thought I was... And then he stopped. He, too, had noticed the figure.

No-one moved, no-one spoke. Even the demons hesitated without Rysto. The stranger seemed satisfied to stand.

To wait.

Wait. With the demons knotting and unknotting their pack of pacing, sniffing, until hunger devoured one entirely and it shrieks into the light, whirls, leaps, drops dead, a five-foot sword flagged in its trunk.

The stranger stepped on its chest, unmired his weapon as vile outpouring sizzled on disgusted steel.

Janu, said Henri and Calan.

Slow was the head unswathed but when silver shone full on the face it was far from remembered. A mask of unconscious hatred, contemptuous of death, criss-crossed by livid scars of conflict like so many worm tracks, and those eyes, almost lost within the bone, at once dead and distant and alive and popping like a rabid dog's in the here and now of all this delicious madness.

Is it true? whispers Rosalia. Is it true? She stands unsteady and the figure begins to turn. Rosalia staggers forward, blinded by an astonishment of tears, but before she can reach into the light a ghost explodes from beneath the altar, flies up and out towards her, a rampage of white rags *fronted by Rysto's blue bruised face, and his oncoming is so violent it knocks her to the ground and his sword would have gouged the heart from her breast but snatches instead at her falling, tears at the ragged fronds and furious momentum carries him straight into Janu.*

The impact of oil thrown against flame for the air is heat and light and at its core two forces crackle in red boiling, spin a maelstrom wherein it is impossible to extricate blades from limbs from heads as they twine, locked fast in a clumsy cogwork of blows and parries. And yet Janu bites deepest, again and again, and strength alone forces the huge man back.

The demons erupt into hideous barking, tearing at one another, ignoring the humans entirely as one by one they dare each other into the storm where they take fleeting kicks and bites at their master's assailant.

In a desperate lunge Rysto falls full forward and Janu grabs the hilt of his thrust, twists so hard that bones snap and now Rysto's neck is strung by five knuckles so that he kicks as a thief on a human gibbet. Wordless choking, how long can he last, when Janu throws him against the altar, spine against spine, and there he folds, divorced fingers twitching but finding no sword.

Janu advances and all around demons shrink into silence to see their master broken. And then Rysto speaks a name.

Rosalia.

Think of Rosalia.

Janu stops. Tests the weight of his blade. Takes one more step.

Rosalia, said Rysto, and the desperate resolve of Janu's hatred stalls. And into its well trickles gold and blue and pearls, and his lips grow crimson with the warmth of her skin softness, and his breath swells with secret perfumes, and his tongue tastes intimate memories.

Involuntarily he turned to see her scrunched in pain by the wasted body of the convent girl. And Rosalia looked up straight into the face of her beloved, for the mask had begun to transform itself, flesh freed into the flowing of love remembered, sculpted by recognition into the face of the young man she had known and dreamed alive.

Janu! she cried, and Rysto laughed. *Yes, yes, she knows you.*

Janu stumbled, Rysto rose.

The shark advanced, stepping down from the dais, plucking a sword from the ground in his left hand.

Janu! cried Rosalia but her voice brought him to his knees.

Ah, you should not have come, said Rysto, shaking his head from the wag of his jaw. *She is killing you.*

The demons sensed the turning and danced around the light. Henri hacked and slashed those who dared too close. Calan swayed, blood oozing from his side. He could not see the devil who stood on the edge of the darkness, halberd erect, intent on putting its hook into the guard's head. Only when the monster fell forward into the light did Calan raise his sword too late.

He was stunned not by any blow but the sight of a man stepping over the demon's body and wiping his sword on the creature's neck. What had been a face was a mosaic of grated flesh and pale patches of skin with an eye socket open and bleeding, the orb gone. Only the grin was complete.

I told you he would come, said Giraud. *Even if delayed by my fall.*

He grasped Calan by the shoulder and the two clung to one another, slumped to their knees, and Henri stepped closer, the only guard standing and yet unable to lift his sword.

Together again, he said, *but no safer.*

Not while Rysto stood over Janu, this bastard wretch who had wronged Heaven with his own death, perverted the powers' by stealing life, forced Rysto himself into abominable communion. Now he would find himself conquered by his own human needs. Wrongs would be righted. S'truth, they must.

Love? said Rysto quietly, and he placed his broken hand lightly on Janu's head. Is love worth this? You see what you have become for her? Thank me, boy. Thank me that I can now grant absolution.

Rysto raised his sword and Rosalia threw herself to the floor and three guards stumbled forward to be met immediately by a wall of red flesh. And this time the heavens sent no visible spirits.

Rosalia, said Janu. I'm sorry.

He looked up into his executioner but even in that face he could not find the hatred that had sustained him, only the frozen laughter of a soul lost to madness, frozen so that his grin was fixed, his eyes white, frozen so that his brow was furrowed deep, frozen, until the blood appeared at each corner of his mouth, ruby tears that became rivers running down his great chin and until his eyes rolled forward and their dismayed pupils saw for the first time the reality of vile offences and the true depth of his soul's corruption.

God, no, said Rysto.

And he fell to the floor with a bejewelled knife hilt proud between his shoulder blades. Far behind him in the circle of light stood Rosalia, the girl whose love could kill.

That day I found out, too, the meaning of Maria's love. After our walk I had stayed down by the Garia tree all afternoon, writing notes, but mostly watching a malachite kingfisher preen its coat. There is a rainbow in every one of its feathers, Maria had told me. Its beauty sleeps then, ah, you see, how it explodes, so many colours.

That thick bill looked too big and unwieldy a tool for grooming such a short body. Many times I thought it would simply slip from its perch and plop into the black flowing without a hint of colour. Only once did it stop, cock its head, listen to the murmur and burble of wind and wood and water. But it was soon insisting its beak between feathers and the day's yellow turned to gold.

I had only just re-entered the camp.

When she saw me, Maria looked up from where she was kneeling by the cold-ashed hearth. Her eyes found mine immediately and I think she tried to smile but was too afraid.

It was as though the Abidar had been waiting until I arrived before he let the knife slide across her throat.

Even now it makes me cry out, a sound I cannot hear, as I fight my way to her, clash without feeling bodies, grapple arms, thump chests and faceless heads with my forehead, the air alive with my hideous scream.

I grasp a blade, twisting the edge into my palm, turning it on end. I think it sticks into the Abidar's chest but there is a tearing sound as he falls and it is back in my own hand as I'm grabbed again and so I swing the blade, knocking someone away and I watch as an Abidar claws at the knife embedded in his face.

Gunshots, bullets, shouts, screams, bodies flying in all directions, but I see only Maria and cannot reach her.

I'm bowled to the ground, dragged along the earth by desperate trampling. Teri falls beside me, both hands wrapped around a gun, which picks her up, points her back into the centre of the camp. There is an explosion and the air is red noise.

I cannot see Maria. I cannot see her.

I see Marcus, huge, alone, stone amid the confusion, and in his arms is the blue and white dress, now red, and the long black hair, now sweeping to the earth, and the soft brown skin of her arms, now red and torn and crooked. A gunshot and Marcus bows, stumbles on to one knee. A gunshot, but first he must lay down Maria. A gunshot. He is lying by her side.

I reach for them. I reach with both my hands but the divide is too great, and now there are hands pulling me, there is swearing, stampeding, and I am fighting against a current.

My fingers find a rifle and I pull a trigger at the advancing black chest but nothing happens until I'm bludgeoning a rifle butt into the eyes of someone who will not let me go.

Sudden branches rip at my face.

Bernie is beside me. She is talking but I cannot hear her through the red. Teri is here, too, shaking her head. Their guns are on the ground and I try picking them up with bleeding fingers, but I am pushed back to the thin edge above the river

Teri is crying. Bernie is on one knee saying something to me. Sorry. Sorry. Sorry.

I think I can remember the shot ring out, a second, third, hot and fire sprays around us, between us, and I hug Bernie, I charge her into Teri, I embrace them both and I hug and push them, push until we are slipping, falling, falling free.

****

Chapter Twenty One

Beyond The Sun

ANGRY is the hosting of the winds which roar 'twixt night and day and rush through hollow halls and batter down doors and tear through here with triumphant howls to sweep away illusions, and the air is flying with terror as all that are vile are sucked screaming back into shadow. Their banishment leaves only silence, caught perfectly in a bauble of air that is empty, cold, and clean.

Rosalia dropped to her knees beside Janu and they clung immediately to the reality of skin on skin, arms and chest, neck and cheek, and eyes, in the eyes, at last, in these eyes the truth. In a million dying sighs their single voice. In a thousand pages unturned their tale ending. Naked truth.

Henri fell too and bundled to his chest the blanket containing the girl.

God's truth, this was the longest night, he said. But his breath froze.

Calan pulled rags around Giraud for this chill had brought raw freshness to wounds. And they sat while the riches of morning waxed silver to gold. And no-one made to move. And around them the chapel was draped in fine red muslin, a liquid veil to dampen offending angles, douse fragments of dome that glowed like pieces of a shattered rainbow.

The day grew bold. Finally Janu's companions were able to stir.

But Janu, clasped to Rosalia, knew he could not move. Never from this embrace in which his body is distilled, his heart humbled to the happiness of one beat, his vision turned back inside itself to the secret place. Slow's his breathing, yet every breath sweet, for Rosalia, he whispers, Rosalia.

Who touches his cheek, he might suspect an angel, but she finds only her own pale image in his unseeing eyes, and the angel says, No. He sinks deeper into the warmth on his lips. No. And he feels an angel's breath when she says for the third time, No. And now he feels the warm life flow from her breast, seeping into his own, melding insubstantial bodies, and the road opens upon a wide shoreless lake.

She nods into his neck and he knows Rysto cut too deep and she says quietly, This time I will follow you.

And so the sun slips numberless fingers down and around them, combing their bodies with a thousand promises, inviting them to be embraced, and Janu's hands are closed by an angel who weaves wings around him until all the air is liquid gold, a gold shimmering under a vast alien sun.

THEY rode in slow procession, mindful of the laughter of children streaming around them with tiny hands reaching up to pull legs and reins, until one caught the gargoyle's eye instead and they screamed away, away below the market stalls. Giraud's face was sombre only from the crackle of old wounds, for he smiled low into his horse's mane and whispered soft words there until her ears twitched and he laughed out loud and slapped her neck.

He led them out beyond the city gates, out among the first fields of gold, among such sudden bounty that the horses snorted and champed and bowed their heads, startled by the strong green scents.

Still their pace did not change, even when they were far above the roofs, breathing deep into themselves pine and honeydew, glad that the hills were in them now and made their bodies tremble, while the arms of the sun windmilled the sky and lapped its waves against their shoulders and soothed the movement of the horses until their roll was the rhythm of trance. The world was awakening, but this journey was paced by the step of their own hearts. At the edges of their beating the day whispered still softly of sleep.

Easy, my girl. You must wait for our friends.

Giraud looked to his companions. Henri, straight-backed and attentive, rode close to the convent girl, who would never speak, was still so weak her fingers scarcely found their way around the straps of leather, until she found Henri's eyes again and her hands gripped tight. At the last she had given everything to the horror but life, now life was entwined with the blood and bone of this man.

Calan was last, bewildered it seemed, for his horse was allowed to wander often into long grasses, head nodding to the flowers. But Calan was alive in his way, gawping and talking the head from a dandelion until he realised he was watched and hid the stem under his tunic.

No need to make faces, he smiled.

Giraud saluted with a finger on his hat.

Exhaustion sucked their frames. But Giraud saw this tiredness was good, too, for all had laid down their weapons, ceased chasing the screaming tunes in their heads or trying to stifle the scream of nightmares, succumbed to the weight of acceptance until the silence of these mountains finally found root.

The burial spot was unsurprising, a cut in the trees leading not far from the path into a bower of tangled hawthorn. A single headstone of granite stood inscribed: Beyond the sun.

Already the soil was well bedded by spring rains and wild flowers had fought from beneath the stones until all there could breath purple scent and were as much part of the earth as the lovers buried in its breast. Immortality is found in such moments.

But is this comfort only, this laughter of streams, lea of trees, lie of rock?

Then know that the tabernacle is transparent as our own flesh and bone because we know this place is not real, that absent hearts can be anywhere they wish and so live in any dream we desire.

Walk softly, my friends, for we tread not only on the dreams of lovers but walk towards our own.

****

Chapter Twenty-Two

Friends And Enemies

HIGHER water had stained the bottom half of the rock so black that not even the sun's day-long censure could suck back the grey. Swollen river flies would not venture across this border but traced confused circles, bumping into one another on the smooth grey slab, slower, slower, until too dizzy they sat. Motionless.

My clothes had creased into the folds of my hunched body. Tucked behind my knees. Furled under my arms. I had lost my boots. Kicked off, I think, as the river roared around my head and wrapped its hundred arms around my legs. I stared at the hole in the right sock. There Detra's darn had caught as I clambered on to the bank, torn as I hauled Teri behind me.

I could hear her little girl sobs from among the shades of the trees behind. She had been crying since the moment Bernie had left us. All through the night. I thought she must never stop. Her soft-moaned grief seemed as natural now as breathing itself.

Once we had heard them moving along the opposite bank. A series of barks and distant replies. They were hunting. Yet neither of us moved. Teri's sobbing continued and I listened. There was nothing more to be done.

When daylight crept on to the bank from the river it brought with it my notebook. Sodden at the corners. Finally dishevelled from its spine. It lay neglected. I did not have to claw its pages open to find words. A verse had been replaying in my mind for as long as I could remember. Dreams and leaves, it told me. Dreams and leaves.

Finally, the kingfisher joined us. It sat patiently above and beyond my eyes. When it torpedoed the sky, rose with the water dancing in its bill, I saw the thousand colours in the splash of its wings, so many wonderful colours, Maria.

The thought made me jump inside myself. I turned to Teri. She was asleep. Slumped aground in the crook of an arm. I had not noticed when she stopped crying for the soft sound continued its lullaby in my head.

I tried to rise. My legs, battered by the river, motionless through night and day, were paralysed. So I, too, for a long time found a deeper darkness.

A touch on the arm roused me. I could not open myself. The touch grew heavy, tightened, pulled me around until my hard body rolled on its bones on the stone that, roused, pushed a fist into the back of my head.

"Jimmy!"

I opened my eyes but could not see.

"Jimmy, please!"

Maria, she has risen from the river, too, and her hair is still wet for I can feel it dripping warm on my chest, or is it blood, is it her blood?

I opened my eyes.

"Come on. Get up."

It must have been night but milk spilled from the river, splashed the white round of Bernie's face, all but the blackness in her eyes.

"It's okay," she said, "there is a way clear, but we have to go. Right now."

Teri was waiting. Her hair had been scraped from the mask of her face where no tears had ever been. Her gaze was intent on the far side of the water. Her eyes may as well have been closed.

I clambered to my knees, my feet, said, "Where did you go?"

"To get this."

Bernie opened the flaps of a muddied satchel to reveal the corner of a portable link.

"We kept some hidden around the Pools, just in case."

"Then you can contact the camp? Maria?"

Bernie said, "The camp had no Link. You know that."

"There is no camp," said Teri. "You know there is no Maria."

Bernie said quickly, "Listen, only Teri and I used the Links. When we had to. Now come on. We have to go."

"Just like that? And it's okay to use that thing now, now that everything has turned to hell, and everyone is dead?"

"Don't! Don't ever!" seethed Bernie. "Not ever. They were my friends. I loved them, too. I was there, Jimmy. Did words save them? Did your words stop the knife?"

Teri stepped between us, grabbed Bernie by her shoulder, said, "Let's go."

Through the milk of the moon our way was slow, for there was no path but the winding way cut and furrowed by bruised forearms. The lengths of my limbs were beyond feeling, but the ground would not forgive my soles and soon I was hobbling, involuntarily limping on to softer patches of leaf and mud though I welcomed the pain. I concentrated on nothing else.

We had been travelling for perhaps two hours when Bernie halted. I stood lame until slowly she moved forward and we found ourselves in a sudden space, a narrow track that on either side faded into the nothing.

"What if he does not come?" asked Teri.

"He'll come," replied Bernie, "He will have picked up the other half of the pulse badge Blue carried from the City," then to me, "I know none of this makes sense right now. Maybe it never will. What happened, at the Pools, none of us could have stopped it. This is the way things are."

I said nothing. There was nothing inside of me left to form words. I sank all my weight into the edges of my feet and watched Teri place a barrier of tiny stones across the breadth of the road, then another parallel, then a third.

"Jimmy?"

I turned to Bernie.

"At least do you want to know who is coming?" she asked

"You're giving me a choice now? Is this when I get to dig up the whole bloody truth all of a sudden?"

She stared into me. I don't know what she saw in my eyes but she shook her head and said, "Come away from the road."

We retreated into the forest and fought our way back through until we were 50 metres from the stones. If Bernie and Teri sat and waited, I did not. I cared only to sink into anywhere where I could concentrate on the intense pain in my feet. I wanted to be far ahead of myself, somewhere I could no longer feel yesterday chasing me. See Maria's face.

I could sense the light long before I could see it or hear any noise. Slowly, it became a white among the trees to our right, a phantom sunrise that, instead of growing, flattened and became twin fans of clarity sweeping the road into existence. With the low hum came recognition. A vehicle was approaching.

Involuntarily I hunkered into the foliage, mindless of the biting and stabbing. Bernie and Teri, too, burrowed further and we bowed our heads as the tide of light and hot air lapped the edge of the road and swept by in a hail of rattle and dust.

A moment only then a soft swoosh. The jets were killed. The light went out. We sat in our blindness until Bernie and Teri rose and stole forward, dragging me by momentum, and we were in the middle of the track.

As we peered into the void an eye blinked bright. Again. At the third signal Bernie said, "Okay," and we walked until a black hulk came into existence. A buzzjeep.

"Well bloody met," said the man who emerged from the driver's seat. He was dressed in huge khaki shorts and an overstuffed, sweat-sodden shirt. He wrapped his thick arms around Bernie, Teri, then looked at me from amidst a wreath of hair that glowed red in the moonlight.

"Mr Blue, at last."

He stretched out a hand. It felt huge and fleshy around mine.

"This is Wardlaw," said Bernie. "He'll get you home."

"You're assuming I want to leave?" I said. "You're giving me a choice?"

Bernie said, "You've always had a choice, Jimmy. This was always your gig. You want to blame it on others? No-one but Jimmy Blue brought you here."

"None of this was supposed to happen, Bernie," I said.

"Then maybe none of it did," said the man she called Wardlaw. "Come on, lad, we can set everything to rights but we've got to be off into the sunrise now."

Bernie grabbed my arm said, "I'm sorry."

"You're sorry?"

Wardlaw stepped closer said, "Listen, girls, lad, not now. None of us is meant to be here, remember?"

Teri looked at me once and stepped back into the darkness.

"When there is time again," said Bernie, "try not to think of the badness, only the good. Maria chose us both for a reason. Always remember that, Jimmy."

She looked at me, lightly brushed my cheek with her lips, and then she too had disappeared.

****

I knew they would be trekking back through the trees, perhaps on their way to the Pools, but I sat too tired to think or move my swollen feet from the cold air vent. I listened to the thrum of the engines, unable to focus much further than the dust-covered dashboard. It was illuminated sporadically by a link screen set on standby.

I could hear teeth clamped tighter between Wardlaw's huge sideburns and guessed he was about to speak.

"Well, lad, you've led us all on quite a merry dance."

I turned to him. Without shifting his gaze from the road, he said, "First of all, remember we're on the wrong side of the river, the wrong side of everything. Whatever happens you're not here and neither am I, okay. None of us were here."

I said nothing. I was thinking of Bernie's words, the way things are, how things might have been had I chosen different paths.

"I still don't understand much of this," I said.

"Ah, now that itself is understandable," said Wardlaw.

"Bernie, Teri, how do they know you? How do you even know Eilidon?"

Wardlaw scratched a sideburn, glanced sideways at me. His eyes flitted to the link.

"Well, see now, the girl you knew has come a long way from Cashelan. You wouldn't have known, of course, but she works for Shipping. You did? No, that means for Siren, lad. Specialist department, if you like. Has done for too long. Yes, too long. Been all over she has, in every viper's nest."

Words swirled from the blood in my head but they felt too big in my throat. I managed only, "Siren? What does she do for Siren?"

"Do?" Wardlaw said, looking at me incredulously. And then he laughed

"Well she does odd jobs, if you like. Here? Yes, odd jobs. Teri, too. Think they met in the City, at a department party, got close, know what I mean?"

The new day was throwing off the weight of the night like an old blanket. Now the dirt track snaked away from us and the trees grew thin and wary of the new road, until finally we were trundling through a hinterland of scrub and grasses.

"Eilidon," I said. "Why were they at Eilidon?"

"Well, it's like this, lad, if you can't beat them, join them."

"Spies?"

"No, not at all. Maria knew who they were, what they were, why they were there. Everything. Marriage of convenience. Those girls knew how to start shit for Eilidon. You see, it suits us all to keep folks like Chavez busy. The mechanics of rule down here are best kept banging along in fits and starts, stops them actually moving anywhere."

I shook my head.

"Chavez tried going down the road of every man that was made before him. Betrayed the plan, lad. Got greedy, went after it all too soon, cutting down Batavia long before there were enough Parks, enough lungs to keep even the germs in his own back yard breathing. Helping Eilidon gave him a party to think about, gave us time for more Hits, more Parks."

"But Bernie must have known. She'd know we'd be attacked? Eilidon would be attacked."

The Morning Parks

"No, lad, what? You don't think she'd have got you out, all of you, eh? That's always the trouble with that girl, too keen to do the right thing by people, even when people don't know what's the right thing for them. Shit, no, she didn't know! But she should have. Burning 221, that was something even for her, oh yes, quite something."

Even as the day rose, my body sank heavier into my seat. It was some time before Wardlaw spoke again. Behind his boisterous, moustachioed bluff there was an anger boiling. I heard his teeth clamped tight, twice, three times before he spoke again.

"You see, it's going to take some doing, working this one out, when Chavez finds out some snake-eye of a jungle Abidar has done his daughter. Lovely girl, Maria. Lovely. Met her at the office once, you know. Petition, I think. That's when I thought it would be good to bring in Bernie. Have to bring her out now, course. Soon as she's Shipped a few heads, got it out her system."

"Shipped?"

"Killed!" cried Wardlaw suddenly, striking the steering wheel. "Dead! Never underestimate the fire in that girl. Long time, long ago, I gave up putting reins on that one. She bends rules, bent them after the first attack on Eilidon, taking you deeper instead of ditching you. Even bent the rules not Shipping you out in a body bag the moment you stepped off the plane."

"Me?"

"Lad, she was supposed to Ship you months ago, when you were still shuffling about in the City, sniffing Siren's armpits and shouting about the smell to anyone who'd read your paper. Shipping is what Bernie does best. God knows why she didn't do you. But she's the only reason you're here right now, even if you wouldn't take the warnings, not even in the Circus House. Yes, you can thank her for that.

"Well, now she's off playing in the jungle, and I wouldn't want to be an Abidar wandering in there."

With a sudden bump the road became steelshod, and the jets readjusted, settling us lower and faster until the grey track widened with the daylight. We were approaching an open space and on the far side was a small bush hopper.

"Right," said Wardlaw. "Time to decide what to do with the loose ends. Tell me, Mr Blue, can you really do something new? Can you keep a secret?"

****

Chapter Twenty-Three

The Beginning

THERE are no ghosts following me now. None trapped in dreams, imprisoned in a notebook or preserved in a holoflask on my desk.

Has it really been a whole year? This winter's sun is unusually low and sharp and white on the walls of Carmelwood Cottage. It offers the reflection of an unfamiliar face in the screen as I type.

What happens now? I don't know.

I know that you call me. We have not met again, but you like to call. I like you to call. Today you wanted to tell me once more about New York. Did I really know already that there are now more than 100 different Central Parks?

"Tom says we should take a look into them. Well, you know, for work, not for real. You could write about it, Jimmy. Someone's going to make a killing with all the law sales. Us probably. There are so many runners being struck down with allergies, like a plague. I guess they're just not used to being near real wildness, the trees and the grass and everything."

"You know, there might be a story in it."

"Juice!" you laugh. "Is that juice, like Charlie used to tell you? I miss Charlie. Does he still sleep in his office? Oh, but the book? I think it was Sam who told me. What happened to your book?"

"The book . . ."

"I miss you, Jimmy," you say suddenly. "Are you sure you're okay? These days you sound, I don't know, you still seem far away."

"I am far away, Anna," I say. "No, it must be an allergy. Too long living with trees."

How can I tell you I've seen people living with dreams pumping in their veins, that their dreams are now feeding the earth?

"What happened? I mean to us, Jimmy?"

"What happened? Oh, I think maybe we just needed to live different stories for a while."

When you laugh again, the sound is soft and familiar, and I find myself glad that you are happy. I'm glad, too, that I don't have a link in Carmelwood. I only want to remember your face.

"There was something, Jimmy, you know, when we were together, in our own story. When I first came here to New York I tried to reach you. I don't know why, it felt so urgent that we should talk. It's just, well, when we made love, everything seemed alive. I thought I needed to feel that again. Isn't that strange? It is strange, isn't it? But everything is so strange and unreal here. That doesn't make any sense, does it?"

"No, Anna, it does."

Later that night you call again. You want to know more about the book, if it will be the perfect love story with perfect lovers. I do not understand why you want to know, so I say only that there is no such thing as perfect lovers, only the perfect love they feel for one another.

There is a pause and you ask me to tell you more and I almost remember something. I tell you that perfect love is the kind that embraces all the mess and the failings in the same arms as triumphs, trails fingers as softly through doubts as hopes. I tell you it will kiss with a yearning, even if this means oblivion in the here and now of a single, forever moment.

There is a longer pause then a burst of nervous laughter, and you say, yes, I've been in the jungle too long, for sure, and what will you do with me? And what do I mean about a forever moment?

I tell you it's okay, we're going to be okay, life tends to move on from forever moments.

Silence again, and then we say goodbye for the last time.

The next morning a parcel arrives at Carmelwood Cottage.

"It's up to you how you play this," says the read-once note. "Not much we can do except Ship you. But Bernie says you know to do the right thing. I guess she means stick to the InfoDats, all that. I know that's what you've been doing anyway, lad, because there are people near you who still have to read the papers. But let's face it, who cares enough to want the truth, right? And I've to give you this. She sent it up by bush hopper, before she heads to Alaska, God knows why, the book and Alaska."

The note is not signed. Slowly, the writing fades and disappears in the sunlight.

I open the parcel. My manuscript falls into my lap. Battered. Brittle. Somehow intact. Held together by a single blue ribbon.

Tucked inside the final two pages is a folded sheaf of paper with these words.

> *Jimmy Blue,*
>
> *The heart is a strange land we visit too rarely. There are mountains there higher than any here in Batavia, taller even than Masota himself. Rivers that are deeper and wider than the mother's vein. There are forests in the heart more vast and beautiful and fertile than any we have seen before, even in this most beautiful place.*
>
> *I'm sure there are cities in the heart, too, filled with people whose faces we do not yet know and whose words, like the dreams and leaves, sound alien to our ears. But we shall come to understand.*
>
> *In the heart there are churches on hills, wild flowers in the fields below. There is a summer of blue skies. In the heart there is laughter in the rain that comes out of nowhere and makes scarecrows of our clothes.*
>
> *In the heart there are huge libraries filled with ancient unwritten books of wisdom and undrawn maps of endless seas and I know Baca sits there yet, telling his stories and chiding Pedro for giggling and talking only of girls.*
>
> *And in the heart, Jimmy, there is blood on the streets, dark labyrinths and secret rooms with locked doors. There*

are faces half glimpsed in the windows of abandoned houses and there are people we know intimately but have neglected so long we no longer recognise them. Please do not forget them.

The heart is a strange land and few dare visit, perhaps because they know many have travelled there and never returned.

Jimmy, traveller, writer, friend, remember.
Maria.

The words leave me in tears, because for a year I have been terrified of travelling back into the land of my heart, to everything I left there, but now Maria has opened the door and reached out.

I should have remembered Janu and Rosalia, sooner, for was it not difficult even for them to travel beyond the sun? Was it ever worthwhile trying to imagine such a journey?

I run my fingers down the last page of the book.

IMAGINE darkness. Close your eyes. No. Now all you see is the mist on the inner window of your eyelids. Imagine the reality of darkness and wrap it in the absence of thought, now drop it in a well of cold neglect until it falls far away from you and is forgotten in unconscious streams, washed away on years until it is past, until it is no more.

Now that we have clarity, let there be light. Sudden daylight with the opening of a door, sharp as the sting of remembered grief, so that the brave new world outside hits your face like the acid spit of a solar flare, pounds your ears with the clamouring surge of a hundred thousand modern lives, the inexorable rage of traffic passing by, and the dull thud of machines. All of this pulls you, pushes you back just as suddenly when the door closes and the darkness returns and only the echo of shock is enough to tell what has passed, enough to light imagination with here and now and the revelation of high cathedral walls.

The figure small and solitary in your mind, standing in this vastness, hesitates. But she is not alone. See how her lonely stance is changed by a companion shadow when she walks on, soft of step, to the rail and where she genuflects and kneels and bows her head that perfect companion is revealed against the flames, fully visible now we have found them together at last, burning patiently in the corners of our imagination.

Two lovers are visiting to offer thanks. Names are no longer important in this tale of horror so fantastic. Their faces we know already for their smiles are in our hearts. They have endured their going and now their coming. Love. That is all. Remember.

I remember, Maria, I remember.

So where do I begin? In the bedroom, of course, on Holy Night last year, listening to the distant thuds of the Hits outside the window, Anna breathing by my side.

****

Printed in the United Kingdom
by Lightning Source UK Ltd.
126082UK00002BA/4-33/A